ST. LUCY'S HOME FOR GIRLS

RAISED BY WOLVES

STORIES BY

KAREN RUSSELL

"A master of tone and texture and an authority on the bizarre, Karen Russell writes with great flair and fearlessness." —Carlo Wolff, *The Denver Post*

"Hallelujah! Karen Russell's work sweeps the ground from beneath your feet and replaces it with something new and wondrous, part Florida swampland, part holy water. A confident, auspicious, unforgettable debut."

—Gary Shteyngart, author of
The Russian Debutante's Handbook and *Absurdistan*

"Most writers her age haven't yet matched Russell's chief achievement: honing a voice so singular and assured that you'd willingly follow it into dark, lawless territory. Which, as it happens, is exactly where it leads us."

—*Time Out New York*

"This book is a miracle. Karen Russell is a literary mystic, channeling spectral tales that surge with feeling. A devastatingly beautiful debut by a powerful new writer."

—Ben Marcus, author of
The Age of Wire and String and *Notable American Women*

"In spare but evocative prose, the 25-year-old conjures a weird world of young misfits and ghosts in the Everglades. Girls are swept off to sea in giant crab shells and fall in love with spirits; boys have Minotaurs for fathers and incurable dream disorders that cause them to live through humanity's greatest tragedies night after night."   —*W Magazine*

"A marvelous book in the tradition of George Saunders and Katherine Dunn."   —*New York Post*

"Karen Russell's fresh and original voice makes this a stunning collection to savor."   —*Pages*

Karen Russell

St. Lucy's Home for Girls Raised by Wolves

Karen Russell, a native of Miami, has been featured in *The Best American Short Stories*, *The New Yorker*'s debut fiction issue, and *New York* magazine's list of twenty-five people to watch under the age of twenty-six. She is a graduate of the Columbia MFA program and was chosen as one of *Granta*'s Best Young American Novelists; her fiction has recently appeared in *Conjunctions*, *Granta*, *Zoetrope*, *Oxford American*, and *The New Yorker*. She lives in New York City.

St. Lucy's Home for Girls Raised by Wolves

STORIES

Karen Russell

Vintage Contemporaries
Vintage Books
A Division of Random House, Inc.
New York

For Mom, Dad, Lauren, and Kent

FIRST VINTAGE CONTEMPORARIES EDITION, AUGUST 2007

Copyright © 2006 by Karen Russell

Some stories in this collection previously appeared in the following: "*from* Children's Reminiscences of the Westward Migration" and "Z.Z.'s Sleep-Away Camp for Disordered Dreamers" in *Conjunctions*; "Out to Sea" in *Five Fingers Review*; "St. Lucy's Home for Girls Raised by Wolves" in *Granta*; "Haunting Olivia" and "Accidental Brief, Occurrence 00-422" in *The New Yorker*; "The City of Shells" in *Oxford American,* under the title "The World's Greatest Sensational Mystery"; "Ava Wrestles the Alligator" in *Zoetrope: All-Story*.

The Library of Congress has cataloged the Knopf edition as follows:
Russell, Karen [date]
St. Lucy's home for girls raised by wolves / by Karen Russell.—1st ed.
p. cm.
1. Everglades (Fla.)—Fiction. I. Title. II. Title: Saint Lucy's home for girls raised by wolves.
PS3618.U755S7 2006
813'.6—dc22   2006045156

Vintage ISBN: 978-0-307-27667-4

Book design by Virginia Tan

www.vintagebooks.com

Printed in the United States of America
10 9 8 7 6 5 4 3 2 1

Contents

St. Lucy's Home for Girls
Raised by Wolves

Ava Wrestles the Alligator

My sister and I are staying in Grandpa Sawtooth's old house until our father, Chief Bigtree, gets back from the Mainland. It's our first summer alone in the swamp. "You girls will be fine," the Chief slurred. "Feed the gators, don't talk to strangers. Lock the door at night." The Chief must have forgotten that it's a screen door at Grandpa's—there is no key, no lock. The old house is a rust-checkered yellow bungalow at the edge of the wild bird estuary. It has a single, airless room; three crude, palmetto windows, with mosquito-blackened sills; a tin roof that hums with the memory of rain. I love it here. Whenever the wind gusts in off the river, the sky rains leaves and feathers. During mating season, the bedroom window rattles with the ardor of birds.

Now the thunder makes the thin window glass ripple like wax paper. Summer rain is still the most comforting sound that I know. I like to pretend that it's our dead mother's fingers, drumming on the ceiling above us. In the distance, an alligator bellows—not one of ours, I frown, a free agent. Our gators are hatched in incubators. If they make any noise at all, it's a perfunctory grunt, bored and sated. This wild gator has an inimitable cry, much louder, much closer. I smile and pull the blankets around my chin. If Osceola hears it, she's not letting on. My sister is lying on the cot opposite me. Her eyes are wide open, and she is smiling and smiling in the dark.

"Hey, Ossie? Is it just you in there?"

My older sister has entire kingdoms inside of her, and some of them are only accessible at certain seasons, in certain kinds of weather. One such melting occurs in summer rain, at midnight, during the vine-green breathing time right before sleep. You have to ask the right question, throw the right rope bridge, to get there—and then bolt across the chasm between you, before your bridge collapses.

"Ossie? Is it just us?" I peer into the grainy dark. There's the chair that looks like a horned devil's silhouette. There's the blind glint of the terrarium glass. But no Luscious. Ossie's evil boyfriend has yet to materialize.

"Yup," she whispers. "Just us." Ossie sounds wonderfully awake. She reaches over and pats my arm.

"Just us girls."

That does it. "Just us!" we scream. And I know that for once, Ossie and I are picturing the same thing. Miles and miles of swamp, and millions and millions of ghosts, and just us, girls, bungalowed in our silly pajamas.

We keep giggling, happy and nervous, tickled by an incomplete innocence. We both sense that some dark joke is being played on us, even if we can't quite grasp the punch line.

"What about Luscious?" I gasp. "You're not dating Luscious anymore?"

Uh-oh. There it is again, that private smile, the one that

implies that Ossie is nostalgic for places I have never been, places I can't even begin to imagine.

Ossie shakes her head. "Something else, now."

"Somebody else? You're not still going to, um," I pause, trying to remember her word, "elope? Are you?"

Ossie doesn't answer. "Listen," she breathes, her eyes like blown embers. The thunder has gentled to a soft nicker. Outside, something is scratching at our dripping window. "He's here."

You know, Ossie's possessions are nothing like those twitch-fests you read about in the Bible, no netherworld voices or pigs on a hill. Her body doesn't smolder like a firecracker, or ululate in dead languages. Her boyfriends possess her in a different way. They steal over her, silking into her ears and mouth and lungs, stealthy and pervasive, like sickness or swallowed water. I watch her metamorphosis in guilty, greedy increments. Ossie is sweating. Ossie is heavy-breathing. She puts her fist in her mouth, her other hand disappearing beneath the covers.

Then she moans, softly.

And I get that peculiar knot of fear and wonder and anger, the husk that holds my whole childhood. Here is another phase change that I don't understand, solid to void, happening in such close proximity to me. The ghost is here. I know it, because I can see my sister disappearing, can feel the body next to me emptying of my Ossie, and leaving me alone in the room. Luscious is her lewdest boyfriend yet. The ghost is moving through her, rolling into her hips, making Ossie do a jerky puppet dance under the blankets. This happens every night, lately, and I'm helpless to stop him. Get out of here, Luscious! I think very loudly. Get back in your grave! You leave my sister alone. . . .

Hag-ridden, her cot is starting to swing.

I am so jealous of Ossie. Every time the lights flicker in a storm, or a dish clatters to the floor, it's a message from her stupid boyfriend. The wind in her hair, the wind in the trees, all of it a whistled valentine. And meanwhile who is busy decapitating stinking ballyhoo for the gators? Who is plunging the Bigtree latrines, and brushing the plaster teeth inside the Gator Head? Exactly. At sixteen, Ossie is four years my senior and twice my height. Yet somehow I'm the one who gets stuck doing all the work. That's the reward for competence, I guess. When the Chief left, he put me in charge of the whole park.

Our family owns Swamplandia!, the island's #1 Gator Theme Park and Swamp Café, although lately we've been slipping in the rankings. You may have seen our wooden sign, swinging from the giant kapok tree on Route 6: COME SEE SETH, FANGSOME SEA SERPENT AND ANCIENT LIZARD OF DEATH!!! All of our alligators, we call "Seth." Tradition is as important, the Chief says, as promotional materials are expensive. When my mother was alive, she ran the show, literally. Mom took care of all the shadowy, behind-the-scenes stuff: clubbing sick gators, fueling up the airboats, butchering chickens. I didn't even know these ugly duties existed. I'm pretty sure Ossie is still oblivious. Osceola doesn't have to do chores. "Your sister is special," the Chief has tried to explain to me, on more than one occasion. I don't cotton to this sophist logic. I'm special too. My name is a palindrome. I can climb trees with simian ease. I can gut buckets of chub fish in record time. Once Grandpa Sawtooth held a dead Seth's jaws open, and I stuck my whole head in his fetid mouth.

There are only two Swamplandia! duties that I can't handle on my own: stringing up the swamp hens on Live Chicken Thursdays, and pulling those gators out of the water. This means that I can't compete in the junior leagues, or perform solo. It doesn't bother me enough to make me braver. I still refuse to wade into the pit, and anyways, I am too weak to get my own gator ashore. Our show is simple: the headlining wrestler, usually the Chief, wades into the water, making a big show of hunting the sandy bottom for his Seth. Then he pulls a gator out by its thrashing tail. The gator immediately lurches forward, yanking the Chief back into the water. The Chief pulls him out again, and again the infuriated gator pulls my father towards the water. This tug-of-war goes on for a foamy length of time, while the crowd whoops and wahoos, cheering for our species.

Finally, the Chief masters his Seth. He manages to get him landlocked and clamber onto his back. This is the part where I come in. Aunt Hilola strikes up a manic tune on the calliope—*ba-da-DOOM-bop-bop!*—and then I'm cartwheeling out across the sand, careful to keep a grin on my face even as I land on the gator's armor-plated scutes. My thighs are waffled with the shadow of those scutes. Up close, the Seths are beautiful, with corrugated gray-green backs and dinosaur feet. The Chief, meanwhile, has taken advantage of my showy entrance to lasso black electrical tape around the Seth's snout. He takes my bare hands and holds them up to the crowd, splaying my little palms for their amusement.

Then he closes them around Seth's jaws. I smile and smile at the tourists. Inside my tight fist, the Seth strains and strains against the tape. The Chief keeps his meaty hands on top of my own, obscuring the fact that I am doing any work at all. The Chief likes to remind me that the tourists don't pay to watch us struggle.

At some point, I must have dozed off, because when I wake up the screen door is banging in the wind. I glance at my watch: 12:07. When Mom was alive, Ossie had a ten o'clock curfew. I guess technically she still does, but nobody's here to enforce it. She lets Luscious possess her for hours at a time. It makes me furious to think about this, and a little jealous, Luscious taking Ossie's body on a joy ride through the swamp. I worry about her. She could be deep into the slash pines by now, or halfway to the pond. But if I leave the house, then I'll be breaking the rules, too. I pull the covers over my head and bite my lip. A surge of unused adrenaline leaves me feeling sick and quakey. The next thing I know, I'm yanking my boots on and running out the door, as if I were the one possessed.

Strange lights burn off the swamp at night. Overhead, the clouds stretch across the sky like some monstrous spiderweb, dewed with stars. Tiny planes from the Mainland whir towards the yellow moon, only to become cobwebbed by cloud. Osceola is much easier than an animal to track. She's mowed a drunken path through the scrub. The reeds grow tall and thick around me, hissing in the wind like a thousand vipers. Every few steps, I glance back at the receding glow of the house.

Several paces ahead of me, I see a shape that turns into Ossie, pushing through the purple cattails. She's used hot spoons and egg dye to style her hair into a lavender vapor. It trails behind her, steaming out of her skull, as if Ossie were the victim of a botched exorcism. The trick is to catch Osceola off guard, to stalk her obliquely behind the dark screen of mangrove trees, and then ambush her with my Flying-Squirrel Super Lunge. If you try to stop her head-on, you don't stand a chance. My sister is a big girl, edging on two hundred pounds, with three extra eyeteeth and a jaguar bite. Also, she is in love. During her love spells, she rolls me off her shoulders with a mindless ox-twitch, and steps right over me.

What is she going to do with Luscious? I wonder. What does she do out there with Luscious for hours every night? I'm more fearful than curious, and now she is waist-deep in the saw grass, an opal speck shrinking into the marsh. At odd intervals, rumbling above the insect drone, I hear one of the wild gators bellow. For a monster, it's a strangely plaintive sound to make: long and throaty, full of a terrible sweetness, like the Chief's voice grown gruff with emotion. Ever since he left us, I am always listening for it. It's a funny kind of comfort in the dark.

As I watch, Ossie moves beyond the clarity of moonlight and the silver-green cattails, subsumed into the black mangroves. A new noise starts soon after.

I pace along the edge of the marsh, too afraid to follow her, not for the first time. This is it, this is the geographical limit of how far I'll go for Ossie. We are learning latitude and longitude in school, and it makes my face burn that I can graph the coordinates of my own love and courage with such damning precision. I walk along the dots of the invisible line, peering after her. There's a syrupy quality to this kind of night: it's humid and impenetrable, pouring over me. I stand there until Ossie is lost to sight.

"Ossie . . . ?" It's only a half-yell, the very least I can do. Then, spooked by the sound of my own voice, I turn and walk quickly back towards the bungalow. It's her body, I think, it's her business. Besides, Ossie likes being lovesick. How do you treat a patient who denies there's anything wrong?

Behind me, the bellows intensify. I walk faster.

Most people think that gators have only two registers, hunger and boredom. But these people have never heard an alligator bellow. "Languidge," Ms. Huerta, our science teacher, likes to lisp, "is what separates us from the animals." But that's just us humans being snobby. Alligators talk to one another, and to the moon, with a woman's stridency.

When you are a kid, it's hard to tell the innocuous secrets from the ones that will kill you if you keep them. As it turns out, I have my own beau. Nothing I tell Ossie, or anybody, about.

When I wake up, I am relieved to see that Ossie is back on her cot. She is covered in scratches, Spanish moss dripping from her matted hair, her nightgown torn in several places, smiling in her sleep. I lie there for a while, watching her face twitch with some happy dream that doesn't include me. Then I go to study the *Bigtree Gator Wrestling Bible* by the inky canal. It's still dark out, the palest smattering of stars in the sky. I swing along the trapeze ropes of the docked boats, dizzy with sleep, the only human awake for miles. Swamp dawns feel like bearing witness to a quiet apocalypse. Infinity comes lapping over, concentric circles on still water. It's otherworldly, a river of grass, and a red needle of light on the horizon.

I curl up in a tiny ball, pretending to be an insect egg. Next to me, the abandoned airboats hunch along the river like giant spiders.

"Nobody in the world knows where I am," I whisper. I chant it fast, under my breath. "Nobodynobodynobody . . ." It makes me feel excited and dizzy—like when I used to look in Mom's mirror and say my name over and over again, Ava-avavava, until the sound didn't belong to my face anymore.

"Nobody in the *world* knows where I am right now. . . ."

That's when I hear the first twig snap behind me.

This is no Prince Charming. He's covered in feathers and bird shit. He's older, and I can tell right away that he is nobody's father.

"Hello!" I yelp. "Are you here to see the show?"

I hate how eager I sound, but I can't help it. It's my Bigtree training—I run up to every adult on Swamplandia! like a dog trailing its leash. "Didn't you see the sign? Don't worry, we're not actually closed."

The stranger looks at me with the flat, lidless interest of the gators. He looks me to pieces. Our alligators are not hunters or scavengers; they are lurkers, waiting to decide if something is worth the lurch. I realize now that I have been glimpsed and corner-of-the-eyed before, by the Chief and my sister and the yawning tourists. But I have never actually been *looked* at. Not like this.

He laughs. "Hello, sugar." His spiny hair, his glasses, make him look like an antlered beetle. If the Chief were here, he would have laughed him off our property.

I'm not scared. I've closed the jaws of eighteen Seths in my bare fist. I've wrestled my fat, love-starved sister to the ground. But I'm not stupid. When the man steps over me and boards one of the busted airboats, I'm on my guard. Never accept airboat rides from strangers. That is one of the Chief's many swamp maxims.

Anyhow, I recognize him now, his type. The heavy, tussocked coat, the silver whistle, the bright eyes in a shingled face. It's just a gypsy Bird Man. There are several Bird Men who travel around the parks, each one following the seasonal migrations, traveling beneath the shadow of his own pestilential horde of birds. These men are avian pied pipers. They call your problem birds out of the trees, and then lead them off your property, waiting for them to alight in someone else's orchard.

"Did the Chief call you to get rid of our honey buzzards?"

"No. What's your name?"

"Ava."

"Ava." He grins. "Can you keep a secret?" He reaches his hairy hand over the canal and holds two fingers against my lips.

Now I'm angry. This Bird Man has ruined the dawn; his clammy touch feels like getting out of a bath and putting your filthy clothes back on.

But I just nod. "Yes, sir," I say politely. I'm lonely, and I want to have a secret with somebody. I picture Ossie coming home to my empty cot, and get a terrible jolt of pleasure.

When you are a kid, you do things for dumb reasons. The Bird Man tells me that he likes my freckles.

"Listen to this, Ava."

I inch forward until I am standing at the edge of the pier.

The Bird Man leans towards me, tilting the airboat so that its hull scrapes against the dock, his thin fingers curled around the rail. The rising sun turns the canal between us a brilliant red. White clouds rinse downriver. The Bird Man locks eyes with me again, that agate, unnervingly fixed stare, and purses his lips.

The first four sounds he makes are familiar. The green-backed heron, the feral peacock, a bevy of coots. Then he makes another noise, keener, as close to an alligator bellow as I have heard a human make, but not quite that, exactly. A braided sound, a rainbow sound. I step closer, and closer still, in spite of myself. I try to imagine what species of bird could make a sound like that. A single note, held in an amber suspension of time, like my art class charcoal of Icarus falling. It is sad and fierce all at once, alive with a lonely purity. It goes on and on, until my own lungs are burning.

"What bird are you calling?" I ask, finally, when I can't stand it any longer.

The Bird Man stops whistling. He grins, so that I can see all his pebbly teeth. He holds out a hand to me over the broth-thin water.

"You."

Much later, I slink into the empty house, feeling skunked and lousy. Ossie is nowhere to be found. Her Ouija board is still sitting out on the kitchen table.

"Mom," I say, "I did a pretty bad thing."

The house is silent except for the neon buzz of the mosquito lamp. I put my hands on the Ouija pointer and squinch my eyes shut. Mom's face swims before me, the way she used to look whenever I told lies or tracked coon shit into the house, her beautiful scowl. I make the pointer spell out what I deem to be an appropriate punishment: "You're in big trouble, missy. I am very . . . d-i-s-s"

I pause, my fingers hovering over the pointer. I can't remember if "disappointed" is spelled with one *s* or two. "Go to your room," I spell instead, "and think about what you did."

"Yes, ma'am." I lie down on the cot in the silent bungalow, and think about what I've done. I close my eyes. I discover that even with my eyes shut, I can still see the black swope of the ceiling fan, the steady scything of the blades, just by listening to the air. The jolly mosquitoes drone on and on. The heat rises like a hand clamped over my mouth.

Sometime around sundown, I manage to get up, and go feed the gators. It occurs to me, in a fuzzy, directionless way, that it is Thursday. When Mom was alive, Thursdays used to be synonymous with Live Chicken Thursday, one of the few Bigtree rituals that I refuse to perform. You have to tie twelve hens to a clotheswire by their hoary talons, so that they're hanging upside down. Then you hoist them over the Gator Pit and stand back. The Seths jump clear out of the water, seven or eight feet high, and snatch at them. Squawking, thrashing, feathers, blood—and then silence, the naked hooks glinting on the line. It's easy to tune out the caged noises if you are a spectator, but the squalling becomes newly horrible when you are its conductor. Usually I stop halfway, overwhelmed by a mercy born of my own cowardice. The Chief used to tease me for being such a little girl about it.

"It's *natural*. It's the food chain, Ava," he'd laugh. "These

chickens are *happy*"—he had to yell, over the squawked pro-
tests of the chickens—"to be fulfilling their chicken destiny."

If the Chief's not around to do it, I usually just thaw out a
bucket of frozen baitfish. I'm nervous around the rooster,
and too squeamish to tie the knots. But today I find myself
walking around back behind the stadium to the red coop.
The swamp hens greet me with a flurry of shin pecks, puff-
ing out their patchy, distended chests. I pick them up, one
by one, and unceremoniously dump them into the wooden
crate. Then I attach the crate to our pulley, ignoring the jab-
bing beaks, and hoist it out over the water.

The hardest part is figuring out how to manipulate the
pulley, and then guessing when to pull the lever to release
the crate. After that, it's all over in a matter of seconds. I listen to the cooing panic, the frantic splashing. I wait, alone in
the concrete half-moon of the stadium, until the splashing
has stopped. Above me, the sun has nearly set. In the distance, the river is the color of a melting pearl. There, I think,
I've done it. When the Chief gets back, he'll make me the
line girl for sure. And still I feel nothing—just a numb surprise at my own lack of affect, like watching your foot curl
when it's fallen asleep. I lie belly-flat on the blue mats. I peer
into the turbid pit, feeling light as the feathers floating on the
rosy water.

On Saturday, Ossie announces that she is taking Luscious to
the Swamp Prom. From her huffy, vaguely French pronun-
ciation of "Swamp Prom," I gather that I'm not invited. It
will be held at seven in the Bigtree Café, she says, and I can be

on the Decorating Committee. She hands me a box of party toothpicks and a bouquet of wilted balloons.

"Can I come?"

"Do you have a date?"

We glare at each other. I nearly tell my sister about the Bird Man, and then bite my lip. She finally agrees to let me go to her dance, but only on the condition that I be the chief musician. Basically, this means that I have to supply a sack of quarters for the jukebox in the Bigtree Café.

"Only love songs, only slow songs, mostly Patsy Cline," she instructs.

I haven't actually spoken to my sister for several days. She comes home from her swamp dates after I've already fallen asleep, and then spends the day in bed. Now that she's with Luscious, she has no free time for me. It's not like I particularly want to chaperone her dates to the underworld, but I'm starting to feel a little crazy, a little like a spook myself, wandering around the park with no one to talk to. I've tried and failed to develop a rapport with the gators.

"Hello, Seths," I say, shaking a bag of alligator flea powder over their pen.

"How is it going? Hot enough for you?"

Sometimes a Seth will sneeze, but mostly they ignore me. In my library books, kids always seem to develop a transcendental bond with their animals, detective cats or injured eagles, stout ponies that save people from drowning. But the gators discourage this sort of identification, by being scaly and reptilian and so thoroughly alien, and by occasionally trying to eat my relatives. At this point, I am grateful for Ossie's company, even if it means I have to share custody of her with a ghost.

In the early evening, we decorate the café with hula lamps and old vanity posters of Luscious. The torchlight casts ivory shadows along the hairy walls of the tiki hut. Patsy Cline croons, "till death do us pa-a-art." Even without a ghost boyfriend of my own, I recognize this phrase to be a stupid fantasy. Is Patsy for real? What makes Patsy think that she'll get off so easy, loving only for a lifetime? I plunk in another quarter, scowling.

I am sitting at a round café table, pretending to do a crossword puzzle, while Ossie waltzes around the room with Luscious. Her head is crowned with an unhappy hydra of geckos. We couldn't decide between Yellow-head, a gaudy meringue, or Tokay, an understated avocado, so she's worn them both. My sister isn't a very good dancer. Yellow-head is livid, envelope-flat against her fancy bun. Tokay is trying to bite his leg off.

"Wanna cut in, Ava?" She holds a hand to my forehead. "You okay?"

"Nah, s'okay. I mean, I'm okay. Maybe later."

"Okay"—she frowns—"just let me know. Luscious doesn't mind. . . . A-va!"

The music has stopped, without my noticing. I plunk in another quarter, scowling.

Soon, Patsy recommences, filling the straw room. Ugh. My sister has retreated to a dark corner, where she is nuzzling into the palm straw of the tiki wall. I chew on my pencil, unable to concentrate. I keep snapping up at every groove in the record, watching the windows for the Bird Man. He's gone; I'm certain of it. I've scouted around, and there isn't a single buzzard left in our mangrove forest. I haven't figured out how to feel about this yet.

The next song is a slow dance. Ossie is struggling with her empty sleeves, trying to slip her own hand under her dress. I stop hearing the spaces between words, every song rising into an identical whine, bright and coppery, the wail of a jukebox banshee. My vision blurs. I'll think I see the Bird Man's face, his long fingers twittering against the glass, and then the panes go dark again. For a terrifying moment, the table melts into numbered squares, rows and columns, all blank.

DOWN
ACROSS
DOWN
ACROSS

Something is going wrong with my eyes, my forehead, my hot, stoppered throat, and I don't know how to tell my sister. What's a six-letter word, the crossword asks me, for . . .

It is way past some kid's bedtime when we finally leave the dance. My head is still pounding, but I'm not about to spoil Ossie's good mood. She is flush with success, already nostalgic for the Swamp Prom. "Did you see those moves, Ava?" She keeps spinning beneath the giant cypress trees, starry-eyed, comparing Luscious to Fred Astaire. We hold hands on the walk home—Ossie's fingers shooting out and linking through mine in the dark—and I feel a joy so intense that it makes my teeth ache inside my skull. It is everything I can do not to clamp down on Ossie's hand, a gator wrestler's reflex.

We sing some silly songs from Ossie's *Boos! Spellbook*, sloshing through the reeds:

> *I loose my shaft, I loose it and the moons cloud over,*
> *I loose it, and the sun is extinguished.*
> *I loose it, and the stars burn dim.*
> *But it is not the sun, moon, and stars that I shoot at,*
> *It is the stalk of the heart of that child of the congregation,*
> *So-and-so.*
> *Cluck! cluck! soul of So-and-so, come and walk with me.*
> *Come and sit with me.*
> *Come and sleep and share my pillow.*
> *Cluck! cluck! soul.*

The palmetto trees look like off-duty sentries, slouching together, gossiping pleasantly in the warm breezes. Fireflies wink on and off. The world feels cozy and round.

"Is Luscious coming home with us?"

"No," Ossie says, unlocking the bungalow door. "He's not going to come to Grandpa's house anymore."

I do my Flying-Squirrel Super Lunge onto my cot, burying my smile in the scratchy pillow. As I hear the door slam shut, I worry that I might start crying, or laughing hysterically. Just us, I grin, just us—just us! I don't want to lie and feign regret, but neither do I want to hurt Ossie's feelings by delighting in Luscious's expulsion from her body. Instead, I make a noncommittal pillow sound: "Hrr-hh-mm!"

"Good night, Ava," Ossie whispers. "Thanks for being the record player."

When I wake up, my sister is not in her cot. Her shoes are gone. Her sheets are on the floor. The glass terrarium, the one Ossie dipped into as her personal jewelry box, usually opaque with lizards, has been ransacked. Only the water bottle and the decorative lichens remain.

"Ossie?"

In the closet, all of her hangers are naked as bones. When I check the bathroom, it's like entering an invisible garden, perfumed with soap blossoms. The mirror is fogged up, and there is a note taped to the corner:

> dir ava
> i am not a bigtree enemore. i am living on my honey-
> moan. don worry we will com back and visat you. i
> will fid mom miself and brig her to. sory ava i haf the
> sownd of more words butt i coud not remember the
> shaps of the letters.
> —ossie robacow

I have to read the letter three times before I understand that she's left me for good. My judgment about these things is getting all the time better, and I know that this is not a secret for keeping. "Ossie, don't go!" I holler. "Wait! I'll . . . I'll stove-pop you some Boos!" Which sounds wincingly inadequate, even to my own ears. What was the thing she was going to do? Eel-up? Earlobe? Elope, I remember. I find Grandpa's dusty, checkerboard dictionary and check it for clues:

elope: [v] to run away, or escape privately, from the place or station to which one is bound by duty

Elope. The word lights up like a bare bulb, swinging long shadows through my brain. Because how exactly do you elope with a ghost? What if Luscious is taking my sister somewhere I can't follow? What if she has to be a ghost, too, to get there? And then another horror occurs to me: What if it's the Bird Man she's been meeting all along?

You'd think I'd start after her right away, but I do not. I put on my rain boots, and then take them off, and then put them on again. I pick up the telephone to call for help, and then drop it back into the receiver, jumping at the blank hum of the dial tone. I try to scream, and only air comes out.

Outside, I can feel the swamp multiplying, a boundless, leafy darkness. The distant pines look like pale flames. Without the Chief to cordon it off, without the tourists to clap politely and commend it to memory, Swamplandia! has reverted to being a regular old wilderness. If the Bird Man were to show up right now, I would barrel into his arms, so grateful for the human company. Where is the Chief, I howl, and where is my sister? My hand hovers above the doorknob. I stand there, a thin wire of fear spooling in my gut, until I can't stay in the empty house any longer. And I'd be tempted to tell Ms. Huerta that *this* is the feeling that separates us from the animals, if I hadn't seen so many of the Chief's dogs die of loneliness.

I pack a flashlight and a Wiffle bat and a steak knife and some peanut butter Boos, to lure Ossie back into her body. We don't have any garlic bulbs, so I bring the cauliflower, and hope that any vampires I encounter will be of the myopic, easily duped variety. And then I open the door, and run.

The air hits me like a wall, hot and muggy. I run as far as the entrance to the stand of mangrove trees, and stop short. The ground sends out feelers, a vegetable panic. The longer I stand there, the more impossible movement seems.

And then comes that familiar sound, that raw bellow, pulsing out of the swamp.

The cubed thing inside me melts into a sudden lick of fear. Something hot-blooded and bad is happening to my sister out there, I am sure of it. And the next thing I know I am on the other side of the trees, crashing towards the fishpond. It's a sensory blur, all jumps and stumbles—oily sinkholes, buried stumps, salt nettles tearing at my flesh. I run for what feels like a very long time. One wisp of cloud blows out the moon.

I wish I could say I gulp pure courage as I run, like those brave little girls you read about in stories, the ones who partner up with detective cats. But this burst of speed comes from an older adrenaline, some limbic other. Not courage, but a deeper terror. I don't want to be left alone. And I am ready to defend Ossie against whatever monster I encounter, ghosts or men or ancient lizards, and save her for myself.

When I break free of the trees and make for the pond, my whole body primed for fight, there is no visible adversary to wrestle with. The Bellower is not the Bird Man. It's not a wild gator. It's my sister, standing stem-naked in the moonlight, her red skirts crumpled around her feet like dead leaves. Osceola, poised over dark water, and singing:

"Cluck! cluck! soul of So-and-so,
come and walk with me. . . ."

On land, Ossie's body looks like an unmade bed, lumpy and disheveled. But in the moonlight, my naked sister is lustrous, almost holy. This is a revelation to me, Ossie's unclothed bulk, her breasts. My own chest is pancake-flat, and covered in tiny brown moles. All this time, my odd-waddling sister has been living in a mother's body.

And something is shifting, something is happening to Ossie's skin. As she walks towards the water, flying sparks come shivering out of her hair, off of her shoulders, a miniature hailstorm. It's the lizards! I realize. She is shaking them off in a scaly shower, flakes of living armor. The geckos fall from her arms, her breasts, they plink into the pond, her hissing, viscous diamonds. I watch, mesmerized. Soon, my sister is completely naked, her thighs ruffled red by the high, prickly grasses. I don't have enough breath left to say a word. And then, still holding the last note of her spell, Ossie walks into the water.

"Ossie, no!" Once I start screaming, I find that I can't stop. But I don't want to wade into the water until I can see exactly what morass I'm getting into. I feel around my overalls for the pocket flashlight, and find Seth's eye instead, my lucky charm. With a biblical wail, I throw the eye at the back of her head.

"Osceola!"

This turns out to be a girly display of strength. The eye falls way short; it barely makes the pond. I picture Seth's eye swirling down and settling in the red mud, its lidless gaze turned up towards Ossie as her legs twitch with the memory, the anticipation, of . . . what? I can't make sense of what I'm seeing. All I know for certain is that she's leaving me.

I wait for what feels like eons for Ossie to resurface, but the pond remains glassy and smooth, that same winking blankness of our mother's mirror. Lily pads coagulate in blots of vapid light. Below the water, I sense more than see Ossie's body, spiraling towards some mute blue crescendo.

"Don't you dare!" I yell at the pond. "Don't you dare go any farther down there!" I charge into the water after her.

I flail around in the shallows, black water pouring through my fingers, seeping into my eyes and mouth and ears, until finally my fingers brush skin. I seize Ossie's shoulders and yank her up. The water buoys her huge body, and I swim with all my strength. No superhuman surge, or pony heroics; it's just me at my most desperate. I splash towards the shore, making this anguished, honking noise, struggling to find purchase in the silty mud.

"Ava?" Ossie sputters. "What are you doing? Let me go!"

We fight each other with all the signature Bigtree moves—the whirligig, the chin thrust, the circumnavigator. Finally, with a triumphant howl, I manage to yank her onto the bank of the pond. I grab the fleshy pads of her feet, black as old orange peels, and try to drag her over a bed of rocks and sticks. Now Ossie is spitting up muck, and I can tell from her filmy, sightless rage that she is still possessed. A lily pad is pasted to her left cheek.

In the process of pulling her out of the water, I've dug these little half-moons into Ossie's arm. Tiny nicks, like the violet impact of kisses, or bruises. They are already darkening, and I watch, fascinated, as they swell into puffy white welts. As if something were still clawing at her from within, pushing outwards, a pressure that is trying to break the skin.

Haunting Olivia

My brother Wallow has been kicking around Gannon's Boat Graveyard for more than an hour, too embarrassed to admit that he doesn't see any ghosts. Instead, he slaps at the ocean with jilted fury. Curse words come piping out of his snorkel. He keeps pausing to readjust the diabolical goggles.

The diabolical goggles were designed for little girls. They are pink, with a floral snorkel attached to the side. They have scratchproof lenses and an adjustable band. Wallow says that we are going to use them to find our dead sister, Olivia.

My brother and I have been making midnight scavenging trips to Gannon's all summer. It's a watery junkyard, a place where people pay to abandon their old boats. Gannon, the grizzled, tattooed undertaker, tows wrecked ships into his marina. Battered sailboats and listing skiffs, yachts with stupid names—*Knot at Work* and *Sail-la-Vie*—the paint peeling from their puns. They sink beneath the water in slow increments, covered with rot and barnacles. Their masts jut out at weird angles. The marina is an open, easy grave to rob. We ride our bikes along the rock wall, coasting quietly past Gannon's tin shack, and hop off at the derelict pier. Then we

26

creep down to the ladder, jump onto the nearest boat, and loot.

It's dubious booty. We mostly find stuff with no resale value: soggy flares and UHF radios, a one-eyed cat yowling on a dinghy. But the goggles are a first. We found them floating in a live-bait tank, deep in the cabin of *La Calavera,* a swamped Largo schooner. We'd pushed our way through a small hole in the prow. Inside, the cabin was rank and flooded. There was no bait living in that tank, just the goggles and a foamy liquid the color of root beer. I dared Wallow to put the goggles on and stick his head in it. I didn't actually expect him to find anything; I just wanted to laugh at Wallow in the pink goggles, bobbing for diseases. But when he surfaced, tearing at the goggles, he told me that he'd seen the orange, unholy light of a fish ghost. Several, in fact, a school of ghoulish mullet.

"They looked just like regular baitfish, bro," Wallow said. "Only deader." I told my brother that I was familiar with the definition of a ghost. Not that I believed a word of it, you understand.

Now Wallow is trying the goggles out in the marina, to see if his vision extends beyond the tank. I'm dangling my legs over the edge of the pier, half expecting something to grab me and pull me under.

"Wallow! You see anything phantasmic yet?"

"Nothing," he bubbles morosely through the snorkel. "I can't see a thing."

I'm not surprised. The water in the boat basin is a cloudy mess. But I'm impressed by Wallow's one-armed doggy paddle.

Wallow shouldn't be swimming at all. Last Thursday,

he slipped on one of the banana peels that Granana leaves around the house. I know. I didn't think it could happen outside of cartoons, either. Now his right arm is in a plaster cast, and in order to enter the water he has to hold it above his head. It looks like he's riding an aquatic unicycle. That buoyancy, it's unexpected. On land, Wallow's a loutish kid. He bulldozes whatever gets in his path: baby strollers, widowers, me.

For brothers, Wallow and I look nothing alike. I've got Dad's blond hair and blue eyes, his embraceably lanky physique. Olivia was equally Heartland, apple cheeks and unnervingly white teeth. Not Wallow. He's got this dental affliction that gives him a tusky, warthog grin. He wears his hair in a greased pompadour and has a thick pelt of back hair. There's no accounting for it. Dad jokes that our mom must have had dalliances with a Minotaur.

Wallow is not Wallow's real name, of course. His real name is Waldo Swallow. Just like I'm Timothy Sparrow and Olivia was—is—Olivia Lark. Our parents used to be bird enthusiasts. That's how they met: Dad spotted my mother on a bird-watching tour of the swamp, her beauty magnified by his 10x binoculars. Dad says that by the time he lowered them the spoonbills he'd been trying to see had scattered, and he was in love. When Wallow and I were very young, they used to take us on their creepy bird excursions, kayaking down island canals, spying on blue herons and coots. These days, they're not enthusiastic about much, feathered or otherwise. They leave us with Granana for months at a time.

Shortly after Olivia's death, my parents started traveling regularly in the Third World. No children allowed.

Granana lives on the other side of the island. She's eighty-four, I'm twelve, and Wallow's fourteen, so it's a little ambiguous as to who's babysitting whom. This particular summer, our parents are in São Paulo. They send us postcards of bullet-pocked favelas and flaming hillocks of trash. "GLAD YOU'RE NOT HERE! xoxo, the 'Rents." I guess the idea is that all the misery makes their marital problems seem petty and inconsequential.

"Hey!" Wallow is directly below me, clutching the rails of the ladder. "Move over."

He climbs up and heaves his big body onto the pier. Defeat puddles all around him. Behind the diabolical goggles, his eyes narrow into slits.

"Did you see them?"

Wallow just grunts. "Here." He wrestles the lady-goggles off his face and thrusts them at me. "I can't swim with this cast, and these bitches are too small for my skull. You try them."

I sigh and strip off my pajamas, bobbling before him. The elastic band of the goggles bites into the back of my head. Somehow, wearing them makes me feel even more naked. My penis is curling up in the salt air like a small pink snail. Wallow points and laughs.

"Sure you don't want to try again?" I ask him. From the edge of the pier, the ocean looks dark and unfamiliar, like the liquid shadow of something truly awful. "Try again, Wallow. Maybe it's just taking a while for your eyes to adjust. . . ."

Wallow holds a finger to his lips. He points behind me. Boats are creaking in the wind, waves slap against the pilings, and then I hear it, too, the distinct thunk of boots on wood. Someone is walking down the pier. We can see the tip of a lit cigarette, suspended in the dark. We hear a man's gargly cough.

"Looking for buried treasure, boys?" Gannon laughs. He keeps walking towards us. "You know, the court still considers it trespassing, be it land or sea." Then he recognizes Wallow. He lets out the low, mournful whistle that all the grown-ups on the island use to identify us now.

"Oh, son. Don't tell me you're out here looking for . . ."

"My dead sister?" Wallow asks with terrifying cheer. "Good guess!"

"You're not going to find her in my marina, boys."

In the dark, Gannon is a huge stencil of a man, wisps of smoke curling from his nostrils. There is a long, pulsing silence, during which Wallow stares at him, squaring his jaw. Then Gannon shrugs. He stubs out his cigarette and shuffles back towards the shore.

"All right, bro," Wallow says. "It's go time." He takes my elbow and gentles me down the planks with such tenderness that I am suddenly very afraid. But there's no sense making the plunge slow and unbearable. I take a running leap down the pier—

"Ayyyyiii!"

—and launch over the water. It's my favorite moment: when I'm one toe away from flight and my body takes over. The choice is made, but the consequence is still just an inky shimmer beneath me. And I'm flying, I'm rushing to meet my own reflection—Gah!

Then comes the less beautiful moment when I'm up to my eyeballs in tar water, and the goggles fill with stinging brine. And, for what seems like a very long time, I can't see anything at all, dead or alive.

When my vision starts to clear, I see a milky, melting light moving swiftly above the ocean floor. Drowned moon-beams, I think at first. Only there is no moon tonight.

Olivia disappeared on a new-moon night. It was exactly two years, or twenty-four new moons, ago. Wallow says that means that tonight is Olivia's unbirthday, the anniversary of her death. It's weird: our grief is cyclical, synced with the lunar cycles. It accordions out as the moon slivers away. On new-moon nights, it rises with the tide.

Even before we lost my sis, I used to get uneasy when the moon was gone. That corner of the sky, as black as an empty safe. Whatever happened to Olivia, I hope she at least had the orange residue of sunset to see by. I can't stand to think of her out here alone after nightfall.

The last time we saw Olivia was at twilight. We'd spent all day crab-sledding down the beach. It's the closest thing we island kids have to a winter sport. You climb into the upended exoskeleton of a giant crab, then you go yeehaw slaloming down the powdery dunes. The faster you go, the more sand whizzes around you, a fine spray on either side of your crab sled. By the time you hit the water, you're covered in it, grit in your teeth and your eyelids, along the line of your scalp.

Herb makes the crab sleds—he guts the crabs and blow-torches off the eyestalks and paints little racer stripes along the sides. Then he rents them down at Pier 2, for two dollars an hour, twelve dollars for a full day. The three of us had been racing down the beach all afternoon. We were sun-burned, and hungry, and loused up with sea bugs. Wallow had stepped on a sea urchin and broken his fall on more urchins. I wanted Jiffy Pop and aloe vera. Wallow wanted prescription painkillers and porno. We voted to head over to Granana's beach cottage, because she has Demerol and an illegal cable box.

Olivia threw a fit. "But we still have half an hour on the sled rental!" A gleam came into her eyes, that transparent little-kid craftiness. "You guys don't have to come with me, you know."

Legally, we did. According to official Herb's Crab-Sledding Policy, under-twelves must be accompanied by a guardian—a rule that Herb has really cracked down on since Olivia's death. But neither Wallow nor I felt like chaperon-ing. And Olivia was eight and a half, which rounds up to twelve. "Stick to the perimeter of the island," Wallow told her. "And get that crab sled back before sundown. Any late fees are coming out of your allowance."

"Yeah, yeah," she assured us, clambering into the sled. The sun was already low in the sky. "I'm just going out one last time."

We helped Olivia drag the sled up the white dunes. She sat Indian-style in the center of the shell, humming tune-lessly. Then we gave her a final push that sent her racing down the slopes. We watched as she flew out over the rock crags and into the foamy water. By the time we'd gathered our towels and turned to go, Olivia was just a speck on the horizon. Neither of us noticed how quickly the tide was going out.

Most people think that tides are caused by the moon alone, but that is not the case. Once a month, the sun and the moon are both on the same side of the globe. Then the Atlantic kowtows to their conglomerate gravity. It's the earth playing tug-of-war with the sky.

On new-moon nights, the sky is winning. The spring tide swells exceptionally high. The spring tide has teeth. It can pull a boat much farther than your average quarter-moon neap tide. When they finally found Olivia's crab sled, it was halfway to Cuba, and empty.

"What do you see, bro?"

"Oh, not much." I cough. I peer back under the surface of the water. There's an aurora borealis exploding inches from my submerged face. "Probably just plankton."

When I come up to clear the goggles, I can barely see Wallow. He is silhouetted against the lone orange lamp, watching me from the pier. Water seeps out of my nose, my ears. It weeps down the corners of the lenses. I push the goggles up and rub my eyes with my fists, which just makes things worse. I kick to stay afloat, the snorkel digging into my cheek, and wave at my brother. Wallow doesn't wave back.

I don't want to tell Wallow, but I have no idea what I just saw, although I'm sure there must be some ugly explanation for it. I tell myself that it was just cyanobacteria, or lustrous pollutants from the Bimini glue factory. Either way, I don't want to double-check.

I shiver in the water, letting the salt dry on my shoulders, listening to the echo of my breath in the snorkel. I fantasize about towels. But Wallow is still watching me, his face a blank oval. I tug at the goggles and stick my head under for a second look.

Immediately, I bite down on the mouthpiece of the snorkel to stop myself from screaming. The goggles: they work. And every inch of the ocean is haunted. There are ghost fish swimming all around me. My hands pass right through their flat bodies. Phantom crabs shake their phantom claws at me from behind a sunken anchor. Octopuses cartwheel by, leaving an effulgent red trail. A school of minnows swims right through my belly button. Dead, I think. They are all dead.

"Um, Wallow?" I gasp, spitting out the snorkel. "I don't think I can do this."

"Sure you can." Squat, boulder-shouldered, Wallow is standing over the ladder, guarding it like a gargoyle. There's nowhere for me to go but back under the water.

Getting used to aquatic ghosts is like adjusting to the temperature of the ocean. After the initial shock gives way, your body numbs. It takes a few more close encounters with the lambent fish before my pulse quiets down. Once I realize that the ghost fish can't hurt me, I relax into something I'd call delight if I weren't supposed to be feeling breathless and bereaved.

I spend the next two hours pretending to look for Olivia. I shadow the spirit manatees, their backs scored with keloid stars from motorboat propellers. I somersault through stingrays. Bonefish flicker around me like mute banshees. I figure out how to braid the furry blue light of dead coral reef through my fingertips, and very nearly giggle. I've started to enjoy myself, and I've nearly succeeded in exorcising Olivia from my thoughts, when a bunch of ghost shrimp materialize in front of my goggles, like a photo rinsed in a developing tray. The shrimp twist into a glowing alphabet, some curling, some flattening, touching tails to antennae in smoky contortions.

Then they loop together to form words, as if drawn by some invisible hand:

G-L-O-W-W-O-R-M G-R-O-T-T-O.

We thought the Glowworm Grotto was just more of Olivia's make-believe. Olivia was a cartographer of imaginary places. She'd crayon elaborate maps of invisible castles and sunken cities. When the Glowworm Grotto is part of a portfolio that includes Mount Waffle Cone, it's hard to take it seriously.

I loved Olivia. But that doesn't mean I didn't recognize that she was one weird little kid. She used to suffer these intense bouts of homesickness in her own bedroom. When she was very small, she would wake up tearing at her bedspread and shrieking, "I wanna go home! I wanna go home!" Which was distressing to all of us, of course, because she was home.

That said, I wouldn't be surprised to learn that Olivia was an adoptee from some other planet. She used to change into Wallow's rubbery yellow flippers on the bus, then waddle around the school halls like some disoriented mallard. She played "house" by getting the broom and sweeping the neon corpses of dead jellyfish off the beach. Her eyes were a stripey cerulean, inhumanly bright. Dad used to tell Olivia that a merman artisan had made them, out of bits of sea glass from Atlantis.

Wallow saved all of her drawings. The one labeled "Glowerm Groto" is a sketch of a dusky red cave, with a little stick-Olivia swimming into the entrance. Another drawing shows the roof of the cave. It looks like a swirly firmament of stars, dalmatianed with yellow dots.

"That's what you see when you're floating on your back," Olivia told us, rubbing the gray crayon down to its nub. "The Glowworm Grotto looks just like the night sky."

"That's nice," we said, exchanging glances. Neither Wallow nor I knew of any caves along the island shore. I figured it must be another Olivia utopia, a no-place. Wallow thought it was Olivia's oddball interpretation of Gannon's Boat Graveyard.

"Maybe that rusty boat hangar looked like the entrance to a cave to her," he'd said. Maybe. If you were eight, and nearsighted, and nostalgic for places that you'd never been.

But if the Glowworm Grotto actually exists, that changes everything. Olivia's ghost could be there now, twitching her nose with rabbity indignation—"But I left you a map!" Wondering what took us so long to find her.

When I surface, the stars have vanished. The clouds are turning red around their edges. I can hear Wallow snoring on the pier. I pull my naked body up and flop onto the warm planks, feeling salt-shucked and newborn. When I spit the snorkel out of my mouth, the unfiltered air tastes acrid and foreign. The Glowworm Grotto. I wish I didn't have to tell Wallow. I wish we'd never found the stupid goggles. There are certain things that I don't want to see.

When we get back to Granana's, her cottage is shuttered and dark. Fat raindrops, the icicles of the tropics, hang from the eaves. We can hear her watching *Evangelical Bingo* in the next room.

"Revelation 20:13!" she hoots. "Bingo!"

Our breakfast is on the table: banana pancakes, with a side of banana pudding. The kitchen is sticky with brown peels and syrup. Granana no longer has any teeth left in her head. For the past two decades, she has subsisted almost entirely on bananas, banana-based dishes, and other foods that you can gum. This means that her farts smell funny, and her calf muscles frequently give out. It means that Wallow and I eat out a lot during the summer.

Wallow finds Olivia's old drawings of the Glowworm Grotto. We spread them out on the table, next to a Crab Shack menu with a cartoon map of the island. Wallow is busy highlighting the jagged shoreline, circling places that might harbor a cave, when Granana shuffles into the kitchen.

"What's all this?"

She peers over my shoulder. "Christ," she says. "Still mooning over that old business?"

Granana doesn't understand what the big deal is. She didn't cry at Olivia's funeral, and I doubt she even remembers Olivia's name. Granana lost, like, ninety-two million kids in childbirth. All of her brothers died in the war. She survived the Depression by stealing radish bulbs from her neighbors' garden, and fishing the elms for pigeons. Dad likes to remind us of this in a grave voice, as if it explained her jaundiced pitilessness: "Boys. Your grandmother ate pigeons."

"Wasn't much for drawing, was she?" Granana says. She taps at stick-Olivia. "Wasn't much for swimming, either."

Wallow visibly stiffens. For a second, I'm worried that he's going to slug Granana in her wattled neck. Then she raises her drawn-on eyebrows. "Would you look at that— the nudey cave. Your grandfather used to take me skinny-dipping there."

Wallow and I do an autonomic, full-body shudder. I get a sudden mental image of two shelled walnuts floating in a glass.

"You mean you recognize this place, Granana?"

"No thanks to this chicken scratch!" She points to an orange dot in the corner of the picture, so small that I hadn't even noticed it. "But look where she drew the sunset. Use your noggins. Must be one of them coves on the western side of the island. I don't remember exactly where."

"What about the stars on the roof?"

Granana snorts. "Worm shit!"

"Huh?"

"Worm shit," she repeats. "You never heard of glow-worms, Mr. Straight-A Science Guy? Their shit glows in the dark. All them coves are covered with it."

We never recovered Olivia's body. Two days after she went missing, Tropical Storm Vita brought wind and chaos and interrupted broadcasts, and the search was called off. Too dangerous, the Coast Guard lieutenant said. He was a fat, earnest man, with tiny black eyes set like watermelon seeds in his pink face.

"When wind opposes sea," he said in a portentous singsong, "the waves build fast."

"Thank you, Billy Shakespeare," my father growled under his breath. For some reason, this hit Dad the hardest—harder than Olivia's death itself, I think. The fact that we had nothing to bury.

It's possible that Olivia washed up on a bone-white

Cojimar beach, or got tangled in some Caribbean fisherman's net. It's probable that her lungs filled up with buckets of tarry black water and she sank. But I don't like to think about that. It's easier to imagine her turning into an angelfish and swimming away, or being bodily assumed into the clouds.

Most likely, Dad says, a freak wave knocked her overboard. Then the current yanked the sled away faster than she could swim. In my night terrors, I watch the sea turn into a great, gloved hand that rises out of the ocean to snatch her. I told Wallow this once, hoping to stir up some fraternal empathy. Instead, Wallow sneered at me.

"Are you serious? That's what you have nightmares about, bro? Some lame-ass Mickey Mouse glove that comes out of the sea?" His lip curled up, but there was envy in his voice, too. "I just see my own hands, you know? Pushing her down that hill."

The following evening, Wallow and I head over to Herb's Crab Sledding Rentals. Herb smokes on his porch in his yellowed boxers and a threadbare Santa hat, rain or shine. Back when we were regular sledders, Wallow always used to razz Herb about his getup.

"Ho-ho-ho," Herb says reflexively. "Merry Christmas. Sleigh bells ring, are ya listening." He gives a halfhearted shake to a sock full of quarters. "Hang on, nauticats. Can't sled without informed consent."

Thanks to the Olivia Bill, new island legislation requires all island children to take a fourteen-hour Sea Safety! course before they can sled. They have to wear helmets and life preservers, and sign multiple waivers. Herb is dangling the permission form in front of our faces. Wallow accepts it with a genial "Thanks, Herb!" Then he crushes it in his good fist.

"Now wait a sec . . ." Herb scratches his ear. "I, ah, I didn't recognize you boys. I'm sorry, but you know I can't rent to you. Anyhow, it'll be dark soon, and neither one of you is certified."

Wallow walks over to one of the sleds and, unhelmeted, unjacketed, shoves it into the water. The half shell bobs there, one of the sturdier two-seaters, a boiled-red color. He picks up a pair of oars so that we can row against the riptides. He glares at Herb.

"We are going to take the sled out tonight, and tomorrow night, and every night until our parents get back. We are going to keep taking it out until we find Olivia." He pauses. "And we are going to pay you three hundred and seventy-six dollars in cash." Coincidentally, this is the exact dollar amount of Granana's Social Security check.

Herb doesn't say a word. He takes the wad of cash, runs a moistened finger through it, and stuffs it under his Santa hat. He waits until we are both in the sled before he opens his mouth.

"Boys," he says. "You have that crab sled back here before dawn. Otherwise, I'm calling the Coast Guard."

Every night, we go a little farther. Out here, you can see dozens of shooting stars, whole galactic herds of them, winking out into cheery oblivion. They make me think of lemmings, flinging themselves over an astral cliff.

We are working our way around the island, with Gannon's Boat Graveyard as our ground zero. I swim parallel to the beach, and Wallow follows along in the crab sled, marking up the shoreline that we've covered on our map. "X" marks all the places where Olivia is not. It's slow going. I'm not a strong swimmer, and I have to paddle back to Wallow every fifteen minutes.

"And just what are we going to do when we find her?" I want to know.

It's the third night of our search. We are halfway around the island, on the sandbar near the twinkling lights of the Bowl-a-Bed Hotel. Wallow's face is momentarily illuminated by the cycloptic gaze of the lighthouse. It arcs out over the water, a thin scythe of light that serves only to make the rest of the ocean look scarier.

"What exactly are we going to do with her, Wallow?"

This question has been weighing on my mind more and more heavily of late. Because let's just say, for argument's sake, that there is a Glowworm Grotto, and that Olivia's ghost haunts it. Then what? Do we genie-in-a-bottle her? Keep her company on weekends? I envision eternal Saturday nights spent treading cold water in a cave, crooning lullabies to the husk of Olivia, and shudder.

"What do you mean?" Wallow says, frowning. "We'll rescue her. We'll preserve her, uh, you know, her memory."

"And how exactly do you propose we do that?"

"I don't know, bro!" Wallow furrows his brow, flustered. You can tell he hasn't thought much beyond finding Olivia. "We'll . . . we'll put her in an aquarium."

"An aquarium?" Now it's my turn to be derisive. "And then what? Are you going to get her a kiddie pool?"

It seems to me that nobody's asking the hard questions here. For example, what if ghost-Olivia doesn't have eyes anymore? Or a nose? What if an eel has taken up residence inside her skull, and every time it lights up it sends this unholy electricity radiating through her sockets?

Wallow fixes me with a baleful stare. "Are you pussying out, bro? She's your sister, for Christ's sake. You telling me you're afraid of your own kid sister? Don't worry about what we're going to do with her, bro. We have to find her first."

I say nothing. But I keep thinking: It's been two years. What if all the Olivia-ness has already seeped out of her and evaporated into the violet welter of clouds? Evaporated, and rained down, and evaporated, and rained down. Olivia slicking over all the rivers and trees and dirty cities in the world. So that now there is only silt, and our stupid, salt-diluted longing. And nothing left of our sister to find.

On the fourth night of our search, I see a churning clump of ghost children. They are drifting straight for me, all kelped together, an eyeless panic of legs and feet and hair. I kick for the surface, heart hammering.

"Wallow!" I scream, hurling myself at the crab sled. "I just saw—I just—I'm not doing this anymore, bro, I am not. You can go stick your face in dead kids for a change. Let Olivia come find us."

"Calm it down." Wallow pokes at the ocean with his oar. "It's only trash." He fishes out a nasty mass of diapers and chicken gristle and whiskery red seaweed, all threaded around the plastic rings of a six-pack. "See?"

I sit huddled in the corner of the sled, staring dully at the blank surface of the water. I know what I saw.

. . .

The goggles are starting to feel less like a superpower and more like a divine punishment, one of those particularly inventive cruelties that you read about in Greek mythology. Every now and then, I think about how much simpler and more pleasant things would be if the goggles conferred a different kind of vision. Like if I could read messages written in squid ink, or laser through the Brazilian girls' tankinis. But then Wallow interrupts these thoughts by dunking me under the water. Repeatedly.

"Keep looking," he snarls, water dripping off his face.

On the fifth night of our search, I see a plesiosaur. It is a megawatt behemoth, bronze and blue-white, streaking across the sea floor like a torpid comet. Watching it, I get this primordial déjà vu, like I'm watching a dream return to my body. It wings towards me with a slow, avian grace. Its long neck is arced in an S-shaped curve; its lizard body is the size of Granana's carport. Each of its ghost flippers pinwheels colored light. I try to swim out of its path, but the thing's too big to avoid. That Leviathan fin, it shivers right through me. It's a light in my belly, cold and familiar. And I flash back to a snippet from school, a line from a poem or a science book, I can't remember which:

There are certain prehistoric things that swim beyond extinction.

I wake up from one of those naps that leach the strength from your bones to a lightning storm. I must have fallen asleep in the crab sled. Otherworldly light goes roiling through an eerie blue froth of clouds.

Wallow is standing at the prow of the sled. Each flash of lightning limns his bared teeth, the hollows of his eyes. It's as if somebody up there were taking an X-ray of grief, again and again.

"I just want to tell her that I'm sorry," Wallow says softly. He doesn't know that I'm awake. He's talking to himself, or maybe to the ocean. There's not a trace of fear in his voice. And it's clear then that Wallow is a better brother than I could ever hope to be.

We have rowed almost all the way around the island. In a quarter of an hour, we'll be back at Gannon's Boat Grave-yard. Thank merciful Christ. Our parents are coming back tomorrow, and I can go back to playing video games and feeling dry and blameless.

Then the lighthouse beacon sweeps out again. It bounces off an outcropping of rocks that we didn't notice on our first expedition. White sequins of light pop along the water.

"Did you see that? That's it!" Wallow says excitedly. "That's gotta be it!"

"Oh. Excellent."

We paddle the rest of the way out in silence. I row the crab sled like a condemned man. The current keeps pushing us back, but we make a quiet kind of progress. I keep praying that the crags will turn out to be low, heaped clouds, or else a seamless mass of stone. Instead, you can tell that they are pocked with dozens of holes. For a second, I'm relieved— nobody, not even string-beany Olivia, could swim into such narrow openings. Wallow's eyes dart around wildly.

"There has to be an entrance," he mutters. "Look!"

Sure enough, there is a muted glow coming from the far end of a salt-eaten overhang, like light from under a door.

"No way can I fit through there," I gasp, knowing immediately that I can. And that the crab sled can't, of course. Which means I'll be going in to meet her alone.

What if the light, I am thinking, is Olivia?

"It's just worms, bro," Wallow says, as if reading my mind. But there's this inscrutable sadness on his face. His muddy eyes swallow up the light and give nothing back.

I look over my shoulder. We're less than half a mile out from shore, could skip a stone to the mangrove islets; and yet the land draws back like a fat swimmer's chimera, impossibly far away.

"Ready?" He grabs at the scruff of my neck and pushes me towards the water. "Set?"

"No!" Staring at the unlit spaces in the crags, I am choked with horror. I fumble the goggles off my face. "Do your own detective work!" I dangle the goggles over the edge of the sled. "I quit."

Wallow lunges forward and pins me against the side of the boat. He tries to spatula me overboard with his one good arm, but I limbo under his cast.

"Don't do it, Timothy," he cautions, but it is too late.

"This is what I think of your diabolical goggles!" I howl. I hoist the goggles over my head and, with all the force in my puny arms, hurl them to the floor of the crab sled.

This proves to be pretty anticlimactic. Naturally, the goggles remain intact. There's not even a hairline fracture. Stupid scratchproof lenses.

The worst part is that Wallow just watches me impassively, his cast held aloft in the air, as if he were patiently waiting to ask the universe a question. He nudges the goggles towards me with his foot.

"You finished?"

"Wally!" I blubber, a last-ditch plea. "This is crazy. What if something happens to me in there and you can't come in after me? Let's go back."

"What?" Wallow barks, disgusted. "And leave Olivia here for dead? Is that what you want?"

"Bingo!" That is exactly what I want. Maybe Granana is slightly off target when it comes to the Food Pyramid, but she has the right idea about death. I want my parents to stop sailing around taking pictures of Sudanese leper colonies. I want Wallow to row back to shore and sleep through the night. I want everybody in the goddamn family to leave Olivia here for dead.

But there's my brother. Struggling with his own repugnance, like an entomologist who has just discovered a loathsome new species of beetle.

"What did you say?"

"I said I'll go," I mumble, not meeting his eyes. I position myself on the edge of the boat. "I'll go."

So that's what it comes down to, then. I'd rather drown in Olivia's ghost than have him look at me that way.

To enter the grotto, you have to slide in on your back, like a letter through a mail slot. Something scrapes my coccyx bone on the way in. There's a polar chill in the water tonight. No outside light can wiggle its way inside.

But, sure enough, phosphorescent dots spangle the domed roof of the grotto. It's like a radiant checkerboard of shit. You can't impose any mental pictures on it—it's too uniform. It defies the mind's desire to constellate randomness. The Glowworm Grotto is nothing like the night sky. The stars here are all equally bright and evenly spaced, like a better-ordered cosmos.

"Olivia?"

The grotto smells like salt and blood and bat shit. Shadows web the walls. I try and fail to touch the bottom.

"Oliviaaa?"

Her name echoes around the cave. After a while, there is only rippled water again, and the gonged absence of sound. Ten more minutes, I think. I could splash around here for ten more minutes and be done with this. I could take off the goggles, even. I could leave without ever looking below the surface of the water, and Wallow would never know.

"Oli—"

I take a deep breath, and dive.

Below me, tiny fish are rising out of golden cylinders of coral. It looks like an undersea calliope, piping a song that you can see instead of hear. One of the fish swims right up and taps against my scratchproof lenses. It's just a regular blue fish, solid and alive. It taps and taps, oblivious of the thick glass. My eyes cross, trying to keep it in focus.

The fish swims off to the beat of some subaqueous music. Everything down here is dancing—the worms' green light and the undulant walls and the leopard-spotted polyps. Everything. And following this fish is like trying to work backwards from the dance to the song. I can't hear it, though; I can't remember a single note of it. It fills me with a hitching sort of sadness.

I trail the fish at an embarrassed distance, feeling warm-blooded and ridiculous in my rubbery flippers, marooned in this clumsy body. Like I'm an impostor, an imperfect monster.

I look for my sister, but it's hopeless. The goggles are all fogged up. Every fish burns lantern-bright, and I can't tell the living from the dead. It's all just blurry light, light smeared like some celestial fingerprint all over the rocks and the reef and the sunken garbage. Olivia could be everywhere.

Z.Z.'s Sleep-Away Camp
for Disordered Dreamers

Emma and I are curled together in the basket of the Thomas Edison Insomnia Balloon, our breath coming in soft quick bursts. I am stroking Emma's cheek. I am spooning amber gobs of soporific dough into Emma's open mouth, cadged from Zorba's medicinal larder in anticipation of just such an occasion. (Sort of a cheat, I know, but it's my first time doing this.) I am trying, desperately, to disguise the fact that this is the closest I've ever been to a girl's face.

I was expecting some ineffable girl smell, dewy and secret, an *eau*. But Emma smells like dinner. Barbecue sauce, the buttery whiff of potato foil. Because it's Emma, it's still sort of hot.

"Just put your head here," I say, in a tone that implies I've nuzzled dozens of sleep-disordered ladies. I try to ease Emma's curly head into the crook of my arm and end up elbowing her in the nose.

"Are you ready?"

"Ready."

What can you do but take a girl at her word? But I hope she really is ready. Being unconscious with somebody, that's a big deal.

I take a deep breath, pull on the rip cord, and plunge the clearing into darkness.

The Insomnia Balloon is in a clearing at the shallow end of the woods. You may have been there; it was public island property until Zorba started the camp a few years back.

The Insomnia Balloon isn't an airship of the literal, sky-flying variety. Zorba says it's for mental flights. The "balloon" part is actually an enormous lightbulb, suspended over a wicker basket by copper wires. It's okay to be awake here, even after Lights Out. Sometimes, Zorba tells us, as a precursor to sleep, you need to let your thoughts dry out beneath the electric light. Eventually dream helium begins to fill your lungs. When you're ready to soar inward, you pull the rip cord and turn the giant lightbulb off.

"How many sleep-disordered campers does it take to change a lightbulb?" Zorba likes to joke, and the punch line is, all of us. Every six months a three-hundred-pound replacement bulb arrives from Norway. The Insomnia Balloon buzzes around the clock, its filaments glowing in a giant glass vacuum bulb. It turns the surrounding forest into an undulant sea of pines. They seem to grow larger when we turn the balloon off, their blue shadows billowing out beneath the low stars. A froth of gully grass pokes through the holes in the wire basket. Emma's blue eye is half open, a quarter of an inch from mine. She is staring at an ant crawling along one moon-limned strand of grass. She won't look at me.

"Elijah, I can't."

"Do you not trust me? If it's that you don't trust me, just say so."

"That's not it! I just . . ." She bites her lip. "I shouldn't have to explain it, you know, I just can't. . . ."

"Well, not with *that* attitude, you can't." My heartbeat thumps in my chest. Not exactly the pace I want to set if I'm going to deliver the eight hours of sleep I've been promising her. After all that big talk, I'm afraid my sleep latency period is going to be eye-blink brief. Slow down, and lengthen, I coach myself, trying to match my breath to hers. Slow down—

"Look, Emma, I've got you. I've got you, okay? Just relax—" And lengthen.

This night is the culmination of weeks of practice. Oglivy has been tutoring me in smooth rock-a-bye technique. I hum a lullaby into her ear, one that Ogli says is guaranteed to make the ladies go limp. She throws her head back in an exaggerated, feline yawn, which I take to be a good sign. I hum louder.

"Are you sleeping?"

"Oh!" she breathes. "Yes!" She makes some theatrical breathing noises that I guess must be Emma's approximations of what a deeply sleeping girl would sound like, but actually make her sound like her trachea is obstructed by a golf ball. I try humming a little more softly.

And then, just when she's started mumbling in that softly demented voice that precedes sleep, Oglivy comes crashing out of the woods, staggering into trees and generally destroying the ambience. Emma bolts upright. "Who's there?" She wriggles away from me and tugs the balloon back on. The light startles her sleep-blurred face back into sociable lines. Damn. All my progress, erased.

"Oh, crap, sorry, guys." Ogli whistles. "I didn't, uh, mean to wake you. . . ." He gives me a big, shit-eating grin.

"Ogli!" Emma looks relieved to see him. She claps a hand over her mouth, but not before she lets out a coy yawn in Ogli's direction. I wish she'd save that stuff for me.

"Annie's giving her Inspiration Assembly." He coughs, averting his gaze with a showy gallantry while Emma rubs her eyelids back to their sentient position. "I thought we could all walk over together. Not that I care, but we're gonna be late, Elijah."

"We'll be there in a second—" But Emma's already clambering out of the wicker basket, tilting the hot yellow bulb. Shadows go spidering out across the clearing.

"Thanks, Oglivy." She smiles. Her curly hair has a rosy glow in the balloon's light. She looks all mussed up and livid and adorably mortal, these violet half-moons under her eyes. "You're right, we'd better get there on time. I heard that last year one of the Incubi—"

"Incubuses," we correct.

"Incubi"—she frowns—"was late, and Zorba put her on laundry duty for a week."

We all shudder. Laundry duty means you have to wash the acrid bed linens for Cabin 5, the Incontinents.

We walk towards the main cabin in silence. It's no easy hike. Sweat and mosquitoes and a purple ambush of nettles. Our bare toes sink into the oxblood clumps of mud.

"Sorry, dude," Ogli says under his breath. "I thought you were ballooning solo. I didn't mean to wake you. . . ."

" 'S okay," I sigh. "She was faking, anyways."

When the trail opens onto the lake, I see that Oglivy's timing was off, as usual. No way are we late. A few Somnambulists are still turning dreamy circles in the poppy pasture, tangling their sleep leashes in the furrows.

"Wait up, Ogli," I wheeze. "We can't *all* be late, retard."

We're all late. The camp director's wife, Annie, is wrapping up her annual talk.

". . . And now, I'm proud to say, my dream contagion has gone into remission, and I've been dreaming my own dreams for nearly three years."

Scattered applause. Somebody bites into an apple. Oglivy and I exchange a bored glance. We have been coming to Z.Z.'s for so long that we're practically de facto junior counselors. We know Annie's spiel verbatim:

"Sleep is the heat that melts time, children. It's a trick that you will practice here. But! We don't expect to cure you of your sleep disorders in these few short weeks."

Oglivy mouths along with Annie, fluttering his eyelids. He has Emma and me laughing with a hot-faced, helpless surrender that has nothing to do with the joke itself. After the white noise of school-year loneliness, I am so happy to be sitting with Ogli and Emma on this pulpy cedar floor again, making the same old jokes.

"That's not why your parents send you here," Annie continues, glaring in our direction. "We just want to provide you with a safe place to lie awake together. And maybe even," she beams at the crowd, "to dream."

"And," I elbow Ogli, "to scream." A veteran Narco sitting near us snickers. They never warn the new fish about all the midnight noises.

At Z.Z.'s, our nights echo with weeping and wailing and gnashing of teeth. Popularity is determined according to an unspoken algorithm that averages the length and volume of your sleep-yodeled terror. Even at a place like Zorba's, there's still a clearly delineated social hierarchy:

Cabin 2: Sleep Apneics
Cabin 3: Somnambulists
Cabin 6: Somniloquists
Cabin 8: Headbangers
Cabin 11: Night Eaters
Cabin 7: Gnashers
Cabin 13: Night Terrors
Cabin 9: Insomniacs
Cabin 1: Narcoleptics
Cabin 10: Incubuses
Cabin 5: Incontinents

And then there's us. Cabin 4: Miscellaneous. The ones whose parents checked the box marked "Other." Our illnesses do not match any diagnostic criteria. That means that we're considered anomalies by Gnasher dudes who have ground their pearly whites down to nubbins, by Incubus girls who think that demon jockeys are riding them in their sleep.

Oglivy is my Other brother, the only other person I have ever met who shares my same disorder. We've been bunk mates for the past three years. Annie calls us her twin boys with this syrupy, slightly unnerving tenderness. She doesn't mean that we look alike. Oglivy is basketball-tall, with these small, pistachio-colored eyes and a pleasantly dopey face. I'm small and dark and inexpertly put together, all knees and elbows and face bones. My mom says I'm destined to be the sort of man who uses big words but pronounces them incorrectly. It's not even like we have that much in common in our waking lives, although we get a lot of mileage out of our few points of intersection—our moonball fanaticism, our mutual abhorrence of grandmothers and cats, our worshipful respect for the hobo. But we are sleep twins, phobically linked by our identical dreams. He is the first and only person I have ever met who is also a prophet of the past.

We would have been friends regardless, even if we weren't the only two prophets in the whole camp. With all due respect to our Other brothers and sisters, Cabin 4 is creepy as hell.

There's Espalda and Espina, the reverend's adopted daughters. They are hunchback twins who giggle at everything and rub their humps together in their sleep.

There's Felipe, a parasomniac with a co-incidence of spirit possession. He caught his ghost after stealing a guanabana from a roadside tree, unaware that its roots had wound around a mass grave of Moncada revolutionaries. He's been possessed by Francisco Pais ever since. This causes him to sleep-detonate imaginary grenades and sleep-yell *"Viva la Revolución!"* while sleep-pumping his fist in the air. He is a deceptively apolitical boy by day.

This year, we've got a New Kid, this Eastern European lycanthrope. He is redolent of tubers and Old World damp. New Kid's face is a pituitary horror, a patchwork of runny sores and sebaceous dips. Ginger fur sprouts from weird places, his chin, his ears. You intuit some horror story—homeschooled, his mother's in a coven, he eats rancid cabbage out of a trough, that sort of thing. His sleep cycles with the moon.

Emma used to be a textbook Somnambulist. She says after her mother died they would find her walking up and down the empty gutters at the Bowl-a-Bed Hotel, her eyes wide open. But her ailment must have mutated into some Other form, because she recently got the wire restraints taken off her bed. It was right around the time when I started noticing that Emma was, in addition to being short and a serviceable moonball shortstop, a girl. She has this amazing tracery of veins around her eyes, like a leaf pressed between the pages of a book. She's the only unknown ailment in the camp. I don't know how exactly I got it into my head that I could save her, or that we could save each other. But now I have this secret fantasy where we sleep together and dream about . . . whatever ordinary kids dream about. And then we wake up together in the morning, in the same bed that we started out in, rested and cured.

And then there's Ogli. I'll never forget the night Ogli and I figured out we had the same disorder. It was the first week of camp, a time when everyone was still skittish and uncertain and we resisted sleep for as long as possible, not wanting to give ourselves away too soon. I hid my ration of soporific dough in a sock under my pillow. Oglivy was sleeping in the bunk facing mine, and I watched him do the same thing. We lay sideways in the dark, eyeing each other like desperadoes in a predawn stalemate. Eventually, we both must have succumbed, because at precisely 4:47, we woke up screaming, staring straight at each other. Oglivy's hair was sticking straight up, his white eyes goggling out in the dark, the mirror image of my terror. Our screams gave way into giggles.

"What did you dream?" he wheezed.

"I dreamed," I gasped, still laughing, "that there was this silver rocket, burning and burning."

He stopped laughing abruptly. "Me too."

I appreciate Ogli's pragmatism about our dreams. He refuses to try to interpret them with me. Like the time last summer when we predicted the St. Louis Zoo Cataclysm of '49: "Who cares what it *means*, bro!" he sighs. "I'm too busy trying to outrun the lions so they don't eat my shins."

"Why don't we get the joyful portents," I want to know, "doves and olives, the Emancipation Proclamation, former paralytics winning Olympic gold? Why?"

Ogli just shrugs. "Look on the bright side, Elijah. At least we don't dream the future."

Oglivy and I have remarkably similar medical histories. For years, we were misdiagnosed as conventional Night Terrors. It's hard to explain your symptoms to adults:

"Mom, I dreamed that fire was falling from outer space. And the fire was headed straight for these long-necked monsters. And oh, Mom, then the whole world was cratered and dark, and there were only these stooped, hairy creatures stealing eggs, and no more monsters. We have to save them!"

"Mom, I dreamed that lava came bubbling out of the ground like blood from a cut. And the townspeople below were just picking tomatoes and singing oblivious Italian folk songs, Mom. We have to warn them!"

"Mom, I dreamed that an 804-foot hydrogen dirigible full of Germans was about to burst into flames. We have to—"

It's just a dream, son, my mother would snap, turning on the scolding overhead light. Just a bad dream. We don't have to do anything. Go back to sleep.

Then I got to school and started to piece things together. I remember flipping through *Our Storied Past!*, eyes agog. The table of contents was like an index to my dreams. Mount Vesuvius, the Bubonic Plague, Tropical Storm Vita—I was a prophet. Annie calls them my postmonitions. Sometimes I think Ogli and I must be like imperfect antennae, the distress signals traveling like light from dead stars.

I guess it wouldn't be so bad, if the dreams didn't have the fated, crimson-tinged horror of prophecy. Or if I could forget them before waking. It's that dread, half-second lapse in the morning that gets me, when time's still just a jumble of tenses at the foot of the bed. I start awake with the certainty that I can actually do something to prevent disaster. *Strengthen the scaffolding, batten down the hatches, don't drink the water, quarantine the sallow man, stay docked in the harbor, wear nonflammable apparel on the subway, avoid the Imperial City today, steer clear of glaciers!* Between the dying echo of a dream explosion and my conscious brain reassuring me, like an alarm bell ringing in a pile of rubble. *Too late: too late.*

Don't get me wrong, there are some perks. I get to go to sleep disorder camp, after all. And I've been runner-up in the history bee for four consecutive years.

It turns out that our tardiness is not a problem, because Zorba himself has yet to show. Annie keeps glancing from her watch to the door. We are just picking teams for the inaugural game of moonball when Zorba bursts into the cabin. He is sweating profusely. His face bulges like an eggplant, shiny and distended.

"*Here* he is," Annie sighs. "Campers, I'd like to present you with our founder and director, my husband, Zorba Zoulekevis. . . ."

"Heimdall is missing!" he thunders in his Mount Olympus baritone. A ripple goes through the crowd. Heimdall is a woolly Houdini, escaping his pen at least once a day. But the campgrounds are small, and walled in by trees. If Heimdall's gone missing, that means he's wandered into the marshy woods, towards the sinkhole.

All the color drains out of Annie's face. "Oh no. Oh, Zorba. What if the dogs are back?" Her voice drops to a whisper. "We musn't panic the children."

The microphone is still on. The cabin echoes with the whine of feedback. Dozens of eyes dart around, searching for unseen dogs.

"Dorry worry," I whisper to one of the new campers. "There aren't any dogs around here. Not that we can see, anyways. Annie's a little, you know . . ." Ogli points at his temple and twirls his index finger like an unraveling kite string so as to indicate *nuts*. Ogli and I know that Annie's just flashing back to her dream contagion again. Annie, prior to her recovery, caught a virulent strand of nightmare from somebody. For years, she dreamed of black dogs, wild dogs, a shadow pack running behind the green screen of trees and killing her lambs. In a separate assembly, Zorba warns us to avoid all mention of our canine pets in Annie's presence.

Zorba eases the microphone out of her hands. "We must find the missing sheep!" he intones. His voice booms through the mess hall with a messianic thunder. Annie passes out flashlights, and we all file out of the main cabin. We split off in pairs to comb the shallow end of the woods. I grab Emma's wrist and drag her towards the shoreline. It's a clear night, and the lake glints mirror-bright in the darkness. I steer her towards our reflection in the water. If I can just get her to *see* how right we look together, I think, see it the way I do, rising out of the lake with the eidetic, rippled force of dreams.

"Emma . . ."

A high, piercing shriek erupts from behind the trees. Emma and I exchange glances. Zorba has found the sheep.

We keep a fuzzy flock of sheep, mostly as a testament to Zorba's melancholy sense of humor. They huddle together in a pen down by the lake, next to the red turkey coop where Zorba fattens the Tryptophan Flock. There are only three sheep, so you can't exactly induce sleep by counting them: Heimdall, Mouflon, and Merino. Even so, they still follow herd logic. Heimdall is our outlier. He was the brazen ram, pushing past the known limits of his grazing world. Mouflon was the bellwether sheep. If Mouflon decided it was safe to follow, then and only then would the rest of the herd, Merino and the occasional disoriented turkey, come trotting over.

We all run to the source of the screaming. And there's poor Heimdall, splayed out like a murdered cloud. He's lying facedown in a puddle of tadpoles and woodsy murk. "His throat is slit!" someone shrieks, but I don't even register this. Somehow, I just keep staring at Heimdall's pink ears. They've flopped inside out, and I have to resist a powerful urge to flop them right side in. They look sad and veiny and indecent. Zorba kneels in the dirt and holds Heimdall's head in his lap, sobbing with an island abandon, a salt-buoyed, voluptuous grief that no Mainland man would permit himself. Staring at Heimdall's furry, triangular face, I feel a pulsing flood of adrenaline. I have never felt more awake than I do right now. Finally, "before" and "after" in their proper order.

"Oglivy," I whisper excitedly. "Something is killing the sheep. Do you know what this means?"

"Gee-ros for lunch tomorrow?"

I point back towards the pen. "It means we have to sneak out and stand watch tonight."

Oglivy frowns. "Couldn't we commemorate the dead sheep my way? With pita, and Annie's moussaka?"

"Ogli, this is serious! Don't you see how great this is? This isn't like the dreams—this is a real tragedy! This is happening right now, in real time. And we can stop it."

I break off abruptly. Zorba comes lumbering out of the crowd, sweeping Annie into an ursine embrace. He buries his curly head into her shoulder. "Oh, Annie, our only ram!" The wiry hairs on his knuckles are flecked with blood.

"My children," he bellows, gathering himself up to his full height of five feet four inches. "Be not afraid. We will sleep through this!" But his roar is all volume and no conviction, the tinderless fire of a faithless preacher. "To your cabins! Lights out!"

"The poor children," we hear Annie sigh, "must be lidless with terror!"

Heimdall's death is the best thing that's ever happened to us here at Z.Z.'s. All night, the air is charged with a giddy, carnival air of terror. The Insomniacs have a reason for their involuntary vigil. The Night Terrors feel justified in their fear. And we Others have another mystery to focus on besides our own disorders. Now that there's an outside threat to unify us, the regular social hierarchy has been suspended. Apneics, Others, and Narcos all gossip merrily on the walk back to our cabins. I'm lucky, because I have Oglivy, so I'm never really alone at night. But you can see how for the other kids, Heimdall's death is a real treat. It's a bridge between our private terrors, this killer skulking around in our woods. Finally, the whole camp has a nightmare in common. It's something to celebrate, like Christmas.

"Who do you think did it, Elijah?" Ogli's ruddy face is hanging upside down in front of me, his tall body arcing over the top bunk.

Lights out was announced over an hour ago. Outside, rain drums down in silvery curtains, pasting the purple ferns against the screen. The walls bulge with it; you can almost hear it humming, the drowned sound of swollen wood. Bullfrogs chorus below our windowsill.

"I dunno. Annie was acting pretty strangely. Did you know she used to be a scryer? She had her spoon out with her tonight. Suspicious. Could be one of the Narcos having a hypnagogic seizure. And then there's—"

"Keep it down over there," the counselor growls from the corner. "Try to sleep. Fake it to make it. Close your eyes and do your lulling exercises." God help him, he would administer a Kentucky sleep remedy if he could, the counselor tells us, and club us over the head. Our jubilant paranoia means that he can't sneak off to refill his flask.

I close my eyes. The cabin is full of comforting sounds, snores and orchestral cicadas, the dromedary rasping of the sisters. But lying in my bunk, listening to the other Others breathe, I get this empty-belly loneliness. It's both too much and not enough, somehow, to be this close to my brothers and sisters in the dark. Espalda and Espina are the luckiest ones. They have a special dispensation to sleep in the same bed. They get to sleep back to back in their matching sailor pajamas, nautical embroidery along the open, lewdly enticing back flaps. I picture their humps sharking together, their vertebrae interlocking in a columnar ladder to their separate brains.

"Are you scared, Emma?" I whisper.

"*I'm* scared!" Espalda says.

"*I'm* scared!" Espina says.

I feel Ogli shift in his bunk, and know he is smirking into his pillow above me. "If you're scared," I continue, more firmly, "you can come sleep in my bed."

"What?" she hisses. "Here? In front of the twins?"

"We don't mind!" says Espalda.

"*I* mind," whispers Espina.

Emma gives me a long, assessing look. Then she fluffs her pillow. She drags her blanket past the bored, whiskey-blurred gaze of the counselor. She crawls into my bed. I annotate the moment with a historian's portentousness. This is it. The event that I've been waiting for all summer.

We spend the next two hours squirming around miserably, trying to get comfortable.

"Elijah, it's just not working," she finally sighs.

"Well, if *somebody* would quit hogging all the covers . . ."

"We just can't sleep together," she says sadly. "Maybe it's your lullaby. . . ."

"Maybe it's *you*," I say, hating and hating myself, "have you ever thought of that? Maybe *you're* what's not working. Maybe *you* can't sleep with other people."

We even lie back to back, fused at the base of our spines, curling out from each other like fetal twins. But it's nothing like I imagined it would be. It's an empty warmth, an only-bodies touching. We listen to the New Kid itching and baying. We watch Felipe flinch beneath invisible grenades. I feel guilty; Ogli has started his midnight divination without me. I shut my eyes, and will myself to sleep.

The following night, I am running towards the sheep pen, flanked by Emma and Oglivy. We take a willfully, gleefully stupid shortcut through the woods. We are Others, I pant to myself, equal to any nocturnal danger. And tonight, we are wide awake. Instead of dreaming about the past while the slaughter continues, we've made a pact to protect the flock.

"Zorba's going to kick us out!"

"Annie's dogs will get us first!"

"You mean the muuuurderer," Oglivy whoops. He mock-stabs us both in the back and then runs past us, vanishing into the marsh.

The forest at night is full of friendly menace. It blurs and ashes all around us, a dark dream of itself. Rain runs down the skinned black hands of the trees, down the white mushrooms that push their tiny faces from the logs. Frogs jump from the branches like spry blemishes. We flinch beneath the leaf-swung shadows, the winged attack of lunatic moths. The forest gives me all sorts of reasons to reach out and hold Emma's hand.

"Blah!" Oglivy yells, pushing Emma and me into a pile of wet leaves. We roll around, a red flail of limbs and hysterical laughter. We are all raccoon-drunk on moonlight and bloodshed and the heady, underblossom smell of the forest. I breathe in the sharp odor of cold stars and skunk, thinking, *This is the happiest that I have ever been.* I wish somebody would murder a sheep every night of my life. It feels like we are all embarking on a nightmare together. *And we will stop it in progress!* I think, yanking Emma and Ogli to their feet and hurtling towards the lake. We will make sure that the rest of the herd escapes Heimdall's fate, we will . . .

Emma lets out a low, strangled cry and stops short. We are too late. The unlatched gate of the pen is swinging in the wind. Ewe's blood glistens on the tiny leaves. She steps aside to reveal the humped form of Merino.

"Oh, Ogli . . ."

This isn't the ashes to ashes of our dreams. This is Merino, our living, bleating lamb, now a heap of meat and sweaters.

"We failed."

When she hears Emma moan, Mouflon comes trotting over from the far end of the pen. She steps blithely over her murdered sister, nosing our palms in search of poppy buns. But Emma is looking past Mouflon, past Merino, to the other side of the fence.

A wraithlike figure is rising out of the mist on the far end of the pen. "Do you think that sheep have human ghosts?" Ogli wants to know. But it's just Annie. She is drenched, her white nightgown sopping wet, water pooling at her bare feet.

"Children?"

She blinks at the dead sheep with a dreamy incomprehension. She stoops and touches a wondering hand to the slick grass.

"Annie, we can ex—"

"Emma," she barks, suddenly all business. "Go back to your cabin. I need to have a word with the boys."

"Yes, ma'am," Emma squeaks. She goes doe-leaping off into the woods without a backwards glance. Blue clouds race past her over the tall pines. Then the clouds part, and the moon blinks open above us.

That's when I notice a bright spatter of blood on the hem of Annie's nightgown.

"Boys," Annie says, "my prophets, I need you to be honest now. Have you had any postmonitions about the dogs?"

We stare down at the blood drying on Annie's hands.

"The dogs, boys," she prods, her hazel eyes shining with a marbled hardness. "The *dogs*."

"Uh, no, ma'am." I cough politely. "We had the Typhoid Mary dream again last night. No, uh, no dogs."

The scariest thing about the blood on Annie's hands is the fact that Annie doesn't seem to know it's there. She's busy scanning the ground for paw prints.

"Oglivy," she asks, taking his hand, "did you dream them? Have you dreamed the dogs? Your dream log has been blank for days."

"Oh," Oglivy gulps, looking down at his clownish feet. "I've been meaning to tell you, Annie. I, uh, I haven't been remembering them. You know, the dreams." He won't look at either of us.

I elbow him sharply.

Annie nods. "Well. We musn't let the little ones see her

like this." She turns to me. "Elijah, I need you to help me to drag Merino to the sinkhole."

"Me?" I ask, horrified. "Um, Oglivy's probably the man for the job. . . ."

But he is already slouching off behind the red bushes. He mumbles a hollow apology over his shoulder.

Annie takes hold of Merino's cloven hooves and grunts. I take up her forelegs, careful not to touch her still-warm body. I nearly drop her, shocked by the tactile revelation that beneath the airy wisps of fur, she is gristle and bone. Merino is easily the heaviest weight I have ever carried.

"Come on, Elijah," Annie huffs. "Good job, Elijah. We're almost to the sinkhole. Unh!" Her muscles shudder. "This is what's necessary, you know, for the little ones to sleep easy."

I wonder which part of this Annie considers to be "necessary," the murder or the cover-up. I wish Ogli had stuck around to help me carry the body. I feel Merino's damp nose brush against my thigh and let out an involuntary groan. When a blood-glutted tick jumps down her haunch and onto the white rim of my thumbnail, onto my sweaty wrist, it's all I can do not to scream.

The sinkhole is a boggy pit on the edges of Zorba's property. Elastic bubbles pop along the puckered brown skin. Lightning-scored cypress trees surround it, a greenish phosphorescence sparking along their submerged roots. And it occurs to me that throwing a dead sheep into the sinkhole, this is not our best idea. The sinkhole is a window to the camp's aquifer. Anything you throw into the sinkhole remains in our water system indefinitely. Eventually, Merino is going to come back to haunt our drinking supply. Annie's not protecting anyone by dumping the body.

"Are you ready?"

Peering over the edge of the limestone cavity, I have an otherworldly certainty that I have been here before. It's one of those rare moments, the air thick and perfumed with memory, when the imagined world and the real world seem to overlap. A catatonic calm takes hold of me. *Oh, no,* I think, staring into the swirling, milky center, the blind eye of the sinkhole. We should not not not be doing this.

"Ready."

With a strength I couldn't have predicted, I help Annie to swing Merino's body into the murk. She hits the sinkhole with an awful thwack, her pale belly facing us. Annie and I watch in a grim, conspiratorial silence as she sinks beneath the surface. I wonder how much of this Annie will remember in the morning.

When we get back to the cabin, I wash my hands eighteen times. Then I loofah them. Then I wash them again. Then I wake Oglivy up and drag him outside and heave him up against the rain-slick wall, my palms still smarting.

"Why did you lie to her?" I hiss. "Were you *trying* to make us look like sheep killers?"

"Jesus, Elijah," Oglivy gasps, squirming away. "Calm down. I was going to tell you, you know." There's a pained expression on his face.

"Tell me what?"

"I think I might possibly be, uh, getting better? Our

dreams, the fires . . ." He gives me a helpless shrug. "I haven't been remembering them."

My hands drop from his shoulders. "What?"

"I mean, I still get the shakes, and everything," he says quickly. "I just can't remember what I augured, you know?"

"No," I growl. "I don't know. You faker! You mean you've been lying to me all summer?"

Z.Z.'s Sleep-Away Camp is divided down all kinds of lines: campers who can't sleep vs. campers who sleep too much, campers who control their bladders vs. campers who do not, campers who splinter through headboards vs. campers who lie still as the dead. Now Ogli and I are separated by one of the greatest rifts: campers who remember in the morning, and the ones who forget.

"You didn't have the Trail of Tears dream, with the ice floes and the frozen squaw?"

He shakes his head.

"The Inundation of Ur dream? All those alluvial, egg-smooth Sumerians?"

He shakes his head.

"What about the Great Peruvian Firequake of 1734—"

"Look, Elijah. It's a good thing."

"Oh, sure. It's great!" I kick the side of the cabin, feeling stupid even as I do it. "You're getting better! You don't remember our dreams! That's a great thing." I blink furiously, glad for the dark. "Really." I reach up to give him an awkward pat on the shoulder. "Really, Ogli. It is."

Ogli grins down at me, relieved. "Look, let's go to sleep? Maybe if I concentrate really hard I'll remember them tonight?"

"Nah, Ogli," I sigh. "I appreciate your volition. But I

don't think the dreams work that way. You go get sleeping without me." I turn back towards the woods. "I need to be awake for a while."

"You're not going back out there tonight, are you?" he yells after me. "After what we just saw?"

You mean what I just saw? I think, a deafening, echoing thought. It roars around me, the new solitude within my own skull. And I am angry, so angry at Ogli, for his forgetting. It's worse, somehow, that it wasn't deliberate, that the dream sickness just left him like a fever lifting. It means I don't even get to hate him. Ogli gets to wake up to cheery blankness and cereal, and I'll spend the rest of my life counting dead sheep.

This time I do a slow, listless shuffle through the woods, crunching into the leaves. All the happy fear has ebbed out of me. The leaves sound like leaves; the lake looks glassy and flat. When I startle a young stag in the middle of my path, I stand my ground and hurl some sticks at it. I climb into the Insomnia Balloon and curl my body like a fist. Now that I really am ballooning solo, I'm afraid to pull the rip cord. At least with Emma I could feel the warmth of another body in the basket.

Far away, I can hear Mouflon, our last sheep, bleating in the dark. I wonder if Annie is still out to protect her, still scouring the woods in barefoot pursuit of those dogs. I feel sorry for Annie, alone with a rabid pack of her own delusions. I feel sorrier for Mouflon. She's alone with Annie.

Eventually the dark gravity of the postmonitions begins to tug at my eyelids, a first oracular shimmer. I shiver and lie flat against the basket. My fingers curl through the holes in the wicker, through the wet grass beneath it, trying to hold tight to the sharp blades of the present. Somewhere in my brain a sinkhole is bubbling over, and each bubble contains a scene from a tiny sunken world: Oglivy erasing his dream log; Annie's blank eyes filling with phantom dogs; Merino's milky gray belly resurfacing with a terrible buoyancy. I have never been the prophet of my own past before. It makes me wonder how the healthy dreamers can bear to sleep at all, if sleep means that you have to peer into that sinkhole by yourself. Oglivy really spoiled me. I had almost forgotten this occipital sorrow, the way you are so alone with the things you see in dreams. Overhead, the glass envelope of the Insomnia Balloon is malfunctioning. It blinks on and off at arrhythmic intervals, making the world go gray:black, gray:black. In the distance, a knot of twisted trees flashes like cerebral circuitry.

The Star-Gazer's Log
of Summer-Time Crime

My job is to be the lookout.

Raffy's job is to give out jobs.

Marta's job is to get Petey choreographed and in costume.

Petey's job is to be the moon.

I didn't come out here tonight expecting to join a Comical Ironical Crime Ring. I'm here because my dad set me up on a date to see Alcyone. Dad made some sly references to her long blue light filaments and her extraordinary nebulosity, and boy was I excited. I polished my pocket planisphere. I read up on all the expert tips for locating her star cluster center in my *Starry-Eyed Guide to the Galaxy—For Kids!* I logged her spectral type prematurely in anticipation of one luminous night. That's how Molly and I got suckered into coming out to the touristy side of the island in the first place. Dad promised us that it would be a Junior Astronomer's beach paradise. But then I crested this dune and saw Petey, and now all my thoughts of Alcyone have been eclipsed.

Petey is dancing on the beach in a puddle of moonlight. He appears to be doing your basic two-step, but he's spiced it up with a spastic little shimmy from side to side. He twitches; he twirls. He lets out a low, gurgly giggle that goes goose-bumpling up my arm.

Petey's not particularly nimble, but he sure is quick. I'm not surprised. The formula bubbles up unbidden in my brain: *Momentum = mass × velocity*. And Petey is a sandy dervish of a man, soft-bellied, at least twice my height.

He is also twinkling like a star.

When I get closer, I find out why. Somebody has tied a trash-can lid to Petey's chest with crisscrossed strings of Xmas lights. It's been buffed to an impressive sheen. The rest of Petey's upper body is festooned with more of the tiny white bulbs. They loop around his arms and neck, blinking on and off at random intervals that seem timed to coincide with his lurching dance. I hypothesize that they must be battery-operated. The nearest hotel is a fifteen-minute walk away, so you'd need a pretty long extension cord.

We've never met before, but I know that this human disco ball must be Petey; after all, what other adult man on the island would look and move and laugh this way? Petey is something of a legend around here. Doreen, the chamber-maid at the Bowl-a-Bed Hotel, told Dad that he's one of the few people who come to the island every summer. Nobody's sure what's wrong with him, exactly, and Doreen says he always shows up at midnight so she's never there to check him in. All Doreen knows for certain is that Petey's at least thirty years old and has wax-white skin and long, color-less lashes. She says that frightened guests always call to report a ghost haunting the hallways whenever Petey comes to stay.

"Is he a friendly ghost?" my sister Molly wanted to know. "Like Casper?"

"Oh, Petey's no ghost," she reassured us. "I told you, I don't know what he is, exactly, but he's harmless. You'll see."

But the ocean mist has fogged up my glasses, and now I can't see a thing. After I spit-shine them, I realize that Petey's arms and hands are covered in tinfoil. He's holding a pair of huge red flashlights in his aluminum-foiled fingertips; he shakes these like maracas. They cast weird shadows across a roped-off square of sand. I can't actually see what's inside the roped-off area; all I can make out is the red plastic tape wrapped around four wooden beams. A triangular sign is attached to a driftwood post behind it. It takes me a couple of Petey's strobe-light revolutions to read it: SEA TURTLE NEST. DO NOT DISTURB! VIOLATORS SUBJECT TO FINES AND IMPRISONMENT.

A boy and a girl are standing next to Petey, staring down at the mound of sand. I recognize the boy as Raffy. Uh-oh, I think. I stuff my stargazing apparatus in my back pocket and turn to go, but it's too late. They've seen me.

"Hey, Raffy," I gulp. "What's up?"

"Hey, cockbag," he says. His tone is unexpectedly genial. "Who the hell are you?"

Raffy must have forgotten that he already knows me. We've had homeroom together since middle school, but Raffy travels in a different social solar system. Raffy hangs out with tattooed graffiti artists who race cars; I hang out with members of the Sci-Fi/Fantasy Club. We discuss the fiery edge of Orion's sword. We wear helmets and reflective knee pads when we ride our ergonomic bikes to school.

Raffy is the reason that we wear protective gear. He demands "loans" from our meager treasury and mocks the size of our genitalia and brags about fornicating with our mothers. If you inform Raffy that you do not, in fact, have a mother, as I have on several occasions, he tells you to go fornicate with yourself. All the girls in the Sci-Fi/Fantasy Club confide to me that they are secretly in love with Raffy. It's not fair. Everybody knows that bullies are supposed to have squat bodies and flattish heads like hammerhead sharks. But Raffy is tall and lean and regal-looking, with these leonine dreadlocks and laughing black eyes. He's bashed me into the gym wall several times and "borrowed" my dollars, but we've never had what you'd call a real conversation.

"I'm Ollie," I remind him. "Oliver White? We have class together. I'm staying over at the Bowl-a-Bed Hotel. . . ."

"You staying on this side of the island too? Small fucking world," Raffy says. He narrows his eyes and gives me the once-over, and I am painfully aware of my dimpled arms, my effeminate blond curls, my collared shirt on which every button has been dutifully buttoned. I feel my planisphere bulging conspicuously in my pocket. But Raffy just nods at me, visibly relaxing.

"Well, Ollie . . ." He turns to the girl, who hands him a big burlap sack. He holds it open for my inspection. "We could use a third. Are you in?"

I peer inside the bag. It's empty, except for one lone potato peel.

In what? I wonder. They're all staring at me expectantly, even Petey. In the uncomfortable silence that follows, the only possibility I can come up with is that Raffy wants me to get in the sack. I try to swing my right leg over, and end up kicking the little girl in the shin.

"No, you retard!" Raffy yells. "Not in the bag. I want to know if you're in on our baby turtle smuggling ring."

"Shhh," the girl says, a finger to her lips. "Don't talk about retards that way in front of Petey."

We all stare at Petey. He's resumed his dance, shaking the flashlights with such gusto that the tinfoil's peeling off, chunks of aluminum big enough to wrap up a ham sandwich. Shimmering bits of foil fall all around him, revealing swatches of Petey's skin. He looks sort of like the Tin Man from the *Wizard of Oz,* were the Tin Man to contract some leprous skin disease. I don't mean to, but I can't help it: I gasp when I first glimpse the skin on Petey's arm. In the moonlight, he looks like he's made of liquid silver.

"We think Petey's an albino," Marta explains.

"And a retard," Raffy adds.

"Mentally handicapped." She frowns, punching him in the arm.

"Special," I say, and it's true. I think that Petey might be the most special person I have ever seen.

"Hi, Petey," I say. "Good to finally meet you."

Petey waggles his silvery fingers at me.

"What about the rest of you?" I ask. "Who are you?"

I smile at the girl. She's cute. She has a freckle-dusted face and these big round glasses with pink frames. She looks like she should be eating vanilla wafers, or pasting evening wear on paper dolls. She definitely doesn't look like she should be hanging around with guys like Raffy. Or even guys like me.

"Who, her?" He pinches her cheek. "This my bitch, Marta."

"I'm his bitch," she repeats happily.

"Oh," I say. "I'm Ollie. Nice to make your acquaintance."

"So, Ollie," Raffy asks again. "You down for some turtle smuggling tonight?"

"Um . . . yeah. I mean, maybe. What is this smuggling ring, exactly?"

Raffy nods at Marta, who hands me a yellow flyer. I recognize it from the lobby of my hotel. They're posted all over the place on the island, in English and Spanish and Creole:

WARNING: DISTURBING A SEA TURTLE NEST IS A VIOLATION OF FEDERAL AND STATE LAWS

As you may be aware, the months of June–August are prime time for sea turtle eggs to hatch. Baby turtles possess an inborn tendency to move in the brightest direction. On a natural beach, they will orient themselves by the reflection of moonbeams and starlight on the water. However, in recent years our hatchlings have become disoriented by artificial lights, which beckon them away from the sanctuary of the ocean.

On the coast of Namibia, a nest of disoriented hatchlings walked into a beach barbecue and were burned to a crisp.

On the shores of Greece, the fatally bright lights of the discotheques lured thousands of baby turtles to their deaths.

Let's not make the same mistake here in Loomis County! Please turn off all outside lights between the hours of dusk and dawn.

REMEMBER: SEA TURTLE HATCHLINGS RELY ON NATURAL LIGHT TO ORIENT THEMSELVES.
DO NOT INTERFERE WITH THE MOON!

"Did you read that first part?" Raffy asks, dreamy-eyed. "A federal offense!"

"You're going to use a mentally handicapped man to help you steal baby turtles?" I ask.

"Yup!" the girl says brightly. "We're going to trick those silly turtles into walking into our burlap sack instead of the ocean. Isn't that right, Petey?"

"Tuuuurtles," he says in his creepy monotone drawl.

"But . . . but why?"

They all stare at me blankly. Raffy shakes the letter in my face, as if it's an open invitation to lure endangered species away from their natural habitat and into a burlap sack of certain doom.

"I mean, what are you going to do once you have all the turtles?"

Raffy waves my question away. "We'll figure that part out later. Don't people keep them as pets? Or eat them in soups, or something?"

"Tortoiseshell accessories are really trendy now," Marta says helpfully. She beams at Raffy.

"Tuuuurtles," Petey says.

"Okay," I say. "But I still don't get why Petey has to wear the trash can and the tinfoil and the festive lights. Doesn't that seem . . . unnecessary?" I want to say *unnecessarily cruel.*

"Why can't we just scoop them up with our hands, or sweep them into a dustpan or something?"

"Because," Raffy says, rolling his eyes at Marta as if I am the mentally handicapped one. "It's *funnier* this way."

Wowie zowie, I think. This is the most truly evil scheme that I have ever heard.

"Okay," I say. "What's my job?"

Two hours later, Petey is sweating profusely, and the turtles have yet to emerge from their nest. His calves quake with exhaustion in a way that makes the dance a lot less amusing.

"These fucking eggs better get cracking," Raffy grumbles. "School starts in a few more weeks." He turns to me. "How long you here for?"

I shrug. My dad is here with a group of his retired astronaut buddies, and my guess is that we'll stay at the Bowl-a-Bed until Dad exhausts his pension or his lunar nostalgia, whichever comes first.

"Well, don't dip out on us, Ollie. Meet us here tomorrow morning. We'll do some practice daytime crimes."

I gulp. "But these crimes . . . I mean, we only commit comical and ironical crimes, right? We don't actually hurt anybody?"

"Please," Raffy laughs. It's not a pleasant laugh—it makes you feel like he's giving you mean little pinches all over your body. "I'm on my summer break here. I save the real crime for the school year." He grins at me. "Hold up, I do remember you. One of the Sci-Fi boys, right? I always had you figured for a fucking dork, kid, but you a'ight."

"Um, thanks . . ." And then, a second too late: "You're

a'ight as well. . . . So, okay, then . . ." I try to keep my voice casual, as if being invited to join a crime ring with a cute girl and the coolest kid in my grade is a routine occurrence for me. "See you tomorrow?" I turn to go, but Raffy grabs me and whirls me around.

"Hey, you dropped something," he says. "Fell out of your pocket." He reaches down and shakes the sand off my *Starry-Eyed Guide to the Galaxy—For Kids!*

Uh-oh. I hope that it is too dark to read. I hope that Raffy is illiterate. I think: *Don't open it—don't read the title— please God just give it back to me.*

Raffy starts flipping through the pages.

The *Starry-Eyed Guide to the Galaxy—For Kids!* was a gift from my father on my twelfth birthday. Molly and I aren't exactly little kids anymore, but Dad hasn't seemed to notice. Besides, it's not like anybody's written a Guide to the Galaxy for Awkward Pubescent Boys yet. Anyhow, I kind of like the glow-in-the-dark graphics.

I'm less fond of the book's other concession to the seven to ten demographic, a bunch of Wowie Zowie! Fun Facts scattered throughout each chapter. As in:

Wowie Zowie! Fun Fact #47:
Q: A shooting star is not a star, how does it shine so bright?
A: The friction as it falls through air produces heat and light!

As in, wowie zowie, we the authors of the *Starry-Eyed Guide to the Galaxy—For Kids!* have never actually had contact with anyone under the age of forty-two. Or, wowic zowie, if kids like Raffy catch you reading this book, they will crown you as King Nerd and announce the glad tidings of your coronation over the PA system.

My dad's version of the book, the staid, declarative *Guide to the Galaxy,* is nearly identical, except that the graphics are a matte black, and the same information is listed as Fact #47. I guess that's what growing up means, at least according to the publishing industry: phosphorescence fades to black and white, and facts cease to be fun.

The planisphere was a gift, too. It's what we Junior Astronomers use to orient us in the night sky. Mine is shiny and compact and has the most accurate star compass on the market. It's fallen out of my pocket and rolled near Raffy's foot, and I quickly stoop down to retrieve it before he can see it flashing in the sand.

"Whatcha found there?"

"Nothing," I squeak. "Just trash."

I panic. Oh God, I think, they are going to pry my fist open and expose me as a law-abiding astronomy lover. And before I've made any sort of conscious decision to do this, I feel myself winding up and chucking my planisphere into the ocean. My weak muscles tense and draw back, and then it's over. Usually I throw like a girl, but tonight the planisphere goes rocketing from my hand. The waves are so dark that I can't even see if it makes a splash when it hits the water.

"You know, weirdo, there's a trash can right over there," Raffy says, pointing at the lidless can. "Say, what's this?" He's turned to the *Star-Gazer's Log of Summer-Time Constellations* section in the back. The half-finished Alcyone page stares up at me accusingly.

"Oh." I blush. "That's not mine. That's my twin sister's."

Raffy pulls out a pen from behind his ear. He crosses out "Constellations" and writes in "Crimes."

"Well, now it's the official log for our crime ring." He grins down at me. "You can be the secretary."

"Hey, Big Dipper," Dad says when I finally get back to our hotel room. He puts down his drink and looks over at me with bleary eyes. "It's past your curfew. I've been waiting up for you for hours." But he sounds more proud of me than angry. "You must have *really* gotten lost in the stars tonight. Did you find Alcyone?"

"Yes, sir," I lie. "Five degrees south of Eta Carinae, right where you said she'd be."

"Great work, son!" he says, beaming at me. His voice drops to a whisper. "Don't tell Little Dipper—it's different for girls—but maybe we can talk about extending that curfew." He winks at me. "There might be a few foxy new clusters around Cassiopeia tomorrow night, if you know what I mean."

I picture my planisphere glinting on the bottom of the dark ocean floor. Right now, I think, schools of tiny yellow fish are probably nibbling at the glow-in-the-dark stars.

"Hubble hubble," I say, raising my eyebrows. "Boy, would I love to get Cassiopeia on the other end of my telescope. Thanks, Dad." We grin at each other, man to man.

Parents can be so dumb.

.   .   .

As I climb into my hotel bed, I have to hold on to the headboard to steady myself. I have the giddy sense that I'm hurtling towards some uncharted corner of space, a world full of bros and bitches and comical, ironical crime. I pull back the covers, preparing to sink into sleep. Then I scream.

"Molly!" She is mummy-wrapped in the hotel sheets and staring right at me, her arms crossed over her flat chest. Anger seems to have inhibited her ability to blink. As usual, I'm dismayed to note that my sister has more arm hair than I do.

Molly and I are twins, but we're not identical, and thank God for that. People often describe me as "cherubic" because I'm blond and fat, but at least I'm well complected. Poor Molly. My sister's like a kiwi fruit—sweet on the inside, but small and hairy and round on the outside. Not to mention her face has more craters than friggin' Callisto.

"Well, well, well," she says icily. "Howdy, Ollie. How was your hot date with Alcyone?"

"Oh," I mumble, "It was okay. . . ."

"Liar!" she howls, throwing back the hotel covers. "Don't patronize me. I know it was a lot better than just okay. We're talking *Alcyone* here." She does a swoony pantomime and collapses against the pillow. "So, are you going to take me with you next time, or what?"

I don't answer. Instead, I pick Molly up and plop her down on her own twin bed. "G'night, Little Dipper."

"I hate you."

I sigh and turn off the lights. Molly's the other fifty percent of the Junior Astronomer Society. At first I didn't want her to join, but I had to capitulate after the Activities Committee told me that I couldn't form a society with only one member. Molly thinks that just because we share the same genome, we have to have matching bedsheets and hobbies and moral systems. I don't want to take her with me tomorrow. The crime ring is *my* new friendship constellation. Besides, Molly's such a goody-goody that she'd probably feel betrayed by my baby turtle smuggling or something. Some people just aren't cut out for a life of crime.

We meet every morning, still bearded with toast crumbs from our continental breakfasts. Everybody assembles in the green shade of the palm trees next to Barnacle Bob's Shrimp Stand. Everybody except for Petey. We don't know where Petey goes during the day. Sometimes we plan crimes and sometimes we perpetrate them. Sometimes we just sit around tic-talking down the hours until we can resume the Great Turtle Stakeout. I keep detailed notes of all our activities in my Star Log.

I guess I'd always assumed that Raffy was a bomb-in-your-mailbox, flaming-bag-of-fecal-matter-on-your-stoop kind of outlaw. But Raffy has a real flair for comical ironical crime. I don't know what he does during the school year, but Raffy's summer-time crime feels good, and clean, and funny. In fact, that's the catchphrase that sparks every crime we commit:

"Wouldn't it be funny if . . . ?"

And Raffy has this magical, abracadabrical ability to transform all his "ifs" into "whens."

. . .

On Monday, we stow away on a glass-bottom boat and then tap out forbidden messages to the dreamy-eyed manatees in full view of the DO NOT TOUCH THE GLASS sign. On Tuesday, we warm up by shoplifting a six-pack of Coke and then throwing the cans away in the PLASTIC ONLY bin. Afterwards we take the bus to the other side of the island—we do not hold on while it is departing—and steal all the pennies from the Children's Hospital Wishing Well. Raffy uses them to buy a Mr. Goodbar candy bar. He seems unperturbed when I point out that *1 Mr. Goodbar = 187 sick children's wishes*.

"Think of it this way," Raffy says, his mouth ringed with chocolate. "We're making *our* wishes come true."

On Wednesday, Raffy makes me use my mechanical expertise to rig up a plastic conch shell so that it makes crude potty noises whenever little old ladies in big floppy hats hold it up to their ears to hear the ocean.

On Thursday, Raffy wants to see if taking candy from a baby is really as easy as the old adage suggests. We walk up and down the splintery boardwalk peering into strollers, but I guess that today's health-conscious parents don't let babies have candy anymore, because all the ones we see are gumming jars of stewed prunes. We take some Ricola cough drops from an elderly sunbather's straw bag instead. It *is* easy, and you can tell that Raffy's disappointed.

"There's just no stopping us," he says glumly.

"Stop her!" Raffy yells, a little over an hour into Night Four of our Turtle Vigil. He points down the beach, to where a shadowy figure is bumbling along towards our nest. "Stop that intruder!"

I peer down the beach at the intruder and stifle a groan. It's Molly. She is engrossed in her star maps, using her birthday planisphere to chart her course. I feel a sudden twinge of remorse. My own star compass is probably all sea-weeded and shattered by now.

"She's just some kid," I say.

"Anybody we know?"

"I told you, it's nobody. Just some girl out past her bedtime."

"Are you *sure* you don't know her?" Raffy asks, turning Petey in her direction and illuminating Molly's startled face. "Because it looks like she's mouthing your name."

"Oh. So she is. That's my little dip . . . sister. I guess I didn't recognize her from here. Hang on, I'll get rid of her." I hurry off to intercept her.

"Ollie?" she says when I run over to her. She pronounces my name uncertainly, as if it's a foreign word. "Is that you? What are you guys doing?" Her eyes are wide and disbelieving. "You're not hanging out with *Rafael Saumat* over there, are you?"

I shrug. "Yeah, and? He's not such a bad guy. He's my bro now."

"Your bro?" she snorts. "He's an asshole, Ollie!"

"Look, you don't know him like I do. He can be really sweet." I try to think of some examples. "Like the other day, these bovine girls with back acne floated by us in the pool—I mean, the kind of girls you wouldn't want to feel up with oven mitts on, Molly—but Raffy gave them these charity cat-calls and politely invited each one to have his baby, even though you could tell that his heart wasn't in it. Why, he'd probably hit on *you*!"

This rhetorical strategy doesn't go over so well. In fact, Molly looks like she's about to burst into tears.

"I bet he doesn't even know your favorite constellation. You probably haven't even told him you're a Junior Astronomer, have you?"

"Well . . ."

"You faker, you phony!"

"Look, I'm not a phony!" I try to huff my voice up to an appropriately righteous volume. "It's just that I choose to accentuate other aspects of myself around Raffy—sort of like how you glob on mascara so as to indicate, Look! I have eyelashes! So maybe I don't mention the Junior Astronomer Society. Well, you don't use mascara on your chin hairs."

"Fine." She sniffs. "Have fun with your new *friends,* Mr. Faker. I've got a date with Vulpecula."

"Does Dad know you're out here? If he finds out, he'll be furious."

"Ha! Dad's been down at the bar with his buddy astronauts for so long now that I doubt he even knows there is an 'out here.' "

I look over my shoulder. Raffy is waving at me impatiently.

"Go back to the hotel, Little Dipper," I beg, whirling her around and giving her a little shove. "You can see Vulpecula just fine from the window of the Bowl-a-Bed."

"I'm ashamed to share your DNA." Molly whacks me with her own dog-eared copy of the *Starry-Eyed Guide to the Galaxy*—hard. Then she stomps off to the Bowl-a-Bed to constellate and sulk.

Molly's pretending to be asleep when I get back that night. She's left me an angry message written on one of the Bowl-a-Bed bar napkins.

Q: What is the constellation that never varies from its position at right ascension seven hours and declination eighteen degrees? Or have you forgotten? (Hint: it used to be your favorite.)

A: Gemini aka The Twins!!!

By the fifth night, the Christmas lights have run out of batteries. Now Petey has a compromised glow. His outfit looks less like the moon and more like a giant prewar nickel. Then Marta decides that we have to put the lid back on the trash can. These huge raccoons have taken up residence inside it, and she's worried about rabies.

"Well, bitches," says Raffy, Boy Scout—resourceful, "I guess we can always get more foil."

So we shoplift some Reynolds Wrap from the Night Owl Mini Mart and triple-wrap all of Petey's extremities. Including his head. It looks like a giant baked potato. Sweet little Marta remembers to make silver slits for his eyes and nose and mouth.

I think I might be developing a species of crush on Marta. It's not sexual or anything, I don't think. It's sort of like what I feel for Molly, and sort of not. I just want Marta to let me lace up her sneakers. I want to rock her and knee-sock her and push her on swings. And, you know . . . I guess I wouldn't mind doing a few other things.

But later, Marta and I have a conversation that effectively forecloses *that* possibility. Raffy decides that we need a get-away vehicle, and he goes off to try to hot-wire a miniature golf cart. I like it when Raffy leaves Marta and me to babysit Petey; it's like we're playing house. Tonight we break open some coconuts and give him the sugary-sweet milk, and then we use the scooped-out shells to dig a shallow little bed for him. We tuck Petey in by shoveling a white blanket over his hulking body. He yawns and smiles up at us, just his downy head sticking out of the sand.

"This should be creepy," I tell Marta, patting down the sand around Petey's neck. "But it's not."

She nods. "Do you ever get that cobwebby feeling when grown-up men look at you?" Marta asks me. "Like you've just walked into something sticky and invisible?"

"Oh, sure." I nod. "Right." I have no idea what Marta is talking about. For all I know, I am giving her this sticky look right now.

"Me too. But it never feels like that when Petey looks at you, you know?" Marta brushes sand off Petey's nose. "Hey, Ollie," she asks me, "can you keep a secret?"

"Sure." I try to sound big brotherly and nonchalant, but my breathing gets all fast and wonky. *Tell-me-that-you-like-me-too!* I think with every exhalation.

"Tonight's my birthday," she says.

"Heeeey!" I give her a noogie. "Happy Birthday! Here . . ." I cup her chin in my hand and tilt her face up at the sky. "Blow out the stars and make a wish."

Dad told me and Molly that our mother used to do this with us when we were very little. We both pretended like we remembered.

Marta shuts her eyes. She smiles. And I am seriously considering leaning in and kissing her.

"Can I tell you what I wished for?" she asks, her eyes still closed.

Kiss her now! I think. But I can't do it; I mean, how do you do it? I just keep picturing my big nose crashing into her smooth cheek like some clumsy meteor.

She opens her eyes. "I wished that Raffy—"

"Don't tell me," I say, and something bee-stung and bitter creeps into my voice. "It won't come true."

Raffy.

I should've known. When Raffy's around, she gets all dumb and honey-eyed. She half parts her pink lips. With me, she turns furry-browed and philosophical, just like the girls in the Sci-Fi/Fantasy Club.

I bet I know exactly what she's wishing for, too. I've already had every girl in the Sci-Fi/Fantasy Club confess the same stupid wish to me. I've been working on a formula to explain this phenomenon. Apparently: *13 cruel comments / 2 not-unkind words = 1 weak-kneed girl*

Raffy returns fifteen minutes later. On foot.

"Watch out for Petey's head!" we call. Petey's still snoring in his sand bed.

"Why is Petey sleeping on the job?" Raffy grumbles. He's grumpy because it turns out there are no golf carts on the island, probably because, as I respectfully pointed out to him several times, there are no golf courses on the island.

I'm about to go help Marta excavate Petey when I get a second chance to prove my worth as the lookout. Two men are power-walking down the beach in our direction, pumping their arms with the frustrated vigor of flightless birds.

"Look out!" I yell. Everybody but Petey turns and obliges.

"It's the environmentalists," Raffy wails. "Shit, man, do something!"

Marta warned us yesterday that a group of environmentalists were holding a conference at the Hostile Hostel, but I told her not to worry about it. I figured that the environmentalists would probably just stay in the lobby the entire time so as not to put any undue strain on the fragile beach ecosystem.

"What should we do, Raffy?" I ask. "If these environmentalists find out about this nest, they'll be here every night with their environmentalist friends, waiting to take digital photographs of one another as they shepherd our baby turtles into the sea!"

Raffy pushes me towards them. "You're a good talker, Ollie. Make with the orating." He can tell he's surprised us with his diction. "I do go to class sometimes, you bitches." He shrugs. "Now go!"

So I orate. I extemporize. I run like hell.

"Hey!" I yell to the environmentalists, leading them far away from the nest. "Over here! I think I hear some beached marine creature."

Then I try to approximate the sound of air wheezing

plaintively out of a blowhole. But I can't figure out how to do this without interrupting my own speech like some ventriloquy school dropout:

"I [bubble bubble] think [bubble bubble] it's a whale!"

A hand clamps down on my shoulder. And it's not the hand of an ovo-lacto vegan. It's a big, red-meaty kind of hand.

"That's no whale," the man growls, whirling me around. "That's a human boy making those noises!"

"Well, you got me, sir," I admit. Then I wriggle out of his grasp and do wind sprints down the beach. I just keep on running, even though neither of the men bother to give chase, until I finally collapse on the sand outside my hotel.

All I'm saying is, Raffy better remember this come school time.

"Sorry, Dad," I say when I get in, disheveled and breathless and over two hours late for my newly extended curfew. "I got a little Milky Way–laid and lost track of time."

"Ahhh, Ollie," he chuckles. "Like father, like son." He shakes his head fondly. "I know it's hard for you kids to imagine, but your old man spent some wild nights up in the Milky Way himself when he was your age." He lifts his glass in my direction.

"Here's to youth! Here's to you, Big Dipper!"

"So what did you see up there tonight?" I ask, and my voice comes out choked and strange. "You, uh, you notice any new nebulas? Any anomalies in the orbit?"

But my father has gone somewhere pensive and inward and doesn't answer. So I get away with it, for the fifth night in a row. I should feel good, I guess, but instead I feel this awful loneliness, an outlaw's loneliness, lying to the person I love best in the world. It's too easy to use his love to fool him. I almost want to be found out and grounded. I don't know why my father believes me. I don't know what the other kids tell their parents they do at night.

We think there must be something wrong with Petey's parents. What kind of parents would allow their adult child to play on the beach at night with kids like us? What kind of parents would bring their mentally handicapped albino son on a beach vacation in the first place?

Nobody knows if Raffy has parents. Raffy's not very forthcoming about these kinds of details. I'm still not sure where he's staying on the island, and we've been hanging out every day for nearly a week.

We know that Marta has a mom, because we keep having these awkward run-ins with her outside the Crustaceous Cocktail Lounge. Marta's mother is always draped across some jowly older individual, and it's never the same one twice. Two nights ago it was a much older man whom she introduced to Marta and me as "my gentleman caller." He had a face like an uncooked steak, pink and unsavory. When Marta's mother got up to use the restroom, I saw him offer Marta a sip of his Coco-Loco cocktail. Marta's mother and her decrepit beaus all look like they came to the island for spring break several decades ago and never left.

"Are you playing nice, honey?" Marta's mother always asks. "Did you make some little friends?"

"Yes, Momma."

"Oh, *good,*" she says, and her smile is as vast and empty as the Gamma Quadrant of space.

You know, it might be my imagination, but it seems like lately our crimes have been getting a lot less comical, and a lot more criminal.

"Wouldn't it be funny," Raffy says idly, "if we got Petey drunk?" He pauses, biting his lower lip, and you can tell he's trying to think of some comical ironical twist. Then he gives up. "You know, it would be even funnier if we got drunk, too."

So we take a ten-dollar bill out of Petey's pocket and close his fist around it and send him into the Night Owl Mini Mart with this note pinned to his lapel:

I WOULD LIKE TO PURCHASE
YOUR LEAST EXPENSIVE BEER.

Five minutes later, Petey gets sent back to us with a new note written beneath the first in prim red letters: NICE TRY, YOU HOOLIGANS!

We peer in the window and see another kid's mother scowling back out at us, holding some eggs and a carton of milk. Her very hair seems to frizz with maternal disapproval. She whispers something to the gas station attendant, and they both shake their heads in our direction. Raffy thinks we could try sending Petey into the Crustaceous Cocktail Lounge, but we can all hear the other mother berating us through the glass—"And if I catch you hooligans out here again, I won't stop at your parents, I'm calling the authorities!!"—and her abrasive voice stops us in our tracks.

"Stupid bitch," Raffy mutters, but he doesn't sound terribly upset. In fact, I think we all look a little relieved. And I am reminded of Wowie Zowie! Fun Fact #52—

INERTIA: Unless an object is acted on by friction from an outside force, it will spiral through space, in the same direction at the same speed—indefinitely!

That night, Molly breaks down and talks to me. She is standing by the bathroom sink and running cold water over her planisphere. She doesn't see me at first. I watch her from the door frame, crossing and uncrossing my toes inside my socks. The harsh bathroom light picks out all the cracks in the mildewed tile between us.

"Ollie! Aren't you going to clean your star compass with me?" She sounds hurt and suspicious. "It's Saturday night."

"Sorry," I lie. "Already did."

"Oh," she says in a tiny voice.

And suddenly my eyes get all hot, and I worry I might actually start to cry. I can't tell Molly this, but I really miss that planisphere. Lately, I feel so lost when I look up at the sky. I've been combing the dunes in the early mornings, checking to see if it's washed up. Maybe some deep-sea diver will find it one day and give it back to me. Dad had it engraved with my initials.

"Sure you don't want some of these scrubbing bubbles? You know what Dad always says . . ." We roll our eyes and repeat it in unison:

"You can't make sense of the universe if you're looking at it through a fogged-up lens!"

And it feels so good to giggle with Molly again.

When I meet up with Raffy on Sunday morning, he's just sent Marta running down the beach to get him a soda. Her little red bathing suit rides up in the back, her white bottom flashing in the sunlight.

"*Damn!*" Raffy whistles after her. "Forget the eggs, yo, wouldn't you love to crack that open tonight?"

(Yes.)

"No! I mean . . ."

We watch her run. The soles of Marta's tiny white feet are always dirty. Even from here, you can see the tar-skunked stripes when she kicks up her heels.

"I mean, it's too bad she's so young. . . ."

"Hey." Raffy winks. "We commit all kinds of crimes together. . . ."

We both laugh a little, and then there's this long pause when neither of us can really look at the other. We stare at Marta's sun-browned legs, the curve of her shoulder blades. I can hear my heart pounding in my chest.

"But, you know . . ." I'm still not looking at him, but I'm not looking at Marta, either. "That wouldn't really be comical, Raffy. Or ironical."

He kicks a sand ball at me. "Where's your sense of humor?"

He's only joking, I think, my pulse quickening. *We're only joking here.*

Marta leans forward to pay the man for Raffy's soda, and we both lean forward with her. Her wet hair is curling down her back like a question mark.

Unless we're not.

Tonight, the other kid's mother is nowhere to be found, and Raffy manages to shoplift a whole case of beer. "Wouldn't it be funny," he burps halfway into it, "if we got Petey to go *skinny-dipping?*"

Nobody thinks this would be funny, not even Raffy. Petey is terrified of the water, and I know we all love Petey.

"Hilarious," I hear myself say.

"If the skin on Petey's *face* is that white, just imagine . . ."

We all look over at Petey.

Marta gives us an uncertain smile, like she wants very badly to laugh but doesn't understand what the joke is.

Please don't do this, I think. *We don't have to do this.* Even as I am helping Raffy pull down Petey's pleated blue shorts.

He grunts and looks up at me unhappily as I pull his shirt over his head. Raffy and I stop laughing and stare. The skin beneath Petey's clothing is whiter than the lunar snow on Io. Whiter than the instep of a baby's foot, before it's learned to walk.

"Atta boy, Petey," I say. "Time to go swimming!"

I know we all love Petey. But we sure have a funny way of showing it.

Petey gets all clumsy and sea-cowed when we lead him to the water. You can tell he doesn't trust the waves to buoy him up. He screams when the sea foam first washes over his long toes. It's a bloodcurdling sound, as if Petey thinks the ocean's actually erasing his foot. Raffy keeps trying to force him in, wedging his fists into the base of Petey's spine, but Petey finally breaks away from him and runs back to sit shivering and naked by the turtle nest. Raffy laughs and laughs—and so do we. The sound of it rings hollowly down the empty beach.

The worst part is, I know that no matter what crimes we do to Petey, he'll always come back the following night. Being with Petey is like being with a dog, or a mother. There is nothing you can do to make him stop loving you.

"He'll go in if you go in, Marta," Raffy says. "Go tell him that you want to go swimming with him." He elbows me. "Marta and Petey—that'll be doubly hilarious!"

"Ha."

Raffy raises his eyebrows at me. "Maybe later Ollie and I will come in, too."

"You'll come in, Raffy?" Marta hesitates for a moment, then starts to unbutton her sweater. She won't look at either of us. Raffy rolls his skullcap up over his empty eyes to watch her, and I watch her, too, a hot cowardly watching. It should be a very easy thing to look away. But this heat feeling that's keeping me watching, it's nothing I can lower like a telescope. And I don't know the mechanics of shutting it off. I resolve to scream, to say something. *We don't have to do this*. Then Raffy grins at me, and I feel myself grinning back.

Now Marta has undone her very last button. Now she's rolling up the bottom of her shirt. The moon gets squeezed to bits by a black fist of clouds. Under the palm trees, our sockets fill with shadows. Marta's skin is just visible in the new dark. I feel itchy with excitement. *Please don't do this,* I wish again. But I wish it in a much weaker register.

"Time to go swimming, Petey!" we say. I can hear his teeth chattering from here.

Now Marta's undoing the drawstring of her butter-colored pants. I can't see her face in the shadows, and I'm glad.

But just as she's started to tug at her elastic waistband, Petey comes bounding towards us, his silvery hair streaming behind him like a comet's tail. *Momentum = mass × velocity.* Droplets of water go rolling down his broad, beautiful back as he flings himself down the beach. He looms huge and naked in front of Marta, one celestial body blocking the light from another, and I think, *Petey's job is to be the moon.* And the word that bursts from his lips like a lunar eclipse is:

"Tuuuurtles." Petey points at the nest. And sure enough, there's something small and black stirring there.

"Shit!" Raffy cries. "I don't believe it! The motherfuckers are actually hatching!"

Petey, slick and nude as the new turtles, is in no position to be the moon. Raffy scrambles off to get the flashlights.

The baby turtles are such funny-looking creatures. They seem so old and so young all at once, with their wrinkly old-man eyes blinking out of these viscous, fragile little shells. As we watch the turtles emerge from their speckled eggs and take their first false steps away from the water, I start to feel disoriented, too. Raffy is grinning and swinging the flashlights maniacally, and Marta is struggling with the burlap sack, and Petey is still wet and naked and shivering beside me. I keep patting my pockets for the reassuring weight of my planisphere, forgetting for a second that it's not there. So then I try this technique my dad taught me for getting your bearings when you get nightmares or nosebleeds or dizzy on car trips. The trick is to mentally pinpoint all the coordinates of your own constellation, and then picture yourself in the swirling center:

Raffy is holding the flashlights, and Marta is holding the burlap sack.

I am holding Petey's hand. I don't think anybody can see this in the dark. Don't let go, Petey.

Petey's still shivering and rubbing at his bare arms. I help him get his shirt back on over his head and whisper part of a lullaby that my mother used to sing. Nobody remembers how the melody goes, not even Dad. But if he's had a few, he'll warble the chorus: "For I have loved the stars too dearly to be fearful of the night . . ."

The baby turtles are turning away from the ocean. It's easy to see why. The black waves lap up the moonbeams, and the starlight on the inky surface of the water gives off such a pale glow when you compare it to the megawatt flashlights that Raffy is swirling in hypnotic circles.

"Are you watching this?" Raffy laughs. "This is fucking hilarious!"

The baby turtles are waddling towards the burlap sack in a silvery S-shaped line. They push their puny flippers into the sand with comic perseverance. Their black shells gleam wetly in the light. I edge closer to Raffy to get a better look.

"Wowie zowie," I breathe, as the first of the turtles files into the bag. Everything is going according to plan. Nothing can stop us now.

"*Look . . .*" Marta says. She has rebuttoned all her buttons, and there is wonder in her voice.

One of the turtles near the end of the line has paused. Some dim instinct must have turned its tiny head back toward the ocean, and now it's turning confused half circles in the sand.

"Get in the burlap sack, motherfucker!" Raffy growls. But I notice that he lowers the flashlight a little.

The turtle blinks up at the too-bright beam of Raffy's flashlight; then it looks back at the starlight on the open sea. It holds up the line, and we all hold our breath.

My job is to be the lookout, so I look past the turtle nest, beyond the flickering confines of Raffy's electric light. Petey has wandered away from us. He stumbles down a long alley of sand, picking up pieces of his tinfoil armor and trying to rewrap himself. Behind him, I can see the distant neon of the Bowl-a-Bed Hotel. I tell myself that I could at any moment start walking towards Room 422 with Dad and Molly, clean linens, buckets of ice; but my inert body doesn't believe this. A mile out from shore, the sea and the sky blend into an infinite blackness. I rub my naked eyes and try to stargaze. The blue Pleiades wink out messages that are illegible to humans. The moon shines down its eerie calligraphy from deep space. Last Sunday, when I was out here alone with my planisphere, this was all still a navigable darkness. That feels like it was a long time ago.

We watch as the single turtle's instincts wither beneath the hot lights. It flips itself back and forth in a miniature of real agony. We laugh harder; we strain our bellies with laughter. We stare at each other pop-eyed over the burlap sack and laugh as if we're afraid to stop. Somebody needs to say the magical, abracadabrical words that will turn tonight's crime into a joke. Marta has buttoned her wet sweater up to her neck. Petey's vanished. Now Raffy swirls the flashlights with true panic. Our joke keeps hatching and waddling forward in a snaky black procession, growing longer and less funny by the second, and this time nobody, not even Raffy, knows the punch line.

from

Children's Reminiscences of the Westward Migration

In the winter, our mother got hold of Fremont's *History of the Western Territories* and brought the book to my father to read, and he was carried away with the idea. Mother said, *O let us not go . . .*

My father, the Minotaur, is more obdurate than any man. Sure, it was his decision, to sell the farm and hitch himself to a four-thousand-pound prairie schooner, and head out West. But our road forked a long time ago, months before we ever yoked Dad to the wagon. If my father was the apple-biter, my mother was his temptress Eve. It was Ma who showed him the book: *Fremont's Almanac of Uninhabited Lands!*

Miss Tourtillott, one of the fusty old biddies in her sewing circle, had lent it to her, as a curiosity. It contained eighteen true-life accounts of emigrants on the Overland Trail, coupons for quinine and barley corn, and speculative maps of the Western Territories. The first page was a watercolor of the New Country, a paradise of clover and golden stubble-fields. The sky was dusky pink, daubed with fat little doves. In the central oval, right where you would expect to find a human settlement, there was nothing but a green vacuity.

Unflattened Pasture! the caption read. *Free for the takers!*

"Can you imagine, Asterion?" My mother smiled like a girl, letting her finger drowse over the page. "All that land, and no people."

You could tell that even my mother, in spite of her sallow practicality, was charmed by the idea. Easy winters, canyon springs. No one to tell the old stories about her husband, or to poke fun at his graying, woolly bull head. She let her finger settle on the word *free,* the deed to an invisible life. She traced the spiky outline of the mountains, a fence that no church lady could peer over.

"Look at that, son." My father grinned. "More grass than I could eat in a lifetime. All that space for your ball plays. Now, wouldn't you want to live there?"

I frowned. Whenever my folks promised me something, it always turned out to be both more and less than what I had expected. My sisters, for instance. I'd spent nine months carving a fraternal whimmerdoodle, and then Ma gave birth to Maisy and Dotes, twin girls. The New Country looked nice enough, but I bet there was a catch.

Besides, we had plenty of grass already. My father had retired from his wild rodeo life, and now lived in quiet retirement. We leased a small farm, raising mostly flowers and geese, where my father had negotiated a very reasonable price on rent. The lunatic asylum was a block away, and the intervening lot was vacant. It bothered my father that we didn't own the land outright, and my mother kept a pistol in the watering can, in case one of our gibbering neighbors ever paid us a visit. But that intervening lot was great for ball plays.

"Don't be silly, Asterion," my mother snorted, a habit she'd picked up from Dad. "Every member of my family lives in this town. Why, if we went west, I would never see them again in this world! My sisters, my mother . . ."

"Now wouldn't that be a tragedy?"

A charged look passed between them.

Since retiring, my father has gotten to be on the largish side for a Minotaur, not fat so much as robust, and now he gathered his bulk to an impressive eighteen hands high. He pawed at the earthen floor. (Ma liked to complain about this, Dad's cloven trenches in our kitchen. "Go do your gouging out of doors, like a respectable animal!")

"Asterion," my mother said, slamming the book shut. "Stop this nonsense at once." Ma is a plain woman, with a petite human skull that calls no attention to itself, but she can be just as hot-blooded as my father. "We have a life here."

Outside, the sun was setting, spilling through our curtains. My father's horns throbbed softly in the checkered light. His ears, teardrop white, lay flat against the base of his skull. His expression was unrecognizable. Who was this, I wondered, this pupiless new creature? I had never seen someone so literally carried away by a desire before. All the reason ebbed out of his eyes, replaced by a glazed, animal ecstasy. If he hadn't been wearing his polka-dot suspenders, you would have mistaken him for a regular old bull.

"And are you happy, Velina, with our life here? Have you stopped hoping for anything better?" This last bit got drowned out by the five o'clock scream from the asylum, which set our blood curdling like clockwork. My mother winced, and I could tell that Dad had a wedge in the door.

"Why not make a fresh start of it? Six hundred acres, and all we have to do is claim it. You will be the wife of a very rich husband. Think of the children! All those unwed miners—your daughters will never want for a dancing partner. Young Jacob will have a farm of his own before his twentieth birthday."

"Asterion." My mother sighed. She gestured around her, palms up. "Be reasonable. You're no frontiersman. Where would we get the money for a single yoke of oxen?"

"Woman!" Dad boomed. He pushed out his flabby barrel chest. "You married a Minotaur. I'll pull our wagon."

"Oh, please!" Ma rolled her eyes. "You get winded during the daisy harvest!"

I was still rocking in the willow chair, slurping up milk.

"Your husband is stronger than a dozen oxen!" he roared. Dad patted his ornamental muscles, the product of flower picking and goose plucking. "Or have you forgotten our rodeo days?"

He tusked his horns at her, with a brute playfulness that I had never seen between them. Then he charged at her, herding her towards the bedroom door. And my mother giggled, suddenly shy and childlike, letting herself go limp against him. I coughed and slurped my milk a little louder, but by this time they had forgotten me completely. "We have each other," he bellowed. "And everything else, we will learn on the Trail. . . ."

I was startled by this, the speed with which one apocryphal watercolor was transforming our future. A minute ago, there had been an opened book, a crazy notion—we could go or we could stay—and now, not five minutes later, the book was shut. We were going. Simple as that.

We have been on the Trail for over a month now. Last night, we camped on Soap Creek Bottom. Down here, it's all soft green mud and yellow bubbles of light. No potable water for our stock, and barely enough for us. The weeds we suck on for moisture taste bitter and waxy. Ma's been complaining of bad headaches, and the twins have been doing most of our cooking. Basically, this means they wake up early enough to beg boiled coffee and quail eggs from the other wagons. Dotes lumps some salt into the yolk and calls it an omelet. Apparently, my sisters still haven't mastered the pot and the spatula, that fiery alchemy, whereby "raw" becomes "food." So help me, if I have to eat another stewed apple, I am defecting to the Grouses' wagon.

We have joined the Grouses' company, at my mother's insistence. Ours is a modest wagon train, twelve families, among them the Quigleys, the Howells, the Hatfields, the Gustafsons, the Pratts, a party of eight lumberwomen, and a sweet, silly spinster, Olive Oatman, who is determined to be a schoolteacher. Olive trails the wagons on a toothless mule, each step like a glue-drip. "Hurry up, Olive!" the men yell, and the women worry in overloud voices that she'll get lost, or fall victim to Indian depredations. But nobody invites Olive to join their family's wagon.

In the beginning, everybody was gushing about the idylls of the open road—look at Hebadiah's children, sitting high on the wagon! Listen to Gus, warbling on that mouth organ! Let's sleep outside! Let's close our eyes, and drink in the cool, violet dune glow with our skin!

But now, we spend most of our time scowling, sunk in our private nostalgia for well water and beds. It is cold and cloudy, with the wind still east. We are on a very large prairie. The few trees are stout and pinky-gray, like swine, and the scrub catches at our wheel axles, as if it wants to hitch a ride with us to somewhere greener. Dad's back is carved solid with red welts. His skin is coming off in patches. Flies twist to slow deaths in the furry coves of his nostrils. Dad shakes his head more violently with every mile, a learned tic, to keep the buzzards from landing on his curved horns.

We keep passing these queer, freshly dug humps of soil. Ma told Maisy and Dotes that they are just rain swells, and the domes of prairie dog houses, but I know better. They are graves. Nobody leaves markers here, Clem says, because there's no point, no chance that you will ever come back to visit the site. We have decided to count them, these tombless losses. It seems like somebody should be keeping score:

Made twenty-two miles . . . passed seven graves.

Everybody is coming to the grim conclusion that we have overloaded our wagons. Our necessities, the things we couldn't have lived without just two weeks ago, are now burdensome luxuries. The whole Trail is littered with cherished detritus: heirloom mirrors, weaving looms, broken loved-up dolls. Maisy and Dotes got Dad's permission to pitch Grandma's empress china set at the trees. Our mother ducked the antique pestle, and cried a little bit.

At dusk, we entered a tall, shadowy belt of timber. Clem

spotted an orange polecat, sinking into the mud, nibbling at the little hand of a giant clock face. Brass kettles glower in the shadows. Empty cradles line the sides of the road, rocking soundlessly in the wind.

During the day, my mother sits on the high chair, shouting instructions to my father. Maisy and Dotes sit inside, shelling peas. Both of my parents continue to implore me to ride in our wagon, but I refuse to. If my dad is sensitive to the weight of a china plate, I don't want to add one bone to his load.

Instead, I walk in the back with the lumberwomen. I love the lumberwomen. They are widowed and ribald and sweat through their tongues, like dogs. Sometimes they let me roll inside the deep tin wells of their hunger-barrels. They ask lots of cheerful, impolite questions about Dad, which are far easier to endure than the frank horror of other emigrant children, or the veiled pity of their mothers.

"Your pa," they holler, "he the one with the . . . ?" Then they scoop at the air above their temples, and whistle. "Whoo-ee! What a piece of luck, that, you children taking after your mother!"

It doesn't feel so lucky. Most times, I wish that I had been born with a colossal bull's head, the bigger the better. People on the Trail act as if it's just as strange, and even more suspicious, my seeming normalcy. We are freckled and ordinary, and it makes every mother but our own uneasy. I could be Clem's brother; my sisters look just as peachy clean as their own daughters. This seems to alarm them. They wrinkle their noses slightly in our presence, as if we are the infected carriers of some hideous past.

My father is doing the heavy labor, sweating through the

traces, plunging into the freezing water, into rivers so deep that sometimes only the shaggy tips of his horns are visible. But he is happier than I have ever seen him. People need my father out here. In town, there was always a distinct chill in the air whenever he took Ma to birthday parties or pumpkin tumbles, barbecues especially. But on the Trail, these same women regard him with a friendly terror. Their husbands solicit him with peace pipes, and obsequious requests:

"Mr. Minotaur, could you kindly open this jar of love apples for us? Mr. Minotaur, when you have a moment, would you mind goring these wolves?"

And I am so proud of my father, the strongest teamster, the least mortal, the most generous.

Ma is, too, even if she won't admit it to him. She told Louvina Pratt that he looks like the Minotaur she married, before he was a father. It's hard for me to imagine, staring at my dad's gray belly hair and blunted horns, but I guess he was a legend once. At the early rodeos—my mother keeps all of his blue vellum posters, hidden inside her Bible—he bucked every gangly cowboy on the circuit. The Pawnee gave him top billing:

The bronco with a human torso, a chipped left horn, and a questionable pedigree!

Back home, people told so many stories about my father! Especially those people who had never seen him perform. That he was a sham man, or a phony bull; that his divinity had been diluted by years of crossbreeding with wild cows and "painted ladies." My own cousins called him a monster. I always wished that they could see my dad just being my dad, covered in goose dander, or pulling a wheelbarrow of poppies. Here on the Trail, people are finally getting to know all the parts of him.

As for my mother: well, things could be better. She spends most of her time gathering twigs and buffalo excrement, and saying terrified prayers with the other women. Her face is brown and wizened, like apple skin left in the sun. She looks shrunken, stooped beneath the absence of small pleasures: fresh lettuces, the seasonal melodies of geese, the anchored bed she used to share with my father. I think she even misses the asylum, its predictable madness.

Ostensibly, the women meet behind the wagons to beat laundry with rocks or plait straw grass into ugly hats. But mostly, they just make implications.

"Velina, you must be so proud of your husband, pulling your wagon." Louvina smiles. "My Harold would *never* consent to walk in the traces."

"Yes, Velina," the Quigley sisters chorus. "Why, he's just as good as any oxen!"

"Our husbands are going to kill themselves out there," my mother snaps. All of her wrinkles point downwards, like tiny pouting mouths. "It makes no difference if they are pulling or driving. We are going to forfeit every happiness we had, for a bunch of empty scrub."

"Don't pay her any mind," my dad laughed later. We were sitting on the outskirts of the campfire, watching the other men dance around its pale flames. Dad was working ancient, alluvial pebbles out of his hooves, and handing them to me for my collection. They are a translucent yellow, pocked by lacy erosion, like honeycomb. Children toddled towards our log, playing slow games of tag. The stars were impossibly bright.

"Velina can't see the West the way I can."

Dad claims that human women are congenitally nervous and shortsighted. "Like moles, son. If your mother is hungry for green corn, or if her bloomers get wet from the dew, she forgets all about the future. Believe me, when we crest those mountains and she sees the New Country . . . listen, everything will be different when we get there, Jacob. I promise."

That much, at least, I believe. . . .

We have lived a string of dull, thirsty weeks. Everybody is irritable, and looking for someone to blame. Our wagons bump along, a pod of wooden leviathans, eaten away from the inside by mold and wood-boring mites. Our road is full of tiny perils, holes and vipers, festering wounds. Today would have been indistinguishable from the twenty before it, except that Clem and I finally got a good ball play going.

As soon as we got done striking camp and picketing the horses, we went exploring. Just north of the campsite, a quarter mile downstream, we found a clearing in a shallow stand of pines. In the center, a shrunken lake, an unlikely blue, was fringed with radish reeds. Behind us, you could see the white swell of the wagon sails, foaming over the trees. And the sky! The sky was the color that we'd been waiting for, our whole lives, it felt like. An otherworldly alloy of orange and violet, the one that meant a thunderstorm at sundown, and night rain for our stills.

"Look!" I pointed to the rising storm, a spider tide of dust and light. Future rain, cocooned in red filaments of cloud. "Clem! See that? My dad says that in the old days—"

"Jacob"—Clem rolled his eyes—"just play the ball, okay?"

Ma had insisted that I take Maisy and Dotes so that they could get some fresh air, which I found infuriating, since they are girls and should be doing girl things, playing mumbly-beans or wearing yellow ribbons somewhere unobtrusive. Clem and I propped them up against some nearby boulders and used them as yard markers.

"Ready, Jacob?"

I swung wide, sending the ball to a delirious altitude, high above the blazing aspens. Maisy and Dotes clapped politely, while Clem ran off to retrieve the ball. A second later, we heard a terrible roar from behind the trees. The aspens started quaking, and I scurried to join him. We peered through the golden leaves.

"Hey," Clem said. "Isn't that your dad?"

My father was shedding his summer hide. His work shirt was hanging from a green sapling. Black fur caught like bits of cloud on the low branches. And there was my dad, rubbing his head right into a bifurcated stump, his horns sparking against the wood. "Uhhhh," he groaned, scratching harder, his back spasming with pleasure.

"No," I lied.

He snapped up when he heard my voice. "Boys!" He stamped. I felt traitorous, and embarrassed for everybody; Dad preferred to take care of his animal functions in private. "What are you doing out here?"

"Hi, Jacob's dad," Clem squeaked. "We were just having a ball play with the twins."

We all turned. The girls had wandered down by the lake, to attend to their own functions. Maisy had unfolded the gingham curtain of modesty, and was holding it up for Dotes. When she looked over and saw us watching, she squealed and let go. The curtain of modesty went flapping off in the wind, revealing a horrified Dotes, bare-legged and squatting in the purple brush.

"Eeee!"

Dotes dove behind a rock.

"Good Christ," my father grumbled, looking away. "Get your bloomers on, Dotes."

On the Trail, propriety is a tough virtue to keep to, even if your curtain of modesty is made of the heaviest fabric—buffalo flannel, or boiled wool.

My father snatched his own thick shirt from the tree, and started buttoning up. He plucked at the pink, scabby spots around his ears and neck—they startled me, these hairless patches, they looked so much like my own raw skin. He avoided our eyes.

"Who told you to take the girls out here, Jacob?" he bellowed. "Who gave you permission to leave the company?"

"Ma did."

"Oh. I *see*. Well." He glanced at Clem, scowling through a nimbus of bull fluff. "I say they go back." Then Dad trotted down to the creek, to where Maisy was wringing out the sodden curtain, and swept the girls up in his arms. He took long, regal strides back towards the camp, poised and paranoid, the way he walks when he suspects that he is being watched.

Afterwards, we couldn't find our ball. We both sat on a

log, sulking, staring into the coming storm, and waiting to be called for dinner. Our bellies grumbled at the same time. A cloud of pollen floated past.

"Hey," Clem demanded, "how come you don't look like your dad?" It was spoken as a challenge, sudden and accusatory, as if we had been fighting all this while.

"What? But I do!" I pulled at my nostrils and blew, a nasally mimicry of my father's anger. "I do! How come *you* don't look like *your* dad?" I tried another wild snort, but it came out sounding like a sneeze.

Clem just smiled at me, aping his own parents' expression, a doughy swell of pity and smug piety. He patted my back. "Poor Jacob. Bless you."

That did it. I charged him with my invisible horns, and suddenly we were fighting in the dirt like animals, dunced into a feral incomprehension. Kicking and scratching and biting, full of a screaming joy, hot and ugly. We kept at it until the dinner bell returned us to our selves; and suddenly, as if by magic, we were back at the camp, gorging on buttered oats and quail cakes, full-bellied, and friends again.

That night, I found my father at the edge of the campfire. The company was having a barbecue, and this always makes my dad uncomfortable. The teamsters tore into the antelope meat like savages. The men wore linen work shirts during the day, but at night they stripped to their bare chests. Then they rushed at each other, half in jest, tipping their bottles back with a taut fatigue. In the center of the corral, Olive had hiked her skirts up, drunk and merry. She was sitting on Gus's lap, slapping a tambourine against her bare knees. The wives sucked air through their teeth, flushed with scandal, and clapping along all the while.

"Dad? Will you cut my hair?"

"Sure, son." This was our favorite ritual. He put on his reading spectacles, and removed a tiny pair of scissors from his belt. Then he started cutting at my curly mop of hair. He cut with a tender precision, squinting furiously, his thick tongue lolling out of the side of his mouth.

When he finished, he held the cold, flat edge of the scissors against my scalp. "Can you feel your horns, son? There?" And I smiled happily, because I *could* feel them, throbbing at my temples, my skulled, secret horns. Ingrown, but every bit as sharp. And I knew that no matter what Ma or Clem or anybody said, I was my father's son.

We had our first true storm last night. Acres of lightning! A smokeless heat, and the choking smell of ash and sage. The wide, roiling prairie announced itself in liquid glimpses, apocalyptic and familiar. We had been sleeping in tents outside, and now we all ran for cover. Blue discs of hail blew into our wagons. The soaked canvas shuddered; and this became indistinguishable from the tremors within our own divided bodies, the hollow vibrato in our spines and human skulls and bellies, during the thunder.

"Mother," I said, to say something.

I had been eagerly awaiting just such a disaster. Storms, wolves, snakebite, floods—these are the occasions to find out how your father sees you, how strong and necessary he thinks you are. As it turns out, I am still just a buff-colored calf to Dad. I watched the older sons and brothers leaping off of the wagon tongues all around me, a shoeless stampede. There went Clem, in a peppery cloud of dust. There went Obadiah, eager to assist.

But none of the fathers called me out of the wagon, least of all my own. I huddled with my mother, nuzzling into her neck, while the men shouted commands to one another, weighting the wagon boxes so that they wouldn't leak or capsize. Our family was in good shape. Months before we set out on the Trail, Mr. Gustafson had come over and treated our cover with linseed oil, until the canvas shone like opal. Now we could actually see the accumulation of each rain-drop, held in an oily suspension above our heads. It was freezing inside our wagon. I peered through the cloth portal, searching for my father, lost in a haze of swung lanterns and the wind. The wagon train blurred and shifted around us, like a serpent uncoiling.

The twins kept on crying in fright, and all around us the treasures we had sewn into the pockets of our wagon cover were shaking loose, pewter spoons and wooden toys, a grainy mess of stone meal, my father's musket. It's a wonder it didn't go off and kill someone. My mother, cold and com-fortless, was cursing "our luck," by which she meant the gods, my father, all fathers. I thought about my hard bed, and the many things I used to hate about our old life—keeping the Sabbath, harvesting the roses, all the honking, stupefying demands of our geese—and wished and wished that we had never left.

. . .

We think the wolves got Olive. When the rain cleared, she had disappeared. The grown-ups all screwed their faces into identical grimaces. They tried to make their sorrow sound as genuine as their surprise. "Poor Olive!"

Jebediah Hatfield found her mule in a ravine eight miles to the west of us, grazing on an abstemious circle of brush, its grizzled snout stained red from the berries. Torn yellow ribbon hung from the low branches. There were bits of a woman's skirt clinging to the currant bushes. My dad volunteered to lead the search party.

"Are you mad?" Mr. Gustafson shook his bushy head. "We could lose a whole day if we send a search party. At this rate, we'll never make it to the New Country."

My dad looked from face to face, incredulous. "What is wrong with you people?" His horns were shaking involuntarily, no longer a mere tic, but an obvious compulsion. His voice sounded small and human. "What about the contract?"

Before we left, we had Reverend Hidalgo officiate our wagon union. Every family had to sign the contract: many wheels, a single destination, all for one until the Trail's end.

Somebody snickered, a thin, hysterical sound. "The contract, Mr. Minotaur?" And I flushed, seeing my father the way the other men did, his puzzled, hairy face, his dumb cow eyes.

Our company took a group conscience, and most everybody agreed it to be hopeless. My father and half-blind Clyde were the only ones who voted in favor of sending a search party, and Clyde later insisted that he had just been stretching.

"Think about it, Mr. Minotaur," Mr. Grouse said with a dark twinkle in his eye, fingering the ribbon. His cheeks were flushed, as if he were telling a naughty joke. "What solution could there be to this mystery? Who wants to waste half a day, burying the answers?"

"Velina!" We all turned. Mrs. Grouse was squatting a few yards away, waving frantically at my mother. She reached into a rain-soaked satchel, and held up one of Olive's lacy, begrimed shirts. "Velina, do you want this? I think it's your size."

Yesterday, my father was the last wagon but one to cross the Great Snake River. We rafted across in the boxes, jowl to elbow, crammed in with albino cats and babies and buckets of bear grease. The men swam alongside their oxen. Clem and I banked first, and sat watching our fathers from the opposite shore. I didn't want to tell Clem, but I was very scared. The cows had churned up a crimson froth of silt and mud, water rising to their necks, and I lost sight of my father in the lowing melee, his ruby eyes, his chipped left horn. For a horrifying instant, I couldn't tell him apart from the regular cattle. I worried that the other men, preoccupied with their own stock, wouldn't know to help him if he started to go under.

"Do you ever worry that your pa won't make it?" Clem asked carefully. His own father was struggling below us, his gum boot caught in the rapids. "I mean, to the end of the Trail?"

I shook my head. "Nope. Of course he'll make it. My father is a legend."

All my life, I have believed only the best parts of my father's myth. But as it turned out, this belief makes little practical difference on the Trail. Dad still got the chills, and had to stop and catch his breath on a small rock island. I got a fire going, and my mother knelt in the sand, wringing the water out of the furry knots of hair around his neck. She murmured something into his wet, mud-rubbed ears. I don't think it was a soothing something. Even now, they are fighting inside our wagon:

"Who do you think you're fooling out there, acting like you're immortal? I should have listened to my mother! I should never have married a Minotaur!"

Ma likes to talk as if she could have done better than my father. All of my aunts married postmasters, and prim, mustachioed mayors.

"Your mother," my father snorted, between a laugh and a sneer. "You women, you're all alike. . . ."

"It's not too late, you know. It's never too late to turn the wagon around—"

"Listen, Velina," my father is saying. "I'm telling you, it's too late. We can only go forward. Our geese have been eaten. There are strangers living in our house. . . ."

There is some wooden clattering that sounds angry and deliberate, and an iron shudder. Then silence on my mother's end.

For the first time, I feel just as sorry for my ma as for my dad. Everybody wants to go home, and no one can agree on where that is anymore.

Today, we nooned in a purple grove, along the dry riverbed of Snail Creek. It was cool and pleasant. After biscuits, I found a dead snake, and skinned it, and made a toy out of its rattler to give to my sisters. They are both quarantined in the wagon, sick with ague. Their heads are swollen and bluish, like tin balloons. Maisy coughs less than Dotes, but Dotes is better at keeping boiled peas down. My parents haven't spoken to each other for three days.

"Hey, Clem?" I asked him. "What does your father talk about with your mother? You know, in your wagon?"

"Huh." Clem frowned. "Your folks talk to each other?" He shrugged. "My mother mostly bangs pans around, or folds the blankets real loudly. Sometimes they pray together."

Without anybody taking verbal notice, in imperceptible increments, we have slipped to the back of the company. After the third time Dad fainted, Mom quietly stepped down from the high seat and slid into the canopied box. Now Ma refuses to drive our wagon. She curls up with the girls on a feather ticking, and sleeps during the day. It has fallen to me, now, to drive my father.

Every morning, I wake up at dawn. The sky is still prickled with stars, and it will be a full hour before the first blue ribbon of smoke gasps up from the first campfire. I shake my father awake, and help him into the traces. It's a special, single yoke, made to order. My father drinks a tiny glass of flame-colored liquid, his breakfast, while I clasp the collar slip around his neck, and secure the nails in his crescent shoes. Then I take the reins. I'm okay once we get rolling, but I'm still uncertain, a herky-jerky greenhorn, when it comes to the commands for stopping and starting:

"Gee? Oh! I mean . . . Haw! Sorry, Dad!"

Even when I close my eyes, now, I see the outline of my

father's back, swaying in front of me: the bent, pebbled steppe of his vertebrae, bruise-purple from sun and toil, the shock of his bull's mane tumbling out of his hat, bleached to the color of old milk.

Gus traded his mouth organ for a sock and a sack of millet, so now we travel in silence. I miss the camaraderie of that first prairie, everybody traveling with a single aim, to the same place, and music even on the worst days. The lighter our wagons get, the quieter our daily sojourn becomes, and the more determined we are to get there and be rid of one another. The lumberwomen are mute and sour, except for the hollow growl of their hunger-barrels. At night, after we make camp, they break long bouts of wordlessness to ask for whiskey and matches and soda crackers, and various other Trail alms.

"Don't you give them anything, Jacob," my mother hisses. "Remember, if you give those women so much as a single cracker, you are taking it from your sisters' mouths."

Lately, my parents can't seem to agree on the value of things. Last night, well after eleven o'clock, my father trotted back to our wagon, bashful and out of breath, fresh from a barter with the local Indians.

"Velina! Open your mouth, close your eyes, I have for you a great surprise. . . ."

Then he put a raw kernel of corn on her tongue, and waited, beaming, for her reaction.

My mother smiled beautifully, rolling the kernel in her mouth. "Oh, Asterion! Where did you get this?"

"I sold our whiffletree," Dad said proudly. He pulled an ear of green corn out of his back pocket and, with a magician's flourish, stroked her cheek with the silky husk.

"You what?" My mother's eyes flew open. She spit corn in his face. "You did what?" Then she took hold of his horns and drew him towards her, slowly, half laughing and half crying, pressing her face against the white diamond at the bridge of his nose. "You did *what*?"

Dad's nostrils flared; he lowered his head and pawed at the caked dirt. I dove into the wagon and slid beneath the blankets with my sisters. The candles had guttered out, but moonlight seeped through the rips in our wagon bonnet.

"Girls?"

Maisy opened one brown eye and held a finger to her lips. Dotes had her fist in her mouth, stifling a cough. I felt proud and sad that my sisters knew enough to pretend to be asleep. Outside, our parents were still arguing:

"Is that what we're worth to you," my mother was yelling, "five dollars and an ear of green corn?"

". . . besides, *you* were the one who said you wanted corn. . . ."

"Do you even have any idea how to repair a whiffle-tree, Asterion? . . . Well, I hope that is some consolation to you, when the wolves are gnawing on your daughters' bones. . . ."

"C'mon," I said, loosening the cinched portal and sneaking my sisters out the back. I carried them over to the Grouses', two wagons down.

"Hey, Clem," I said. "Can we sleep in your wagon tonight?"

"No," Clem said sadly. "No, my ma says that we're only allowed to be friends in church now. They think your dad gave me lice." He brightened. "You can sleep under the wagon." We all peered beneath the hickory box. The undercarriage of the wagon was white and wormy. Light leaked through the planks, a palsied glow, sopped up by a dark mosaic of soil. In the dead center, the darkness pooled and shifted. Dotes gasped. It was a clotted mass of dogs, spotted dogs, yellow dogs, swimming dogs, all huddled together for warmth.

"You first," Maisy said.

Today I was poking at the fringes of the campfire, gathering stones for my collection, when I overheard some of the other men talking about my father.

"That Minotaur is spreading sucking lice to the children!" Mr. Grouse said, shaking and red, with a rage out of all proportion to his insect allegation. "He is titillating the milk cows, and curdling our children's milk!" I flattened myself against the ground and inched forward. The other emigrants were all frowning and nodding. Watching them, I could see the way Mr. Grouse's anger spread from man to man, the hot, viral coil of it, a warmth the men breathed in like a welcome fever.

It's enough to make you hate people.

I ran off to find Clem. He was out back, catching lizards behind the corral.

"Howdy-howdy, Jacob . . . Ow!"

I butted him in the ribs, sharply, wishing fervently that I had inherited my father's antlered might. I butted him once, twice, and then stomped on his buckskin shoes.

"What was that for?"

"If you don't know, I am not going to tell you." I ran off into the sunset, crying hot, frustrated tears, cursing the

Grouses at the top of my lungs. Then I lost sight of the wagons, and got scared, and ran back. I hoped Clem wasn't watching.

When everybody was ladling soup at the bean cauldrons, I snuck into Clem's wagon. I stole his sisters' dolls, the ones the Grouse girls have been making out of cornhusks since Fort Charity, and ate them. In my vengative fury, I forgot to remove the button eyes. My stomach is still cramping.

I hope the West is big enough for us to really spread out. It's a terrible thought, one of my worst fears, that we are going to get there, and these people will still be our neighbors.

Three nights ago, I was sleeping under my own family wagon, my bare arms and face covered in a fine cedar dust from the box, and dreaming of the most ordinary things, chalk and pillows and ceiling boards, pitchers of lemonade and gooseberry pies, when I woke to a hand—not my own—pinching at my cheek.

"Wake up, Jacob."

I rolled over, eye level with the tip of my mother's caulked boot. I slid out from under the wagon. Ma had Maisy in one arm and Dotes in the other. Their eyes looked shiny and protuberant; their throats bulged with the echo of swallowed coughs. I felt the danger, too, sensed it with an animal intuitiveness, and froze.

"Come out of there, Jacob." My mother spoke in a low, careful tone. "Come gather your things."

"Why?" I was surprised at how alert I sounded, wide awake, without a trace of grogginess.

"Circumstances have obliged us," she glanced nervously over her shoulder, "to part ways with your father."

I gaped up at my mother, and let her words sink in. I'd

known for some time that a change was coming; I welcomed the idea of it, I *wanted* it, almost, or tried to want it, like my ambivalent prayers for rain in open country. But *parting ways!* This was a lunatic move, ghastly and extreme, like digging up coffins because we needed some wood.

"Jacob," she pleaded. "Now."

We stared at each other for a long moment. I drew my blanket up around my chin, flat with panic, and wedged myself under the carriage.

"No."

Ma bit her lip miserably. She squatted in the dust, inches from my face. I could see my name, two puffs, in the chilly air.

"Ja-cob!"

I linked my arm around a wheel axle, and glared at her, daring her to try to grab me. The spokes shifted, ever so slightly, sending up a pearly exhumation of sand and flint. A light came on in our wagon.

"Velina? Is that you?"

With a soft, defeated cry, my mother rose to her feet. She glanced down at me a final time, pressing her hand to her cheek. Then she stumbled back towards my father's voice, the amber penumbra of our wagon.

The Trail is full of surprises. The following morning, Mr. Grouse announced that two wagons had deserted our party, the Quigleys and the Howells, heading back east. My mother was seated by the campfires, boiling water for porridge, and she received this news without so much as a *huh,* an anesthetized murmur. I waited for her to look up at me, but she just sat there, staring blankly at the bubbles.

And then, just when I was at my most muddled, besieged

by all sorts of flickering, waxy fears, another surprise. Through the orange transparency of our tarp, I saw my parents' silhouettes, blurring together into a single, monstrous shadow. I held my eye up to a hole in the cover. Dad's head was in my mother's lap. His great eyes were shut. My mother had an iron bucket, and a thin, dirty kerchief. She was daubing a whitish solution of borax, sugar, and alum onto the sores beneath his fur. My dad was running his long, rough tongue over her boots, licking up the lichens and the toxic-colored spoors. His horns scraped against the floorboards. "I love you," my mother kept muttering, over and over, pushing the rag into his wounds, "I love you," as if she was trying to torture the true meaning out of the words. My father groaned his response.

So much of what passes between my parents on the Trail is illegible to me. It's as if they speak a private language, some animal cuneiform, pawing messages to each other in the red dirt. During the day, my father continues to pull our wagon forward. My mother hasn't spoken of that evening since. . . .

Mr. Grouse's oxen died in their traces today. They were a team, his beloved blue-ribbon leaders, Quick and Nimble. It took three men to cut them loose. All I could focus on was the coiled rope, slack and slick with blood, and the thought that Clem would probably not be interested in ball plays for a while. All the mothers shielded our eyes, and scooted us towards the wagons. They said that the oxen had "failed in the traces," their euphemism to protect the youngest children, which seemed a little silly to me, since everybody had to step over a big dead ox.

"Ma," Dotes asked, making a paper daisy chain in the wagon, "if I die, promise you'll dig a grave deep enough so the wolves can't get at me?"

My mother looked up from her knitting with a bleary horror. "Oh, sweetheart"—she poked her head out the wagon—"are you hearing this, Asterion?"

We all looked outside, to where Dad was standing in high, dun-colored grasses with the other men. They directed, while he used his hooves to tamp down some perfunctory dirt over Nimble. Lately, the men's requests have grown a lot less obsequious. Just the other day, Vilner Pratt persuaded my father to wear a silver cow bell so that the company will know when he's coming. ("You have a tendency to sneak up on a man, Mr. Minotaur." Vilner shrugged, with an aw-shucks sort of malice. "And to tell you the truth, it spooks our women.")

At the sound of my mother's voice, our father looked up, and waved. His horns and hide have darkened to a dull yellow-gray; the skin hangs loosely from his arms.

"Ma," Maisy asked, sucking on the fizzled wick of an old flare. "Is Dad going to fail in the traces?"

There was a time when my mother would have said no, and reassured us with shock or laughter. These days, she leaves our hair unwashed and our questions unanswered. "How should I know, Maisy? What can I know? You go and ask your father. You go and tell your father," Ma said, her eyes glinting like nail heads, "what you are afraid of."

Finally, we have reached the bluffs. From up here, we can see the midway point, the alkali desert of the Great Sink. It's a tough landmark to celebrate. The Great Sink is a weird, treeless terrain. Even the clouds look flat and waterless. A wide, dry canal cuts through the desert, a conglomerate rut, winnowed out by a thousand wagons. It looks as if someone has dug out the spine of the desert. The Great Sink reminds me of home, an Olympian version of the trenches that Dad used to paw in our kitchen. When I mentioned this to Ma, she laughed for the first time in many days.

This patch of our journey feels like a glum, perpetual noon. The lumberwomen are in low spirits; there is no wood for them to hack at. Suddenly, their curses sound hoarse and sincere. Wolves skulk around our wagons by day, just beyond rifle shot. Clem and I scare them off by singing hymns and patriotic ditties. Above us, the pale sky is greased with birds.

Inside our wagon, Dotes shivers beneath three horsehide blankets. Maisy sleeps and sleeps. Yesterday, Ma wanted us to stop, but my father was afraid of losing the company. At night they stepped outside again, to take a spousal conscience. Ma made me hold up the curtain of modesty, now soiled and tissue-thin, as a courtesy for our neighbors.

"Do you see any doctors around here?" Dad asked, making a big show of looking under a rock. He squeezed the rock in his fist, crushing it to powder. "Any medicine? Be brave, Velina. We have to press on now, we are over halfway there—"

He broke off abruptly. I had lowered the curtain. My arms were tired, and I had to itch my nose. Our eyes met, and my father saw something in my expression that made him trot over.

"Jacob." His teeth were shining. He wobbled a little, eyes burning, his hair on end, full of a radiant, precarious cheer, like our town drunk. He touched the nick in his horn to my cheek.

"Don't pay her any mind, son. We'll get there. Have a little faith in your father."

Then he picked me up and waltzed me through the ashes of our campfire. "Hold on, son!" He charged around and around the corral, making his shoulder muscles buckle and snap like oilcloth, an impromptu rodeo. "Gee!" I pleaded, giggling in spite of myself, "Haw!"

"Don't let go!" I yelped, even though I was the one holding on to his horns.

Then Dad spun me away from my mother, beyond the edge of our camp. We waltzed straight to the edge of the bluff.

"Look at that, Jacob." He whistled. "Look how far we've come."

Viewed from my father's shoulders, the desert stretched for eons, flat and markerless. It was an empty vista, each dune echoing itself for miles of glowing sand. A silent, windless night, where any horizon could be the West. The heat made me mistrustful of my own vision: I couldn't be certain if the blue smudges I saw in the distance were mountains, or mirages. The wagon trains camped below us were no help. With their snubbed, segmented ends, they looked like white grubs, curling into themselves, each head and tail identical. Tiny fires spangled the dark.

"Do you see, now?"

I peered into the desert.

I had no idea what my father saw out there, or what he wanted me to see. Still holding on to his horns, I pivoted, slow and halting, in a direction that I desperately hoped was West.

"Oh! Yes!"

Dad grinned. The firelight limned the absent places in his hide, the burn marks in his skin. Some of his bull's hair had come off in my fist. He lowered me to the ground, and then whispered directly into my ear, as if this was a secret between men:

"They say the clover grows wild all over the West, Jacob. So *green,* so lush and dense! So high, son, that when you wade through it, it covers your face. . . ."

Lady Yeti and the
Palace of Artificial Snows

"So what happens," Badger wanted to know, "during the Blizzard?"

Badger sidled up behind me during recess with no introduction, stepping across a yellow line and onto the rubbery surface of the tether court. We'd never spoken before. Badger's father had given me a ride home from school a few times, and even then we didn't speak. We sat in a hot, awful silence and waited for the lights to change.

"I dunno." I shrugged. "It's Adults Only."

Badger slammed his fist into the tethered ball. It swung between our faces.

"What do you mean you don't know? Your father works at the damn place!"

He grabbed me by the shoulders and rocked me a little bit, back and forth on the balls of my sneaks, and it was like we were dancing.

"I dunno."

Badger's breath smelled like egg sandwich. He had zillions of blackheads on his pug nose.

"I don't think my pops knows, either." My pops mostly did maintenance work at the Palace of Artificial Snows, fixing up the giant snow fans and rewiring the Zamboni. Sometimes he'd bring me along. I'd feed cherry snow to the orangutans and pretend not to notice when Pops flirted with the Ice Witch. (All of the fathers flirted with the Ice Witch, not just mine. I think it was a nervous reaction to her leotard. Her flesh-toned tights and all those rhinestones.) He got me certain perks, sure. Free skate rentals, gelatinous bags of sno-cone mix ("Liquid breakfast!" Pops grinned in the a.m.). But the Blizzard was Adults Only. Even if Pops could have finagled a pass for me, I wouldn't have wanted to go. Adults Only was shorthand for boring, or scary, or some combination thereof. I'd heard the rumors, and I wasn't interested.

"Well." Badger nodded. "We're going. Next Wednesday. Bring some money."

"Hey, Pops?" I called out. He was spattered with oil, pretending to be asleep on the couch. "How was the Blizzard?" Flakes of snow or dandruff were stuck to his jacket. I ruffled his hair. I lifted a twenty from his wallet. "Guess what? I made a friend today."

The bus let us out across the street, by the line of wilting palm trees. We stared at the ugly domed building in front of us: the Palace. It looked like a rusty spaceship, surrounded by filth and Buicks. Humid exhaust floated around the dingy blue stucco. From its nondescript exterior, you'd never guess that the Palace housed two thousand square feet of winter inside.

The Palace of Artificial Snows
Skating Rink
Perennial Snow Banks
Den of the World Famous Apes on Ice!

We walked across the long parking lot. Waves of heat broke against the ugly cars. Black asphalt. Sunlit metal. Secrets locked in trunks. A thirsty Saint Bernard whimpered as we passed, her tongue lolling out a crack in the driver's-side window. What sort of sadist would bring a Saint Bernard to the tropics? I reached two fingers through the crack and tried to pet her.

"Poor old pup. Shh," I whispered. My petting was pretty ineffectual. "Shhh . . ."

Badger drew up behind me with a metal pipe in his hand. He swung it once, twice, smashing through the backseat window.

"There you go, doggy!"

Often it was scary to hang out with Badger.

We saw Badger's father's Datsun in the parking lot. He must've been in some kind of hurry to get inside—the driver's-side door was hanging open. What a cheap, evil car. Whenever they drove me home from school, I would sit tall on my coccyx bone and try to resist the slickery vinyl. It smelled like cigarettes and women's shampoo; or else it smelled like subterfuge and aerosol blasts of lemon. Dark windows, the leering grille of the Datsun.

"See?" Badger said. "I knew he'd be here."

I nodded. It's not like there had been any debate about this. Everybody on the island knew that Badger's father practically lived at the Palace. My pops said we shouldn't begrudge him this, an icy reprieve from Badger's mother.

"Looks like a lot of people are here."

The Palace of Artificial Snows became extra-popular in summer, when it was a frozen oasis on our island. Outside, the world was all melt and swelter. But inside! Sweat froze on your face. Gherkin served fizzy sodas with names like Hoarfrost and Red Penguino. I loved it there. I would skate in tight, contained circles, and dream about winter.

The doors slid open, and we stepped into a polar centigrade.

"Hurry up, Reg." The doors slid shut. The sun vanished behind us. "We might as well pick our hiding places now."

We hid under the booth, chewing on yellow stuffing from the torn upholstery until the lights went low. It felt especially chilly over there, in the roped-off section of the Palace: UN ER R NOV T ON. The old snack bar had a pleasant, homey dilapidation: split cushions, ancient popcorn on the tables, the flickering blue and violet bulbs. A nice contrast, I thought, to the newer sections of the Palace, and the hideous perfection of the Ice Witch. From our damp square of carpet, we had a view of the whole rink: the plush DJ booth, the rental lockers. To our left, you could hear the hooting of the apes.

They kept the apes in a metal warren of cages by the shoe lockers. To the extent that you can love a mute and captive monkey, I loved those apes. Gorgeous pelts! The orangey red of starfish and pigeons' feet. Unlike the Blizzard, the Apes on Ice! Show was a treat for all ages. Five o'clock, every Wednesday. Pops and I used to go together all the time when I was younger. Nowadays, that sort of thing would never be legal. It was a pretty appalling extravaganza, even then.

"Hey, Reggie, check out that big 'un!"

Badger pointed at Cornelius, who caught us looking and rattled the bars. But it was an affected rattle—as if he were only pretending to feel wild and dissatisfied for our benefit. Cornelius beat his chest once, and winced. His gray, heart-shaped face frowned beneath a red corona of hair, like a jilted king on stupid rental skates. Those orangutans never tried to escape—they were inbred captives who knew only this artificial winter, the choreographed dances that we bribed them to do. But they'd bite your fingers, if you provoked them. They'd fidget and scratch.

On the other side of the Palace, Lady Yeti was riding the pink Zamboni. She puttered around the rink, one furry hand on the steering wheel. It could have been a Sunday afternoon on an alien planet, and Lady Yeti was out mowing the lawn.

Lady Yeti's real name was Reba. She worked as the DJ, and the Modulator of the Snows. She had wide, hairy hips and maternal bags under her eyes. I never saw her without her Yeti suit. She was abominable in the best way, a bipedal gorilla with a moon-white pelt. We all loved her. Unlike many employees at the Palace—Gherkin with his split lip, the Ice Witch, my balding pops—Lady Yeti was spectacularly ugly. She was sort of lazy. She got winded from eating. "HI, REGGIE," she'd roar in my ear, breathing heavy and covered in nacho crumbs. She was the most generous of us; her very body was warm and generous. Kids clambered all over her and hid in the baggy folds of her costume. Spit and candy matted her fur. We liked her much better than the Ice Witch.

The Ice Witch was the daytime supervisor at the Palace of Artificial Snows. Lady Yeti worked nights. We'd arrived right at the transition.

There were rumors that the Ice Witch and Lady Yeti were sisters, or that they were actually the same woman. And it was true that you never saw one with the other. But in every bodily respect, the Ice Witch and Lady Yeti were opposites. The Ice Witch was a skeletal beauty. Cold, quartz eyes, an anemic complexion. Once I caught her licking salt from the Big Soft Pretzel machine. She wore blue earmuffs and pearl-seamed gloves. She chain-smoked Sir Puffsters in the parking lot. The Ice Witch could work a sequined hypnosis on the male skaters, sure. But babies and primates don't disguise their terror. Infants howled. The alpha orangutans lobbed bricks of ice at her; the orange runts cowered; and the medium-sized apes mostly ate their own feces and sulked.

Lady Yeti's voice growled over the loudspeaker. "Now presenting . . . the World Famous . . . Apes on Ice!"

All at once, fourteen orangutans slid down chrome chutes into heaps of artificial snow. Poof! Poof! Lady Yeti dusted the grainy powder off of them and swung them around the rink. The two alphas, Cornelius and Tang, held on to Lady Yeti's gloved hands, and the lesser apes knit their skinny gray fingers together, forming a staggered V of monkeys. In a peculiar inversion, the apes wore human costumes: tailored boleros, gold helmets, these special Velcro skates. They must've done this act a hundred times, and they still looked terrified.

From the arena seats, if you squinted, you could pretend that the orangutans were skating of their own volition. But Badger and I had a privileged vantage point, low to the ground. We could see Lady Yeti's tugs on the sequined leashes. We could hear her huffing and cursing:

"Goddamn it, Cornelius, you milquetoast bum! A little help? Pick it up, Tang!"

When I was a kid, I used to get weirdly aroused imagining this, Lady Yeti's face beneath her mask, her cheeks turning rosy from the strain. She spun the apes in sad pirouettes beneath the colored lights. A neon disco ball freckled their bodies. Their helmets kept slipping over their eyes. The roving spotlight turned the apes weird and beautiful colors, and even Badger crept closer to watch. Pink light danced across their white fur, their golden fur, burgundy, blue, brown.

You know, on the eve of our first Blizzard, we weren't even friends yet, me and Badger? Which seems impossible to me now. But I could feel us becoming friends, our friendship freezing and solidifying with each hidden minute that we spent together beneath the dark booth. Our legs were tangled. Our round faces parted the red fringe.

"Closing time!"

After the Apes on Ice! Show and the Senior Hockey Hour, the Ice Witch banished everybody from the ice. Usually, this was the time of day when I would unlace my skates and trudge back to the bus with the other kids. But tonight Badger and I watched as the seniors headed off the ice, winking and gossiping, to change out of their uniforms. Most of them, we knew, would be staying for the Blizzard.

The blinds came down. The wind piped up. Lady Yeti was already ensconced in the DJ booth, assembling her records. Peabo Bryson, Chaka Khan. We watched her flip a switch. The Indoor Weather Manufacturer lit up, an industrial palette of yellows and grays. Unseen instruments began to rumble. The temperature ticked down by degrees. My stomach roiled, and I got the vertiginous suspicion that we were descending down, down, down. Frost blurred the windows.

Badger shifted onto his knees. "Did you hear that? They're coming!"

Adult laughter echoed through the Palace. Footsteps were headed towards us, toward the skate rental counter. I stifled a gasp. These were shoes that we knew: Herb's galoshes, Mayor Horacio's suede boots, Sister John's square-toed oxfords, Chief Bigtree's gator leather. Half the staff of our school was here: Cafeteria Midge, Principal Yglesias, Mr. Swanson. When I spotted the cheap, tasseled loafers that I knew belonged to Badger's father, I looked over at Badger. His breath sounded funny. He looked like he was trying not to sneeze.

The adults knelt down and stepped out of their familiar shoes. They grunted into their ski socks, their anonymous skate rentals. Nobody said a word.

"Psst! Badger!" I asked stupidly. "That your father?"

Badger shoved crumbs of popcorn into his mouth and

didn't answer. He was staring straight ahead. His father was bending down on one knee pad in front of us, doing up his laces.

"When I found out he was coming here, I tried hiding his skates." Bits of kernel gleamed between Badger's teeth. "I took his gear and shit to the pawn shop."

"And then what happened?"

Quivering fingers, inches from our noses. Tying double, triple-knots.

"It didn't matter. He comes anyways. Rentals are three dollars."

"How did you find out that your pops was coming here?"

Badger didn't answer. Lady Yeti had spotted us. She was skating over. Those legs! Lady Yeti looked like she could kill a man with her woolly quadriceps. Now she had seen us, there was nothing to be done. She'd have to extradite us to the Ice Witch. We curled in our spines and tailbones, paralyzed, and prayed for mercy.

Lady Yeti got down on her knees with us. She blinked out at us from inside her shaggy costume.

"Huh!" she chuckled. "Shouldn't be here!" Her tiny eyes looked sad inside her mask. She reached into a secret pocket and emptied out its contents: mostly fur, and peppermints with fur stuck to them. "For when you get hungry, huh! Stay put." She skated away.

Badger's father was one of the first men on the ice. He shoved away from the railing, his arms wheeling in the rising wind. His face made me want to like him more than I did. He had black, slicked-back hair and startled eyes. Poor form for a skater, I thought: hunched and eager. A funny buckle at the knees. Something about the way he was moving across the ice made me feel a little sick inside.

Badger's father was skating towards a stranger. A stranger to us, anyways. She had on a figure skater outfit—diaphanous skirts, ruby spangles, purple tights. It was the show-stopping garb of a petite Olympian. She looked to be about forty.

"Huh," I said. "She somebody you, uh, you know?"

Badger's eyes went small and mean. He crushed a soda can in his fist.

"This is all your fault, Reg. Right now if it weren't for you, he'd be home."

"I'm sorry?"

Badger pounded and pounded. The can was horseshoe-flat.

"Wouldn't even *be* a Blizzard if your pops didn't work maintenance, and your pops wouldn't need to work maintenance if *you* didn't exist."

Often it was hard to argue with Badger.

I tried anyhow: "Uh-uh. Don't you put this on us. My pops doesn't have anything to do with the Blizzard. He just unstuffs the pipes." This was true. Pops rarely even needed his tool box. Mostly he just pulled scarves out of the fans. "Somebody else would maintain the Blizzard if he didn't. It's a popular event."

Badger wasn't listening to me. His eyes were glued to the ice.

"I wondercould you burn down an ice arena? Or would you have to, like, explode it?"

"Explode it, I guess? But, um, you know, you probably shouldn't do either."

Badger was staring from his father to the strange woman and back again. We watched her stoop and pretend to smooth her seamless tights. Badger's father turned a teenage shade of red. He pulled the woman closer.

"But I wondercould you do it?"

Badger had invented a new word, *wondercould,* a lexical bridge to all sorts of ugliness. *Wondercould* came out in one exhalation. It didn't leave either of us much room to reflect. Even now, Badger was stroking the red tip of a match.

"Badger . . . ?"

Now Badger's father and the woman were skating together. She was a good skater, I guess, but I thought Badger's mother had a more beautiful face. She circumscribed his hurried, hungry slide forward with a lithe figure eight. Her lips were red and parted. Her skirts swirled to a stop.

The match had burned down to Badger's fingers. I touched a flake of snow to the stick.

"Badger?"

"Shhh!" Badger said. "It's starting."

The first snowflake of the Blizzard fell at 7:03. Isolated snowflakes came piping out of the vents, shy, single flakes, and then Lady Yeti flipped some invisible lever. The snow got faster. It got colder and thicker, and we felt a raw tingle in the air.

She turned the knob up to "wintry mix." Phil Collins crooned his mellow sorrow out of the loudspeakers. Snow blasted our faces. Factory snow. It fell in sheets, these uniform hexagonal crystals. Less unique, I guess, but more reliable than nature. You could taste the hard, mica falseness on your tongue.

At this point, everyone had laced into their skates. Most of the adults were spinning in excitable circles, orbiting one another, sliding forward, colliding, collapsing—then skating quickly back to the snow fans, to hide beneath the starry blasts of snow. From our spot on the ground, we could see their faces. Mayor Horacio kept falling backwards and cursing. Midge did accidental splits. Suddenly ice-skating seemed like the most ludicrous of all human endeavors. What a stupid innovation! Skate blades. Indoor lakes. It had a perverse, fairy-tale logic, I thought, tying knives to your feet and carving out over frozen water.

The Blizzard got going, the adults picked up speed. All that fake snow was disorienting, and we could only pick out about one face in twenty—Badger's father, then Annie, then old Ned—their features blurred and fleeting, like faces from a dream. Scrawled-on eyes, a black declivity where their mouths should be. Badger's father was skating with his head thrown back, laughing, letting the ice carry him forward. The music changed to Men Without Hats, and the adults went slamming into one another with a new violence. When it got to be too much, they skated for the "safety snow," the dry, banked heaps along the outer edges of the rink. From what Gherkin had told me, I knew that this stuff was neither snow nor safe. It was a cold chemical foam trucked in from a plant in Scranton, glowing an unreal, satiny blue. Everybody seemed eager to collapse into it, to tumble into one another. I watched women roll around in it until their bodies became anonymous. Sister John dove headlong into the safety bank and emerged looking like a shrunken yeti, disguised and dripping with snow.

Lady Yeti presided over it all from the raised dais of the DJ booth. Every few songs, a man would skate over to the DJ booth to "make a request." He would slide Lady Yeti an embarrassing bribe: $5 in quarters, lotto tickets, raspberry cake gooed into napkins. She always accepted. Then the entire rink got that much wilder, that much whiter with snow. At first this confused me: *this* was what they were paying for? And then I got it. I saw it. What these men were purchasing was blindness: a snow cloak of invisibility. They could grab at the passing women without penalty, taunting them, tugging at their skirts. What the women wanted was less clear to me. To be grabbed at, I guess, without judgment.

Mayor Horacio, in a holey, slush-crusted orange leotard, skated over to the DJ booth. He started complaining to Lady Yeti. He had to crane his neck to look up at her, black hair tufting over the sagging elastic. His Adam's apple looked bulbous and indecent. "Do you see that clear patch over there? Yeah? Of course you do. Because there is no snow there. Because somebody is too busy eating nacho cheese to do her goddamn job. . . ."

This was true. The part of the rink that he pointed to looked weirdly unaffected by the Blizzard. Snow dripped down the walls, melting to a new and worrisome clarity. A short, chubby woman was standing there in full view, exposed in the pitiless winter light. She was trying to fan the meager flurries around her. When she caught Horacio looking, she sucked in her belly. Badger and I recognized her: Midge, who ladled cold noodles onto our plates five days a week. She looked pink and nervous. Carroty curls

144

were pasted to her face. Someone—Badger's father? Mayor Horacio?—had clawed runs into Midge's tights. She waggled a wet, uncertain mitten in his direction.

Horacio groaned. "Jesus, would you hurry?" He shoved damp singles at Lady Yeti. "Would you get me some big flurries over there, stat?"

"Hold on!" Lady Yeti growled. Her control panel fizzed and sparked. "Problems. Let me give Maintenance a buzz."

Uh-oh. I'd been on the receiving end of the emergency calls from the Palace. The "Pops, it's for you" end. Pops belting up, stumbling out to fix the midnight world.

"Badger? Hey, Badger? We gotta go."

But Lady Yeti wasn't dialing my father. Instead, she pounded her hairy fist on the control panel. "There we go! Never mind!"

She cranked the wind up to a 6/7 on the Beaufort scale, just shy of gale force. She turned up the precipitation. And then a white curtain swirled around Horacio and Midge, blotting them out. I breathed a sigh of relief.

"That was close, huh? I thought she was going to call in my pops."

Badger looked at me dully. "Oh. Where does he think you are right now?"

"Your house. What about you? What did you tell your father?"

Badger snorted. "I'm supposed to be at my house too. Babysitting Mom."

"Oh." *If you're here, then who's watching her?* But I didn't want to know the answer.

Badger's mother was very, very sick. It looked like she caught a bad dream from somebody. She slumped in a motorized chair, heavy with sleep. If you saw her from a distance, she looked like an extension of the machine, a fleshy covering for the machine. Nobody on the island knew the specifics of her disease, but we could see its sly effects. It turned you into some nightmare centaur, a robot in a woman-blanket. Coughs, whirs, beeps, moans, but no movement. So—not that I condoned what Badger's father was doing during the Blizzard, but I could see why he'd pay to go snow-blind for a while.

I said as much, in my mincing way, to Badger.

"You shut up now, Reggie. Shut up. I'll bet your dad comes here too and what's his excuse? There is no excuse. I wondercould you go to hell, Reggie?"

He sent popcorn jumping up from the damp carpet with his fist.

"Look!" Badger dragged me out from under the table. "It's her!"

Lady Yeti was helping a woman off the rink. It looked like she had taken a nasty spill into a snow fan. Head to toe, she was dripping with it.

". . . and he hurt me, he hurt me *bad*," the woman was sobbing into Lady Yeti's fur. "He pushed me and he just let me fall. . . ."

"You just told me that story, ma'am." Lady Yeti was careful to modulate her own booming alpine volume. "Remember? You just got done telling me that very same story."

"Really?" The woman touched the hollow of her throat and shivered a little. "That same story?"

"Word for word."

A look came over the woman's face then, a confused and

terrible look. As if she had just stumbled on a set of her own footprints in the snow, and realized that she was lost.

"Well! It's a good story, anyways! Let's get ya cleaned up, huh!" Lady Yeti beat the wet flakes out of the woman's hair. "You better sit this one out. . . ."

We followed the snow-drunk woman into the bathroom.

They even had flurries going in the bathroom, a phony violet-blue, piped in through the high vents. Somebody—my pops?—had rigged up the hand dryers to spew translucence. It must have been a nightmare for Gherkin to clean up. Frost limned the mirrors. The sinks were bowls of freezing slush. All the toilet paper was damp. We could see our outlines in the glass, but not much else. The woman's face materialized behind us, her eyes shiny and rimmed with red.

"You," Badger sputtered. "You." You could tell he hadn't really planned this far ahead.

The woman fell forward and pressed her nose against the mirror. She gave us a scary, sidelong smile. The flurries blew around the room like tiny moths.

"Should you boys be in here? This is the ladies' room. . . ."

"Y-y-you." His teeth were chattering. "You! You're not my mother. You're nobody. . . ."

The woman wouldn't even turn to face us. She was unsteady on the blunt edge of her skates, and allowed herself to topple backwards. Badger held out an unwilling arm to support her.

"Why were you skating with my father?"

The woman giggled. She yanked at her soaking tights.

"Which one's your father?

Badger shoved her away from us, hard. She fell backwards

into one of the freezing sinks, her head thunking against the mirror. Chunks of snow bobbed around her like little icebergs.

"You're nobody! You're just some able-bodied bitch. . . ."

He yanked me towards the door. Behind us, we could hear the woman shouting for Lady Yeti. I hoped that she hadn't gotten a good look at our faces. Now we had our own reason to flee the bright lights.

Beyond the thin halogen glow of the bathroom, the Blizzard raged in earnest. Downdrafts, snowfall, the black sparkle of the rink. The Palace had grown subzero cold. I thought we must be near the cages—you could hear the monkeys howling above the wind.

"Badger, wait up! What was that . . . ?"

"Forget it, forget her. Anyhow, I don't think she was the right one. Come on. We need to get on the ice. We need to turn this dumb storm off." He hopped the counter and grabbed us skates.

"Are you nuts? We can't go out there. Look how dark it is. I can barely see you!"

Which was a lie. Badger was kneeling in front of me, forcing my feet into skates.

"There, stand up. Lace those up. I wondercould you wiggle your toes?"

"I don't think so; I don't think—"

And then it was too late, we were right in the thick of it. I could feel the Blizzard working on me, too. As soon as we got on the ice I felt a cold thrill of happiness, an instant forgetting. I flung myself into the wind. So this was the Blizzard. It looked different once you were inside it. Snowflakes rushed in jet streams all around us. It was wonderful, the speed, the shocking cold of it; it was like outskating an awareness of gravity! We let the gales push us forward and double us back. Sparks leapt from our skates, tiny flecks of light on the black ice, the blades cutting quick and faster beneath us. Overhead, machines were sharpening the wind.

Shortly thereafter, though, the chill grew intolerable. I think that windchill was a deliberate effect, one of the Ice Witch's spells for profit. It goaded us forward, towards one another. It turned each skater into a heat seeker, a human comet. There was a terrible pleasure to this, getting pelted and bruised, pelting and bruising in circles. All of us went crashing around the rink. Midge was flat on her back with her skates in the air. Coach Crotty did a series of unsightly lutzes. Mrs. Saumat slid into Badger and pulled him down into the safety snow with her, roaring with laughter.

Where was the DJ booth? We'd been around the rink a dozen times now, and we couldn't find it. I felt a cold, dark lunge in my throat.

Phil Collins started playing from the speakers again. For a while I could still make out Phil's tinny optimism, threaded through the Arctic winds: "You can't hurry love, oooh, you just have to wait. . . ." And then it was just shrieking and the screech of fan blades and black ice on the sides of the rink, wind and darkness, snow-drunk faces screaming out at us, distorted beyond recognition. Walls and bodies came at us out of nowhere.

"I got you, Reggie." Badger's hands on my shoulders felt warm and secure. "Hang on, Reg, I got you. . . ." We skated forward. Dodging and swerving, bodies whizzing into us and then contracting back. We'd be rounding corners and briefly alone; then lunging forward, helpless, towards another stranger on the ice.

"Sorry!" I slammed into somebody and slid forward. Badger got knocked facedown beside me, jostling a tooth loose. I watched the tooth slide away, too dazed to stop it. When I looked up, Badger was gone. I caught a glimpse of him blowing backwards across the dark rink, his face a diminishing oval.

Something had gone very wrong with the Blizzard. Bodies collided, borders vanished. The spindrift sent freezing eddies through the air, and for the first time I was afraid of real blindness. After a few more loops around the rink, I couldn't tell where the room ended and my own body began. I struggled to regain my balance. Women sped by me with their makeup running. Men collapsed into the safety snow with their bruised legs tangled together. Poor Badger, I thought, and my pity warmed me. To know your father was a participant in this kind of weather!

And then I heard a laugh that I recognized.

Fear blurred the glass. Not my pops! I thought. Definitely not. It was Mr. Swanson, Mr. Yjonsun, some other kid's father. But I didn't stick around to investigate. Backwards skate! I used muscles that I didn't know I had to push myself backwards, into the dense white center of the Blizzard. I wasn't like Badger, I didn't want some monster confrontation. I didn't even want to be there.

After many numbing, numberless revolutions, I finally spotted the DJ booth and skated towards it. But Lady Yeti had vanished. She'd left a huge white suit with no obvious zipper. Wisps of fur and snow, and no clues. A few mints. I didn't even know who to look for. Lady Yeti could be anybody out on the ice.

The Indoor Weather Manufacturer was ablaze with tiny lights, making its own manic music of beeps and adjustments. I ran my finger over the hot pointy bulbs. I picked up the headset and pushed the button marked MAINTENANCE. It rang four times before somebody answered.

"Lady Yeti?" My pops sounded sleepy, and far away. I could hear some dumb sitcom on our TV behind him. "That you?"

Snowflakes were erasing the headset, my left hand, the coiled black wires. I grinned into the receiver. The Blizzard whirled around me, but it didn't matter now. All this time my pops had been asleep, at home.

"There some kind of malfunction? You need me to come out to the Palace?"

"Huh!" I did my best to imitate a Yeti bark. "No! Thanks!"

Then I hung up the phone.

You know, in retrospect, I probably shouldn't have tried to Modulate the Snows on my own. It was an abominable technology, that control panel, full of riddles and switches. But I didn't know then that the Blizzard was on a timer. If I'd known that we were only minutes away from the Meltdown, I would have waited it out.

Instead, I pushed the biggest, most luminous button. And I knew from the first iron shriek, the clang of unseen metal, that I'd made a mistake. Somewhere, the doors to the metal warrens flew open. The apes shook off their malaise.

Within moments I saw orange shapes, blue feet flying in the Palace rafters high above me. Coppery twinkles went shooting through curtains of ice. The orangutans were brachiating around an invisible network of pipes. Every few moments, I'd catch a glimpse of their feet dangling and grasping above me. The indoor world had gone very wrong tonight. An ape fell shrieking into the snow.

Maybe the pipes had grown too cold for the apes to hold on to. Maybe Phil Collins's percussion was shaking them loose. Whatever the trouble, they were falling all around me, the orangutans, in twos and threes. They made inadvertent snow angels where they fell. Their bodies flailed into one another; and when they tumbled up, you could see their wide simian wingspan, red hair in the white trenches. *Pffft!* spat one of the fallen orangutans. It was Cornelius. He looked the way I felt: the blue sag of his face in its wild red frame. Frost hung from his arms. He'd been too cold, for too long, too far from his jungle home. I was sorry I'd released him.

Now great sheets of sleet pelted the rink in waves, hard pellets clattering to the ice. Bodies were whistling all around me, behind the snow, and I could feel the dense atomic wake of them as they passed. They made their own music, a darker weather.

One woman was skating stark naked, her red hair flaming out behind her. Or possibly I was watching an escaped orangutan; inside the ice clouds, it was impossible to judge.

"Lady Yeti?"

I skated after her.

As I whipped around the rink, I got periodic jolts of

color. A few of the orangutans were stirring in the safety snow. They stared at me from the melting heaps, looking battered, bright-eyed, alive. Snow spattered the males' gray cheek pads. They slid forward in crazed ochcr maneuvers, eager to return to their cages. A lucky few made it safely to the other side. Tang went skidding past me on all fours, clawing at the ice with her long spindle fingers.

Whcre was Lady Yeti? The Blizzard was getting louder and wilder. The music was getting louder, too, until I thought my sternum would burst with it. I forgot about Badger, his father, Lady Yeti, my failure at the control panel, everybody but my own. Everything conspired to convince me that the storm was on the verge of swirling us somewhere better: the music rising and the music swelling, the deceptive up-tick of rhythm, the smooth give of the ice, a roaring white sound that made me think that the storm was breaking, that some crescendo was coming, a final mechanical gale that would white-out the entire Palace. . . .

It never came. The vents sucked back the snow. The wind switched off. I couldn't believe it: the Blizzard was over.

A neon sign blinked on the far wall: MELTDOWN!

When the fluorescent lights came back on, I saw Lady Yeti first. She was newly costumed, standing in the center of the ice. Glassy bits of factory snow winked down around her. One of the men was embracing Lady Yeti, the soft citadel of Lady Yeti, taking shelter behind her bulky silhouette. Her back was turned to me, and I could only see the man's short, thick arms straining to close around her. His fists were lost in her fur. The knuckles looked familiar. Lady Yeti looked over her huge shoulder and saw my face.

"Don't worry, baby, huh?" she said. "We're just finishing up here."

I skated around her to get a better look. Next to Lady Yeti, Badger's father looked like a stout, wizened child. He was standing on his tiptoes, his face lost in the white curls of Lady Yeti's chest. He fumbled for a zipper that he couldn't find.

Lady Yeti was ticklish. She chuckled off gray clumps of snow. Her big shoulders shook in ripples, seamless, of luster and muscle. It amazed me that Lady Yeti had been able to shed her fur and rearmor so quickly. She moved as if her costume were sewn onto her skin with invisible stitches. Badger's father tugged harder. His own workshirt was missing buttons, and I pictured Badger's father skating with Lady Yeti, both of them flying naked and weightless over the ice. Behind me, I heard a new roaring begin.

"I wondercould you get out of my way, Reg?"

I turned and saw Badger sitting high astride the pink Zamboni. He wasn't smiling, so I couldn't tell which tooth was missing. Badger had black, snow-blind eyes and no hat. His face looked stung and frozen. Snow was melting down his hair, his cheeks. He was bearing down on his father.

The auger bit down on the ice with a fresh menace. A very large, very sharp blade, similar to those used in industrial paper cutters, shaved up the ruined surface of the rink. My fevered shouting *No!* and *Please!* and *Stop!* got swallowed in the Zamboni's engine. Badger's father never even saw him coming—he was still burying his face in Lady Yeti's costume. At the last minute, Badger swerved. Blue light bounced off the metal blade. Then Badger drove the Zamboni in careful circles around the entire surface of the rink. Dirty ice and russet orangutan hair flew backwards into the Zamboni's vacuum. Water sewed up the white cuts behind him. Badger filled in the gashes from so many skate blades, line by line, until the rink became a perfect mirror once again, frozen and blank.

The City of Shells

Barnaby is busy hosing down Paundra, that hoary old carapace, when he first hears the screaming. He tells himself that it's just the wind. Barnaby has spent the whole day scrubbing seagull excrement with a Sisyphean fury, and now it looks like the storm is going to hit after all.

"Goddamn it," he mutters to the smirking gulls. "Never fails. As soon as I suds up these bitches, it pours."

The City of Shells closed to the visiting public over an hour ago. Now the boardwalk is deserted. Silent, except for the medleyed roar of the waves and the distant rumble of thunder. Gray, rain-bellied clouds are rolling in. Farther out, the sea is sluicing into night. There's a hushed, tingly feeling in the air, as if the whole world is holding its breath. Only the silvery gulls dot the horizon. They peck at used condoms and empty Dorito bags with a salt-preened serenity.

Barnaby stares at the massive thunderheads, full of misgivings. Ever since closing time, he's been on edge. He generally tries to punch out right at seven. You've probably heard the rumors, too: there are strange noises in the City after dusk. Legend has it—if you can use *legend* to describe the booze-fueled tales that get passed laterally within a janitorial staff of two—that the Giant Conchs are haunted. On stormy nights, they echo with the radular skitterclatter of their extinct inhabitants. The teenage kid who works this job on weekends, Raffy, gets all lyrical-hysterical on the subject. "This place turns into a motherfuckin' ghost town after hours! The shells start *singing*."

Raffy says that if you hear the ghost music, it earworms into your brain and infects you like an auditory virus. It plays at subliminal levels, alien and resonant as insect song. The boss dismisses Raffy's reports as inner-ear dementia. "Had an uncle who suffered from musical hallucinations," the boss once told Barnaby sadly. "Poor bastard. Spent the last decade of his life deaf to everything except the opening bars of 'Who Can Be a Toucan? You Can!'" He shook his head. "I don't envy that Raffy. Must be a tough row to hoe."

The screaming is coming from inside Cornuta. *Not real,* Barnaby thinks. He leans on his broom and wonders, for a delicious, sky-tilting second of vertigo, if he might be going crazy. But this is no phantom music. This sound is scary in a different way. Too real, too human.

Cornuta is off-limits to guests, roped off on the other side of the park. She got banged up during Tropical Storm Vita and is currently under repair. The boss rented a crane and lowered her so that she's lying sideways on the beach. Now she's a bitch to clean, cracked at the tip of her nacreous dome and always filling up with trash and irascible crabs. For a Giant Conch, Cornuta is one of the island's tiniest, forty-five feet from end to end, about the size of a small trailer. The overlapping whorls that lead into the shell never widen beyond the circumference of a sewer pipe. It's not exactly the kind of rabbit hole you can tumble down by accident.

"Who goes there?" The ancient elocution bubbles up out of nowhere, making Barnaby blush. "I mean, is somebody in there?"

Abruptly, the screaming stops. Barnaby takes a shaky breath and peers inside the Giant Conch. All he can make out are two glittery eyes, blinking out of the preternatural darkness at the bottom of the shell. *It's back,* he thinks, feeling foolish even as he grips the toilet brush like a weapon, *the thing that used to live in the shell is back.*

"Excuse me!" a child's voice honks miserably. "I'm stuck. Do you have any Band-Aids, or food?"

Big Red had been looking forward to this field trip all month. The City of Shells is touted as "A Merman's Stonehenge!" They have to take the ferry to get there. It isn't, technically, a city: it's a megalithic formation of Precambrian Giant Conchs. The brochures make it look like some Neptunian version of Easter Island. The cover illustration shows a dozen of the Giant Conchs, arrayed in a weird half-moon formation along the beach. Each of the shells is a swirly, pearly licorne, some the height of a house. Gulls wheel in wicked circles around their marble parasols. Salt-bleached skyscrapers, the caption says, cast onto the shore by Cretaceous tsunamis, and set upright by our very own island progenitors! And there they are, in a photo inset: the ancestors. A small, furry people, their cheeks swollen like those of prudent rodents, lighting holy fires in the shadow of the giant shells.

Grades five through seven take a field trip there every August. The City of Shells is owned and operated by Laramie Uribe's father, and he gives the kids paper conch hats and a special discount. Laramie sat next to Big Red on the bus ride over. She and Big Red are best friends by default. Although she is only two grades above Big Red, puberty has been inordinately kind to Laramie. Teachers refer to Laramie as "sophisticated" and "mature for her age," but Big Red knows that Laramie is neither of these things. Laramie still snorts milk through her wide nostrils. She reads at a fourth-grade level. She defends herself against bathroom calumny by flicking snot berries at her detractors. What the teachers actually mean is that Laramie has huge boobs; that she smells like coconut oil and unfiltered Camels; and that she gives it up to high-school boys named Federico.

"Wait'll we get there." Laramie grinned slyly at Big Red. "I'll give you a tour of all the shells where we did it."

Big Red bit her lip and stared out the window. She had only a squeamy, abdominal sense of what "it" could be.

When they got there, Big Red pushed past Laramie and thundered off the bus. She raced down the beach, raced right into the sunlit center of the City, and then stopped short. She shielded her eyes and blinked up at the Giant Conchs, oblivious to the other children swarming around her. She thought: *What the heck is this?* These conchs were giant disappointments. The City had fallen into seedy disrepair. The pinky-white turrets were covered with seagull excrement; the interiors shimmered with grout. Mayo packets and pickle sticks slimed the axial ribs. Mr. Uribe had rigged the conchs with miniature speakers so that the tourists could hear the roar of the primordial seas—but the electricity was on the fritz. Tintinnabula was the only one working. She sounded like a giant refrigerator. If these shells had ever been the Fourteenth Wonder of the World, as touted on the tattered banners, they had definitely slipped in the rankings. Sweaty women took glamour shots in front of Sweet Venus. A froggy man rubbed his cigarette out on her speckled ventral side.

The kids yawned through a lecture on conchology. They ate a picnic lunch of corn dogs and strawberries. A hairless woman snapped their class photo in the City center—"Say chelicerae," she rasped—below the barnacled awning of Possicle. They gathered their things to go.

"Wait a sec!" Big Red interjected, tugging at sleeves. "When do we get to go inside the shells?"

"Well, of course we're not going inside them, Lillith." Sister John patted her head affectionately, as if Big Red was a sainted retard. "Who promised you that we were going inside the shells?"

Big Red bit her lip. She couldn't remember who had made her that promise, although she felt certain that someone had. Big Red felt a dull, cuckolded rage, but she wasn't surprised. For her first nine years on the planet, Big Red had lived a life of compromise. She wanted to be beautiful, but she'd had to settle for being nice. She wanted to see the Aquanauts for her birthday, but she'd had to settle for the gimp lobsters at the Crab Shack. She wanted a father, but she'd had to settle for Mr. Pappadakis. Mr. Pappadakis smells like Just for Men peroxide dye and eucalyptus foot unguents. He has a face like a catcher's mitt. The whole thing puckers inward, drooping with the memory of some dropped fly

ball. Big Red's mother has many epithets for Mr. Pappadakis: "our meal ticket," "my sacrifice," "vitamin P." He is an
obdurate man, a man of irritating, inveterate habits. He
refuses to put down toilet seats, or quit sucking on pistachio
shells, or die.

Laramie tells Big Red that she is lucky. Mr. Pappadakis
doesn't know when she's home in the first place, so she never
has to sneak around. Laramie sneaks out every Monday, Wednesday, and Friday afternoon. Laramie bragged to Big Red
that she had personally defiled eight out of thirteen Giant
Conchs.

"See that big 'un over there?" she whispered.

They're all big, Laramie.

"That's where I sucked off the chlorine vendor." Her
voice got low and slurry. "See that curly black hair stuck to
your shoe? That's his son Lyle's—"

Laramie shut up abruptly. A second later, her father came
striding down the boardwalk. At five feet three inches, with
wrinkly skin and a bright, bald face, Mr. Uribe looked like an
animate peanut. Too short, too fat, Big Red thought. He
couldn't even be the understudy for a TV dad. But at least he
didn't look like cadaverous Pappadakis.

"All right, kids," he said, clapping his hands. "Tour's over.
Don't forget to buy your plush conchs and conch accessories
in the gift store. The ferry is waiting for you." Most of the
kids went stampeding towards the dock. Big Red hung back.
She stared over the railing, sucking salt from her braid. Her
orange hair was knotted with sand. Below her, the sun was
drowsing on the surface of the water.

"Look!" Big Red breathed. She pointed at the marina.

Manatees were pushing their bovine wings through the water, emerging in ones and twos from under the pier. They swirled through motor oil in slow, graceful circles. "How beautiful . . ."

"They look like giant turds!" Rogelio squealed. "Giant turds, giant turds!" The other children sniggered.

Infidels! Big Red thought. She had just learned this word in social studies, and liked to walk around thinking it with religious furor. Sometimes, she fantasized about a great pyre, where she burned all of her heathen classmates. Manatees are God's creatures, not turds! she would roar. And my . . . name . . . is LILLITH!

"Get it, Big Red?" Rogelio elbowed her.

"Ha-ha," Big Red laughed. "Turds."

She followed the others into the store. Much more excitement was generated by the Giant Conch sea-salt shakers than by the shells themselves. Big Red didn't even have to wait until the coast was clear; nobody was looking. She slunk back down the dock to where the toppled shell was hunched on its side. She took a darting look around, then slipped under the yellow CAUTION ropes. Big Red crouched on her hands and knees and inched forward along the crimson outer wing that spun into the shell. Cornuta's inner chamber seemed to pulse with light, purpling inward to some effulgent, unreachable end point. Down below, the scooped-out hollow looked irresistibly snug.

Sucking in her stomach, knowing better, Big Red pushed her way inside. She slid down the canal and oomphed onto the floor. It was a much bigger drop-off than she had expected. Inside, the shell had a clean, blue smell, like the memory of

salt. It took a while for her eyes to adjust to the twinkly dark.
The shell body bowled out to the size of a walk-in closet. Big
Red wished that it was even smaller, the width of a cabinet, a
cupboard. She pressed both hands to the parabolic sides of
the shell. She closed her eyes and smiled—it felt like being
parenthesized. When Big Red looked down at her palms, she
saw that they were covered with beach grit: sand and cigarette butts, wet gull feathers. Someone had covered the
white, harp-shaped ledges with graffiti. Nasty words, bad
words. It was a language that Big Red recognized without
understanding. She mouthed the words to herself: ————
————. They made her feel too many things all at once,
hot-faced and dizzy and scared and ashamed. She didn't draw
a total blank; instead, the words smudged Big Red's mind
with fleshy blurs. Something opaque and darkly familiar, like
two bodies moving behind steamed-up shower glass. On the
far wall, she noticed more scrawled graffiti: LARAMIE ♥ RAFFY
4EVA!

Big Red stared up at the opalescent canopy above her. The
spines radiated outwards, pink to puce to a speckled orange.
She could see tiny perforations in the walls. Good. Big Red
pressed her cheek to the cool floor of the shell with a mar-
tyred glee. I hope the Giant Conch has one million gajillion
cracks and fills up with rainwater and I drown. Then they'll
be sorry. It gave her a smug satisfaction to picture beating
Mr. Pappadakis, the come-from-behind victor in a race to
the grave.

Ever since they moved into Mr. Pappadakis's cavernous
house, Big Red has sought out tiny spaces. She climbs into
the clothes hamper and pulls the lid on behind her. She sits

for hours under the sink, eyes closed, listening to the gurgling of the pipes. Some nights she crawls into the neighbor's dog house and holds Mr. Beagle's tight, squirmy body until she can feel all of its bones. And sometimes, if she sits long enough, it happens. Beneath the hum of her own blood, beneath the hum of the world itself, she thinks she can hear the faint strains of another song. It's a red spark of sound, just enough to cast acoustic shadows of the older song that she has forgotten. It sounds like this:

When Big Red opens her eyes, long-jawed shadows have overtaken the shell. Outside, the tide is coming in. The foamy rush of unseen water laps at her ears. Big Red shimmies to the back of the conch and holds her eye up to the fist-sized opening like a telescope. The visible sky is purple and clobbered with stars. Lightning licks the palm fronds. The whole conch hums with the promise of rain.

At first, Big Red is just pretending to be trapped. It isn't until she tries to get out of the Giant Conch that she realizes she really is stuck. She can belly-crawl back down the spine of the shell, no problemo. But when she tries to pull herself onto the calcite ledge that angles up and out of the siphon, she keeps sliding back down. The opening of the Giant Conch seems to have narrowed, somehow, and Big Red can't find purchase on the slippery shell walls. She tries to backtrack, but she can't wedge her pudgy body through the crack in the tip of the shell. Oh God, she thinks, how embarrassing. Please just leave me here to die.

But as the minutes tick by, she starts to feel increasingly uneasy. The fear of being found, of the sisters' wimpled censure and Rogelio's fat jokes, melts into a new fear: What if nobody is looking for her at all?

Don't panic, the grown-up voices in Big Red's head say sternly. They sound a little bit like Coach Crotty, the phys ed teacher, and a lot like Margarita, the TV mother on *Guess Who Loves You More? Stay calm.*

But the next thunderclap undoes her. Suddenly, the prospect of spending the night here seems too terrible to bear. Big Red's body heaves with panic. She bloodies her hands on Cornuta's horny clefts; she writhes on an invisible hook; she goes salmon-leaping towards the top of the shell, again, and again. And again and again she slumps back, battered and exhausted.

"Help!" Big Red squeals in the empty shell. Hot, oily tears roll down her face. "I'm stuck, I'm stuck, help!"

Nobody is coming, the grown-up voices intone, a tribunal of icicles. *Correction: the rain is coming. So you'd better help yourself get out of this mess before it storms.*

But then there he is, looking inside the shell with a worried expression. Big Red stops blubbering. Those piercing blue eyes, that gosling-soft hair. The doomed, affable face of the World's Greatest Sensational Mystery.

"What are you doing in there, kid?" Barnaby barks. "Park's closed."

The first raindrop hits the tiny hairs on the back of his neck. The sky is a seething, cobalt blue; it's going to start coming down any minute. What a nightmare. Barnaby knows that a better man would be feeling sorry for the kid, a roly-poly redhead who is staring up at him. Instead, Barnaby is thinking: *I'm going to miss the big game, and possibly the last ferry. The boss is going to find some way to pin this fat kid's misfortune on me. And I'm not even getting paid overtime.*

"Didn't you see the sign? Cornuta's out for the count."

"I just wanted to look around," she squeaks, "but now I can't get back out."

"Well, you got in, didn't you?" Another raindrop slides down his nose. "Why don't you give it another try?"

Big Red holds up her bloody palms and shakes her head. And Barnaby finds himself in an awkward sort of hostage situation, negotiating with the prisoner for her own release.

"Listen. Do you hear that?" he says through gritted teeth. "It is going to start raining any minute, kid. And we will have many sodden problems if we miss that ferry. So I need you to give it one more try."

She puts a hesitant hand on the jagged underlip of the ledge out. She tries to do a pull-up and winces.

"Careful! Can you move your leg? Can you wiggle your toes? You may have sprained something."

Big Red wiggles all five of her toes inside of her sneaker. She looks up at her Houdini and says nothing.

"Well? If you can't move them," Barnaby sighs, "I'll have to come in and get you myself."

Big Red withdraws her hand. "I can't."

He groans. "This oughta be good." Barnaby has never worked hard enough to develop the tawny musculature of a career broom pusher. His muscles have long since gone soft and turned to fat.

"Okay, kid, you've got to help, too. . . ."

Barnaby finds himself thinking many ungenerous thoughts.

"I can't get you out of there if you don't cooperate, you know. . . ."

Thoughts such as: I probably can't get you out of there at all, you goddamn butterball. He is thinking: winches, pulleys. Goggled men blowtorching the chubby lass out, the boss somehow blaming Barnaby for the lost revenue.

"Jesus, kid, would you just—"

"You're hurting me!"

"Put your right foot there, and push with your . . . god-*damn* it!"

Barnaby looks at his watch. Seven minutes till the ferry leaves.

"Okay. Clearly, this isn't working. Just hang tight. I am going to go tell the ferry driver to wait for us. And then I'll call for help. . . ."

Thunder booms through the City and they both jump. Barnaby watches the poor kid bang her head on the chitinous dome of the shell. Her gray eyes are filling with tears.

"I . . . I'm sorry, sir," she gasps. "I can't. Please, please don't leave me here."

Barnaby stops in his tracks. Oh, he wishes the kid hadn't called him sir.

"All right," he hears himself saying. "Let's give it one more shot in the dark."

They seesaw together in a sweaty dance: Barnaby pulls, and Big Red pushes. Big Red pushes, and Barnaby pulls. And in the middle of their pendular wrangling—while Barnaby is pulling, the blue tendons throbbing on his spindly arms, and Big Red is pushing, pigeon-toed on the polished floor—she falls backwards for a second time. And pulls Barnaby in after her. Cornuta reverberates with their strangled cries, and the splintery crunch of bone.

"Are you still angry with me?"

It's been almost an hour since they heard the last ferry engine gunning in the distance. Night seeps into the City, an implacable blackness. Barnaby's face is inches from her own. Big Red is acutely aware of every pore on her face, every follicle of hair on her head. Her smile feels huge and strange.

Barnaby doesn't answer. He is rubbing his leg and staring morosely out the small portal where Cornuta's spiral opens to the sky. A few fat raindrops plink into the sand. Goosebumps prick up along his arms. He shivers, snaps up his top two shirt buttons. The floor, the walls of the shell have become freezing to the touch.

"How long till your boss comes?"

"I told you, kid. At least twelve hours." He is holding his curly brown head in his hands. "Jesus. Any guesses as to when your parents are going to sound the alert?"

Big Red tugs at her shoelace. "Hard to say."

Big Red's mother is away on business. She is "on call," and often has to leave at a moment's notice. This is confusing to Big Red, because her mother is also unemployed.

"You'll understand when you're older," her mother sighs. Then she gives her the scary, slack tightrope smile, and Big Red knows not to press.

Mr. Pappadakis is estranged from lucidity. On his bad days, he thinks Big Red is a figment of his imagination. On his good days, he lives around her, in the polite, damning way that he will eat around certain loathsome foods on his plate.

"What about your dad, then?" Barnaby asks. "I mean, your real dad?"

Big Red has never met her biological father. She heard her mother refer to him once, with a dismissive wave of her hand, as "a rainy afternoon at the Bowl-a-Bed." She's never even seen a picture. But Big Red hates him just the same. She is learning about genetics, and she envisions her father as a big, bow-legged X. Pumping out the evil chemical that accounts for Big Red's glandular woes, the orange injustice of her stupid hair.

"Kid? What's your name anyways?"

"Big . . ." She bites her lip. "Lillith."

"Big Lillith?" He smiles. "You look like a Lillith."

"Really?" Her face mushrooms out of the darkness with a terrible hopefulness. "I do?"

Lillith is the name of her old self, the one she left behind when they moved to the island. On the Mainland, her nickname used to be Lil. That was before her body swelled into something loafy and unrecognizable. Now the kids at her new school have rechristened her: BIG RED—BIG RED!

They chaw imaginary wads of gum like truckers when they say it. They chaw it so often that even she has started to think of herself this way, "Big Red," in the cheery singsong of her tormenters.

Sometimes Big Red can hear the ghost of Lillith haunting this new body. At night, Lillith goes wailing down the corridors of Big Red's limbs. She swings angrily in the belfry of her hips, the nave of her breasts. "Growing pains." Her mother shrugs. Hearing her real name spoken aloud, Big Red sheds her awkwardness like a mantle.

"You know," she grins, "who you look like?"

Barnaby looks at her blearily and shakes his head.

"Harry Houdini."

"Houdini, huh?" He grins in spite of himself. "That's a first. I guess you could call me a magician. My name's Barnaby. I'm the janitor. I make the trash disappear." His laugh echoes hollowly in the dark conch. "It's a limited bag of tricks, kid. I'm no great escape artist, clearly. I couldn't crack us out of this shell."

"Houdini is my favorite," she says shyly.

He snorts. "Shouldn't you have a crush on one of those boy bands? Gregorian Chowder, or whatever their name is?"

Big Red makes a face. "Everybody will come to their senses and stop liking them in three months, tops. Houdini is perennial."

For a ten-year-old girl, Big Red has a rich fantasy life. Pirates tie her to their tattooed shoulders and stroke her parrot feathers. Impish, asexual jockeys named Nate or Stan nudge their heels into her flanks with a stirrupy gentleness. Zookeepers put her in cages filled with clean, soft straw. They ask simple things of her—Honk this rubber ball with your nose! Eat a banana!—and applaud softly when she succeeds. "Even better than the ocelot!"

But her favorite is the Houdini fantasy. Big Red disagrees with his biographers, who say that he was driven by his longing to shuck off this mortal coil. She knows that he was all the time just searching for a box that could hold him. In the Houdini fantasy, she is curled inside an iron nautilus that sinks slowly to the dark sea floor, sending up silvery columns of bubbles. She has shackled dreams in blue meadows of sea grass, an inert argonaut. The nautilus is nothing like this porous, polluted shell. It is a seamless wedge of stone, impregnable. The keyhole subsumed back into the metal, and no suggestion of a lock.

"Do you think that's normal?" Big Red asks Barnaby. "To daydream about that stuff?"

"Sure." Barnaby shrugs. When he was her age, he fantasized about robots and cartoon mermaids.

Outside the shell, Barnaby can just make out a single star, hung low in the violet sky. Now that he has lost all feeling in his left leg, things are much more pleasant. The pink island moon bounces off the whorled roofs of the City. Intermittent moonlight makes the spiraled domes appear to be moving, somehow, spinning to the beat of an off-kilter carousel. The whole skyline ripples in jolly waves, as if the invisible world is casting material shadows.

Raffy was wrong, though, Barnaby thinks; there are no ghosts in the City of Shells. It's been dark for hours, and the only thing that's materialized so far is a cloud of mosquitoes. The storm has held off for longer than Barnaby dared to hope. Even so, he can't take much more of this. His leg is bent under him at a wrong-feeling angle, and it's colder than a meat locker inside Cornuta. He wonders if his injury qualifies him for workman's comp. *Surely we'll hear the ferry motoring up at any moment,* Barnaby thinks. *Surely* somebody *is out looking for us.*

Big Red, however, seems downright jubilant. She is squidged up under his right elbow, staring up at him with a moony grin. He smiles back at her uneasily.

"Are you hungry?" Barnaby fishes around in his pocket. "Here." He produces five lint-furred peppermints and a silver flask. "It'll take the edge off."

Big Red takes a sip and blanches.

"Well, hand it over if you're not going to finish it."

She stares up at him and takes a long swig.

Barnaby takes the bottle back and downs a few gulps himself. He hasn't spent any real amount of time inside the shells. It's depressing. He can see all the spots he's missed. The hose reaches only so far, after all, and Barnaby isn't known for his janitorial scruples. The dark stains are like Rorschach tests, each one diagnosing his professional shortcomings. Even by Cornuta's muted glow, Barnaby can see the tarry footprints where his boots slipped, a monument to his most recent failure.

"Geez," he coughs. "Pretty filthy down here." He doesn't tell the child that he, Barnaby, is the reason that these ancient shells resemble waste receptacles. Sponging baby oil and bleach onto Giant Conchs all day—this is not his vocation. When Barnaby was a boy, about Big Red's age, he wanted to be a real forest ranger. He wanted to be the steward of eternal landscapes, gashed rock and petrified woods. He would protect the cud-chewing noblesse of the buffalo; he would wear a badge and a hat. Now here he is, scraping expletives off Possicle for minimum wage. One thing never led to another. Mr. Uribe would have fired him long ago, if he hadn't made himself indispensable by hiding all the cleaning supplies.

Barnaby tries not to think about this too much. He looks

at Big Red, her eyes welling with some dopey-kid sentiment, and he gets a sudden image of a jack-in-the-box with its crank broken off. A child's box with no handle. That's how Barnaby feels when he thinks about his own kid ambitions. This cold, coiled music in the pit of his stomach and no hope of release.

"Yup. Pre-tty filthy . . ."

Keyhole light spills through the minuscule cracks in the conch. The kid is moon-spattered and covered with dust. She just sits there, staring and staring at him.

"Say, you know what we're sitting in, kid?" Barnaby does his nasally tour guide impression. "A megalithic exoskeleton. Why, we can only conjecture about what used to live here—" He breaks off abruptly. Hearing his own voice echo in the dark, he has accidentally terrified himself. All of a sudden, the shiny penumbral walls seem oddly malleable.

"Say, kid?" Barnaby coughs. "You haven't, uh, heard any strange noises out here, have you?"

Her ears turn bright pink. "Why?"

"Oh, nothing," he says with a whistling nonchalance. "My, er, colleague says he hears funny noises sometimes. Coming from inside the shell."

"Oh." Big Red says flatly. "That."

"Oh, what?"

"That's just Laramie." She scrunches up her nose. "You know. Doing it."

"Laramie Uribe? Doing . . . it?" Now Barnaby blushes, too. He is going to give Raffy some major shit about this in the morning. Leave it to Raffy to mistake that terrestrial yowling for a ghost song. Unless Raffy was just messing with him all along—Raffy has a bad reputation around the City for pranks that are more cruel than funny. And Laramie! She can't be older than twelve. He almost preferred the ghost explanation.

"So the boss's kid sneaks into the conchs." He shakes his head. "What about you? What's your story? Were you going to meet a boyfriend, too?" Barnaby elbows her in the side, perhaps a little harder than is strictly necessary. "Playing hide-and-seek? Pretending to be a sea slug?"

Big Red sniffles once. Her eyes get that melty watercolor glaze. *Jesus,* Barnaby thinks. *Here come the waterworks.* He pats her shoulder uncomfortably. "There, there." She nuzzles into his shoulder, tentatively at first, and then with a purring abandon. "There, there." He watches a single louse walking a white path through her frizzy red thickets of hair. He reaches over, tender as he can manage, and flicks it off her. And out of nowhere, Barnaby feels a rush of love for his pudgy shell mate. He's full of wild fantasies: *I'll adopt her, I'll raise her as my sister-daughter. We'll go to magic shows on the Mainland.* It's unexpected, and deeply reassuring, this feeling. *I'm a good person,* Barnaby thinks wonderingly, stroking her hair. *I'm an okay person.*

"Don't worry, kid." He burps, patting her damp back. A drop of water plashes onto the grimy shell floor. "You're safe."

Big Red smiles like she believes him. She doesn't know how to answer the man's question about why she snuck into the conch. She just feels like there's something she needs to protect. Some larval understanding, something cocooned inside her, that seems to get unspun and exploded with each passing year. Big Red curls up in a cold recess of the conch. *That's the way to do it,* the grown-up voices whisper. *Wear your skeleton on the inside out, and keep your insect heart secret.*

Outside, the wind has died down; the water is tinged with a firefly light. In the illusory calm that precedes the storm, everything has quieted. Blue moths make rococo loops in the watery glow of the City. The moon glints like a clock face with no hands. A quick, ticklish thrill monkeys up Big Red's spine. Something's going to happen, Big Red thinks, heart pounding. It feels like an invisible hand has turned up the volume inside the Giant Conch. She hears the humming with her bones. If Big Red closes her eyes and really listens, she can hear a boxed-in roar beneath the ocean. The shell air crackles. The grown-up voices inside Big Red have vanished. Please God, let something happen, she prays. She stares at the black, gnawed-on nails of Barnaby's hand. She isn't even sure what to hope for. Something.

Big Red has felt like this only once before. It was her first evening in the new house with Mr. Pappadakis. Mr. Pappadakis was watching TV, and she'd skirted his chair on her way to the kitchen. Without warning, he did a pincerlike crab-grab and pulled her onto his lap. Big Red was too surprised to resist. His liver-spotted hands went limp on her thighs. That had been the worst part of it, his palsied, noncommittal grip. And Big Red just sat there awkwardly, staring straight ahead, all the way through two commercial breaks. *Who Loves You More?* was on the TV, and she remembers laughing crazily at a joke that wasn't even very funny. Very slowly, Mr. Pappadakis craned his neck to look at her. He stared at her in a blank, idle way. Then he pushed her away, his lips curling with faint disgust. It was identical to the expression that he wore when he looked inside the fridge for a long moment, sniffed at something sour, and then shut the door.

For the next few weeks, Big Red walked around full of wonderment and confusion. A damp furry rage like a rag in her mouth. She took to parading by Mr. Pappadakis's recliner, her watermelon skorts hiked high, half daring him to grab at her again.

That unshucked, unsafe feeling. It was with her all the time, now.

"Um, kid?" Barnaby asks. "Everything okay? Do you have allergies, or something?" *There is something wrong with her face,* he thinks. Her eyes are shut, her cheeks are swollen, she's pursing out her tiny lips. She looks like a rhesus monkey miming human passion. And then suddenly she comes hurtling towards him in the dark. She smells like a white mix of things, soap and clean hair and grass and apples, so much like a kid that it makes his heart lurch. Her baby teeth click against Barnaby's crowns, a porcelain, tea-party clink.

"Kid?" he says, pushing her off him. "Lillith? What did you do that for?" Outside, the City reverberates with a low growl of thunder. The wind picks up. Their labored breathing echoes up the walls.

Barnaby never gets an answer. Big Red goes sliding away from him, cringing like a kicked dog. The wind swells into an apocalyptic howl, as if the world can't keep its secrets any longer. Some celestial artery opens up, and rain bursts from the sky. The whole conch rings like a tuning fork. And then the sound that Barnaby had forgotten he was waiting for trumpets in the dark.

The Giant Conchs start to rumble in tandem. Big Red has heard her mother say, "That struck a chord with me"; and it is one of the many phrases that she only thought she understood. Because now her bones really do ache and snap as if her body is a tendon-strung instrument. Her spinal column feels like a xylophone, each vertebra trembling in a mute vibrato. Cornuta quivers with columns of air. Big Red discovers that if she slides forward or backwards, she can alter the pitch of the long canal, using her body like a fist in a brass instrument. All of the Giant Conchs blast the same low note. It throbs through the City of Shells like an ancient alarum, bouncing around the circular monoliths. The music moves in a logarithmic spiral, spooling around Cornuta. And below it, Big Red can hear the other song. Ghostly tones, a minor key that goes silking through the membrane of her skin. It sounds like seagulls and cymbals and rainfall flashing into dark water. It comes whorling out from deep within the shell, and it would be terrifying if it wasn't so familiar.

"Do you hear that?" Big Red yells over the din, her eyes round and horsey white. Barnaby is shouting something and waving his hands, and Big Red thinks of Houdini again, conducting a magical escape. The sound is getting louder all the time. Cornuta throbs like the fisted pumping of a heart, amplified to unbearable volumes. Barnaby holds his skull as if it is about to split apart.

"C'mon, kid," he hollers. "We've got to get out of here."

Already, the floor of the shell is filling with cold water. Bits of sand and ashes float up to the surface. Barnaby starts to drag his busted leg through the rising tide of rain.

"Kid? What are you doing? Get back here!"

Big Red ignores the man's cries. She doesn't try to worm her way out of the shell, but deeper, until the pain in her head pulses like song. She pushes her soft body as far back into the shell as it will go. Back, back, through a curtain of stinging salt water. She can hear the man clambering after her. Wind and rain come piping through the cracks, peeling her lips away from her face, lifting her wet hair. She reaches blindly along Cornuta's rain-slicked sides, searching for the origins of the music. Her knuckles rap up against the seahorse coil of Cornuta's apex. But Big Red finds only angled walls and blistered pearls, the small bumps where the shell plates have puckered and fused together, like vestigial knobs to vanished doors.

Out to Sea

At first, Sawtooth thought it was a damn fool program. All of the residents at the Out-to-Sea Retirement Community got letters about it in their mail buckets:

> Dear Mr./Ms. <u>SAWTOOTH BIGTREE</u>,
> We are pleased to announce that you have been selected to participate in the No Elder Person Is an Island Volunteer Program! You will be paired with one at-risk youth from the Mainland who is completing his/her court-ordered community service. All aboard the "Friend Ship" to intergenerational rapport! Your Volunteer Buddy is <u>AUGIE RODDENBERRY</u>.
> Sincerely,
> *Out-to-Sea Management*

"Volunteers!" he'd grumbled. It didn't sound to Sawtooth like there was anything voluntary about it. And the last thing Sawtooth had wanted was some juvenile scoundrel barging onto his barge. Sawtooth stuffed the Suggestions Buoy with complaints about the program. He bottled threats and floated them towards the Administration Ship. He flat-out refused to participate—until the day the girl showed up at his cabin door.

"Augie's a damn fool name for a pretty girl" was all he could think to say when he found her standing on his deck. Sawtooth still refuses to call her Augie—that ugly, braying sound. He thinks of her as, simply, "the girl."

The girl has a child's face, round and guileless, and eyelashes so long that Sawtooth thinks that he could fish with them. She reminds Sawtooth of someone from his past, a wife or a mother, possibly one of his own granddaughters. Someone whose name he can no longer remember, but whom he feels certain that he loved very much.

"Are you the amputee?" she'd asked that first afternoon on his deck. "I told Miss Levy that I wanted the amputee."

"Are you blind?" he'd glowered, shaking his left crutch at her. "See any other one-legged mariners around here?"

But he'd smoothed his empty pant leg and smiled as she came aboard.

The girl is an apple-cheeked high-school junior and a convicted felon. She won't tell Sawtooth what crime she committed, and he doesn't ask. All he knows is that the Loomis County Court System has sentenced Augie to fifty hours of visiting him. In the beginning, fifty hours sounded like a bleak ocean of time, more hours than Sawtooth wanted to spend with himself, let alone with another person. Now he *needs* the girl to sit and measure time with him, the way the neighbor woman needs her prescription mirror so that she doesn't forget her own face.

Increasingly, Sawtooth's own memories are a loud bright

muddle, like opening the door on a party full of strangers. He lies awake at night, limping down the long corridors of his memory, trying to find the girl's hands, her slack mouth.

The girl is coming today, and Sawtooth wants everything to be perfect. So when he looks outside his porthole and sees Miss Markopoulos strewing a bucket of fish entrails across his property, he gets understandably irate.

"I seen you!" Sawtooth wheezes. "I seen you feeding them!"

Sawtooth uses his aluminum crutches to carefully swing himself over to the starboard side of his houseboat, to where she can't ignore him. His amputation gives Sawtooth a flamingular majesty. He rears up before her on his one remaining leg, feather-ruffled and pink with rage.

The neighbor woman, Miss Markopoulos, fills her days with a steady diet of black olives and soap operas and, most recently, the maternal nurture of stingrays. Like most of the residents of the Out-to-Sea Retirement Community, Miss Markopoulos has spent decades hoarding a secret cache of love, shelved and putrefying in a quiet cupboard within her; and now, at the end of a life, she has no one to share it with. No one but the rays, Sawtooth grunts, a bunch of wall-eyed invertebrates. He would pity her, if she wasn't such a damn fool.

Today she is grinning over the railing of her deck. Her teeth are as yellow and uneven as calliope pipes. Her hands are clasped to her heaving bosom. Tiny fish scales and bright spots of blood glint along the webbing of her thick fingers.

"You better cut it out, you hear me?" Sawtooth narrows

his eyes and swings his free arm like a cudgel. His height gives him an impish quality that's become only more pronounced with old age and his amputation. Lately, Sawtooth has the uneasy sensation that he's shrinking—even as, perversely, parts of him have started to grow at a delirious pace. His hairy ears boomerang out from the sides of his head. His eyebrows have overtaken his face like milky weeds. When he confronts Miss Markopoulos, he furrows them into a single white line and draws himself up on his one remaining leg.

"My buddy is coming today," he repeats, "and I don't want those goddamned strays in my backyard when she gets here." Miss Markopoulos feigns deafness in whatever ear is facing Sawtooth to avoid confrontation. She smiles blankly up at Sawtooth. She continues to strew bloody fistfuls of krill like wedding rice.

Between their two boats, the water is alive with stingrays.

At the Out-to-Sea Retirement Community, all of the elderly residents live in individual houseboats. Like their occupants, the boats themselves are retired. They are battered cargo ships and naval jalopies; boats whose iron hulls are liver-spotted with rust; boats with mud-clogged pipes, with barnacled rudders, with unhinged portholes that hang like broken eyeglasses—all of which have been refurbished and converted into "independent living units." Sawtooth is living in a Biscayne star-fishing barge. Zenaida Zapata, Sawtooth's neighbor to the right, is living in *La Rumba,* a former Venezuelan party rental. She complains that the smell of limeade and fornication has saturated the wooden walls. These are boats that fought in foreign wars, that survived wild hurricanes, that carried young lovers along moonlit currents. Now they sit on short tethers in shallow water, permanently at anchor. After two of the residents tried to elope, they sent Gherkin from maintenance around to remove all the engines.

Man-made waves lap gently against the sides of the boats, controlled by a machine that hums like the rise and fall of a giant respirator. But the Out-to-Sea Retirement Community has been sealed off from the real ocean. A stone seawall extends under the water and wraps around the marina like a giant gray honeycomb. Spidery crabs scuttle down the sides and disappear through the cracks.

The perfect balance, the brochure advertises, *of privacy and community!* Most residents spend their afternoons peering into one another's houseboats with prescription binoculars. On weekend afternoons, Sawtooth can sometimes hear the siren song of children playing farther down the beach. The sound lures even the saltiest old codgers out of their cabins, pale and vulnerable as shucked clams. They all turn their deck chairs to face the seawall, even though there's nothing to see.

Thanks to the wall, there's no danger of the residents setting out on the open sea anymore, but things occasionally drift in: golden coils of kelp, an old bowling pin, a colorful potpourri of jellyfish and used condoms, and, most recently, the stingrays. There's a nearby cove where they congregate, dozens of them swooping around submerged stalagmites like aquatic bats. Their flat bodies glide easily through the narrow openings in the seawall.

Sawtooth doesn't mind the stingrays, personally. He grew up on the swamp, and he has a gator wrestler's respect for wild things. But the girl is coming today, and the stingrays terrify her. "They look like monsters," she'd squealed the first time she saw them. "They're *horrible*." She'd clutched at

Sawtooth's moist palm reflexively, watching them sponge the clotted fish chum into their smooth white bellies. "They're like one giant mouth."

At the time, he'd just blinked at the girl with a glassy-eyed incomprehension. But watching the stingrays now, Sawtooth decides that there *is* something unsettling about the way they feed. Their bodies reinvent themselves below him, a boneless dance of empty appetite. They've eaten all the shrimp, but they continue to noiselessly storm around imagined food.

"Listen, woman—"

"They are my angels." Miss Markopoulos sniffs. "You go away now, please." Miss Markopoulos feeds the stingrays with the same fanatic devotion that other elderly women lavish on pigeons or cats. Chumming the water, it's called, and it's strictly prohibited by the Out-to-Sea Code. Sawtooth keeps leaving copies of the code in her mail bucket, with "Policy 12: Zero Tolerance for Chummers" circled so many times that the paper's torn through. Miss Markopoulos feigns an ignorance of written English. She continues to spend her entire Social Security check down at Don Barato's bait shack. Sawtooth watches as even more stingrays come flying their way. First there are only two or three, ink-blotting towards them; then they coagulate into a dense black mass, like a fast-moving cloud under the water. They flap their pectoral fins like yellow wings. Whenever the clouds part, spasms of light go rippling over their spotted backs.

"You better quit chumming up my water before the girl gets here," Sawtooth bristles, "or I'm calling Gherkin."

Sawtooth gives her a final scathing glance and swings

himself back inside his cabin. He doesn't have time to fool around with her. He has to get ready for the girl.

First he sheds his pajamas and worms his way into faded dress pants. He pins his empty left trouser leg into a dapper crease. He scatters tiny flecks of orange rind around the boat—a trick he's learned to cover up his sickly sweet old-man smell, to mask the black stench of seaweed curling in the sun. There's not much left to tidy in Sawtooth's cramped houseboat.

There is a mustard-yellow kitchenette and a window-less commode. A gator skull hangs on the bathroom wall, a smirking memento of Sawtooth's able-bodied youth on the swamp. In the main cabin there is a lint-furred sofa, a gimp table, a captain's chair that doubles as a geyser of yellow stuffing. Wavy ribbons of light fall across the carpet. In the far corner, hidden in the shadows, sits a cardboard box full of Sawtooth's useless left shoes.

Sawtooth scans the room for something he thinks the girl might like, something she could fit easily in her pocket. His gator skull? His egg timer? There's not much left. He drapes a grimy pair of overalls over the chair and stuffs a ten-dollar bill so that it hangs half in, half out of the pocket. Then he takes his Demerol off the high bathroom shelf and counts out his remaining pills—twenty-two. He puts them in the center of the table. Too obvious, he thinks. He slides them over next to the lamp, hoping that she'll see them. He positions the money and the medicine with painstaking care, the way he used to bait fishing hooks in the swamp.

The girl has been stealing from Sawtooth for some time. When things first started to go missing around the cabin,

Sawtooth chalked it up to the onslaught of dementia. He was relieved when he realized that it was just Augie. He does little experiments to test her. He'll leave something small on the table, a pack of Sir Puffsters or a withered red starfish, and go crouch in the bathroom. When he comes back, the table is always empty, the girl smiling with her hands folded neatly in her lap.

Sawtooth likes it best when she takes sentimental things, objects with no resale value whatsoever. She steals his left socks, his grocery lists; she pries the little hand off the wall clock. Once he watched her surreptitiously sweep his gray whisker clippings into a plastic bag. Probably for hoodoo love spells, he flatters himself. Probably for a locket.

On her last visit, the girl stole one of his family photographs right out of the frame. He thinks this means she is starting to care about him, too. Now whenever he looks at the empty frame, Sawtooth is moved to tears. He has to stare straight up at the ceiling, a loophole that prevents fluid from falling out of the eyes, thus saving a man the embarrassment of crying like a damn fool infant.

And then, a little over a month ago, Sawtooth noticed that his pain pills were disappearing in small increments, two or three pills at a time. Even before Augie, Sawtooth was reluctant to take the Demerol. "Highly addictive stuff, Mr. Bigtree," the doctor had cautioned. "For emergency use only." Once he realized that the girl was stealing his meds, he stopped taking them altogether. Now he's begun hoarding the pills for her. He tells himself that this isn't so different from those old women who set out dishes of candy to bribe their grandchildren.

Sawtooth is lucky. The other residents willingly endure

far worse indignities at the hands of their buddies. Mr. Kaufman has been paired with a junior arsonist, a boy with sinister ears and a face like a waffle iron. He keeps setting kitchen fires. Mr. Kaufman recently confessed to Sawtooth that he's started stocking up on lighter fluid. "Keeps him interested." He'd shrugged.

Zenaida had a buddy, but she kicked him out after his frank appraisal of Undersea Mary's erect nipples. Some buddies! Sawtooth harrumphs. Fat boys with slitty eyes like razor blades. Skinny girls with hyena laughs and spotted faces. Burly girls who break into the liquor cabinet after being invited to make themselves at home. Old ladies smile their sweet, terrified smiles while the buddies ransack their pantries and rock their boats.

The program, overall, has been hailed as a huge success.

After he finishes shoving his dirty dishes in drawers, Sawtooth settles in to wait. And wait.

When Sawtooth first arrived at the Out-to-Sea Retirement Community, the silence seeped into his lungs like water. Whole days whispered by, a stillness broken only by the ticking of Sawtooth's clock, the intermittent cries of the sooty gulls, the asthmatic gasping of the sea. But today, the silence is made bearable by the knowledge that a sound is coming.

The sound comes sooner than expected. A low moan of pain causes Sawtooth to jump in his chair. He grabs his cane and goes outside to investigate. Two boats down, Ned Kaufman is sprawled on his deck in staged agony, mispronouncing the names of various organs. Sawtooth shakes his head and looks away. Damn fool Ned. Everybody knows that Ned is a shameless faker. He just wants someone from the Medic Ship to row over and take note of his vital signs.

Sawtooth won't admit it, even to himself, but he has come to look forward to his own visits to the Medic Ship. It's one of the few pleasures left to him, the pressure of a gloved finger on his pulse.

"Mr. Ned," comes a woman's quavery voice. "*Que te sanes!* I will light a candle for you!"

Sawtooth groans. His neighbor to the right, Zenaida Zapata, has started praying to Undersea Mary on the prow of her boat.

In her previous incarnation, Undersea Mary was *La Rumba*'s plaster figurehead. Her pert breasts used to greet Sawtooth every morning, until she fell into the water after a tropical storm. For months, she lay sideways on the ocean floor. Needlefish nibbled the paint off her lemon meringue bikini. Then Zenaida moved in. She fished the statue out and installed her on a pedestal made out of floral Kleenex boxes and the cushion of a rusty Exercycle.

Now Zenaida courts Mary's attentions like a lover. She has robed her in sateen bedsheets, celestial blue. She leaves Undersea Mary bouquets of napkin roses in nightmare shades of red and ocher. Today she is lighting waxy votive candles that she stole from the Hurricane Supply Kit. Sawtooth tries to hobble back inside his cabin without acknowledging her.

"You buddy coming today, Mr. Sawtooth?" she calls.

None of your goddamn business, Sawtooth thinks. He glowers at her.

Zenaida nods smugly. "I don't need no buddy," she tells him. "The Virgin visits me. I see her in the morning and in the afternoon. I see her during the news shows and during the commercial breaks. Everywhere," she says, gloating like a child, "I see her everywhere. She is always with me. I am never alone."

Zenaida turns around and lights another candle. Sawtooth watches as tiny plumes of smoke go curling up to join
the gray clouds. What could she possibly have to pray for, at
her age? he fumes. Whose lungs does she think she's filling
up there with all her damn fool prayers?

Sawtooth hurries back inside his cabin. He doesn't understand how he came to be adrift in this sea of crackpots.

Around three-thirty, Sawtooth's heart starts pounding at
a rate that poses a serious health risk at his age. The girl is
scheduled to arrive any minute now. He hops around the
room like an agitated stork, making imperceptible adjustments in the placement of the lone sofa cushion, the crumpled bill, his pain pills.

He wonders what the girl does with the pills, if she takes
them or sells them. He wonders if there's a chance that she
might get addicted, too.

Finally, at a quarter past four, Sawtooth can hear the
squeal of tires pulling into the boatyard, followed by a chorus of multilingual obscenities and the chaperone's cries for
order. From his porthole, he can see the buddies come streaming down the dock, in ones and twos at first, then the whole
raucous flock of them.

"Permission to board?" the girl chirrups. She is right at
the edge of his boat slip.

Sawtooth swallows his chewing tobacco. He licks his
fingertips and fluffs his hair into a wispy, silver crown—"the
rooster gawk comb-back," somebody used to call it. An
uncle or a brother, possibly a wife. A wife. Sawtooth takes a
deep breath and reaches for the door.

"Hiya, Pops." She grins, pushing past him. She laughs her
wind-chime laugh and plops onto the sofa.

"Hello, girl," he grunts happily.

Today Augie is wearing a potato-colored T-shirt that says DAPPER CADAVER and a baseball cap pulled down over her blue eyes. Sawtooth doesn't understand why she always dresses like a boy, in slouchy black pants that billow around her legs like garbage bags. Sawtooth's even tried to give the girl shopping money himself on several occasions—although she never accepts money if it's offered to her.

"Whadda you think, Pops?" Augie pulls off her baseball cap and shakes out her hair. Augie has short, auburn hair, but Sawtooth sees that the damn fool girl has gone and streaked it through with flamingo pink. Sawtooth doesn't want to like it, but he does. It sparks like copper wire, like the fiery ball of sunset over the swamp.

"You look like a damn fool Easter egg," Sawtooth snorts.

He's pleased to see that she's in one of her penny-bright moods. Some days she just sits on his couch, prickly as a sea urchin, while Sawtooth reaches feverishly for something to say. Some days she arrives seething with a formless rage, a heat that Sawtooth can feel radiating from her pale skin. Once she didn't come at all. On that day, Sawtooth watched the ebb and flow of the artificial tides and felt like he was evaporating.

The girl pouts and puts her cap back on. She settles back on the couch, and they spend the next few minutes playing a round of This Object Is Older Than You Are. It's Sawtooth's favorite game.

"How old are you today, girl? Fifteen? Ha!" He chuckles, his eyes thin and steely as dimes. "You see that flounder thermometer? It's older than you are. You see this carpet stain? It's older than—"

"Say, let's cut to the chase, Pops," Augie interrupts. "Are you going to show it to me today, or what?"

Sawtooth grins with a childlike pleasure. "Sure it don't make you squeamish, girl?" Then he starts fumbling with the pin to his trousers.

Ever since Sawtooth mentioned his phantom-limb syndrome, the girl has been fascinated with his scarred left stump. He feels flattered by the attention. Most people look anywhere but his lower body. They pretend not to notice when he limps down the docks. It makes it worse, somehow, everyone pretending that he's still whole.

Sawtooth rolls up his pant leg coyly, with the practiced languor of a showgirl. They both stare down at the white nub of his thigh.

"So you can still feel it?"

The girl's fingers hover gingerly over the place where his left leg used to be, shaping it in the air.

"I mean, you'll be looking at it, you can see it's not there, and you feel it?"

Sawtooth nods. "You think I'm pulling your leg?"

The girl smiles wanly.

Then she gets down on her knees. Sawtooth holds his breath. He will never grow accustomed to this, but now his uneasiness is spiked with a hot, wincing thrill. It makes him feel like a much younger man, this sort of attention. He learned early on that he could use his own mangled body as a kind of bait, something the girl would keep coming back to nibble at. The girl flicks her pink tongue at the very tip of his stump. She circles around it, once, twice.

"You feel it," Augie repeats. She smiles up at him, her eyes glinting with a dull satisfaction.

Sawtooth grunts. She is tracing the outline of his ghost leg with her tongue, and he feels it, by God he *feels* it. If Sawtooth could verbalize the hitching in his chest, he would tell her exactly what he feels. He would thank the girl, for making his pain meaningful. Before he started saving his pills for her, his phantom limb used to infuriate him. It was a senseless aching, a bad neural joke. Now the pain reminds him that the girl has been here.

"Your body is haunted," she intones, with an adolescent portentousness. "Like a house."

"That's one way to look at it, I guess." Sawtooth frowns. The girl has a funny way of romanticizing things.

"So, how much time you got left to serve, girl?" He feels grateful that at his age, the tremors in his voice pass unnoticed.

"Oh, I was meaning to tell you," Augie says. She stands, smoothing her hair. "Miss Levy got them to lessen my sentence. I'll be out of your hair soon." The girl keeps her voice casual, but she still won't meet his eyes. "Which reminds me, look at the time! I guess I'd better get going. Sign my form?"

Sawtooth stares dumbly at the form that she's waving in front of him. He tenses, half expecting his ghost leg to cramp up, but there is nothing.

If Sawtooth could put words to the brambled knot forming in his throat, he would tell her: Girl, don't go. I am marooned in this place without you. What I feel for you is more than love. It's stronger, peninsular. You connect me to the Mainland. You are my leg of land over dark water.

"Do you want an egg?" he asks instead. He grabs her hand desperately. "Do girls still eat eggs? I could fry you up an egg."

"No thanks," she says, withdrawing her hand. "No, I really should get going, the bus will leave without me. . . ." Her smile darkens. She taps at the blank space on the bottom of her form.

"In a minute, girl," he rasps, panic sealing off his throat. "In a minute . . ." Sawtooth gets up to go to the narrow bathroom. He leans his cane against the door and squats on the lidless commode, feeling the mechanized sway of the waves beneath him. One, two . . . he can hear the girl bumbling around outside. Sometimes he has to resist the urge to lecture her on the proper way to burgle your elders. Kids today don't know the first thing about theft, he thinks. He hopes the girl doesn't have trouble with the damn fool childproof lid on his Demerol. Three, he breathes, four . . .

On the other side of the marina, one of the stingrays slides dangerously close to the Wave Assuager. It struggles against the machine's currents, its stinger pointed like an arrow towards the undertow. The ray gets sucked into the whirring underwater fan, silvering between the blades like a quarter into a slot. The accordion pump of the Wave Assuager lets out an elastic sigh. It sparks and groans. It vaporizes clouds of minnows with its electric death throes.

Then the Wave Assuager sends a final, renegade crest coursing up beneath the houseboats.

Ned Kaufman cracks skulls with his buddy and lets out a howl of real pain. Undersea Mary gets swept back overboard, her votive candles extinguished. When the wave hits, Sawtooth is squatting in the bathroom, his carbuncular car pressed against the bathroom wall. If he had two legs to stand on, he might have been able to regain his balance. Instead, he spills out onto the living room floor.

"Fuck!" Augie falls backwards into the box of left shoes. The pain pills go flying out of her hands, raining down on Sawtooth's prone body. Sawtooth grunts and struggles onto his knee. Augie is regarding him with a stricken expression, still holding the empty orange bottle.

"I didn't see anything," he wheezes. He sweeps the nearby pills into his clammy palm and holds them out to her. "I didn't see a damn fool thing. . . ."

"Oh, God . . ." She starts scrambling to grab her things.

"I know you been stealing from me, girl," Sawtooth cries. "I know and I don't care. . . ."

Augie already has her hand on the doorknob before Sawtooth realizes that she's leaving.

"Girl," he sputters. "Girl . . ."

Even as a young man, Sawtooth had a hard time talking to women. Since moving to Out-to-Sea, he's become tight-lipped as an oyster. But he can feel the words pearling on his tongue: Girl, you are my moon. You are the tidal pull that keeps time marching forward.

What comes out is: "I used to steal muskrats."

Augie struggles with the handle. "Fuck."

"During the Depression."

The door swings open.

"Stole 'em right out of the bigger boys' traps."

Sunlight spills into the dim cabin. Sawtooth takes a shuddery breath.

"Girl," he says in a low, throaty voice, not unlike a bullfrog in heat. "I love you."

Augie pauses, one foot out the door. She whirls around,

slowly, and comes to stand over his prone form. Her eyes have narrowed into hard, bright kernels.

"You *love* me, Pops?" Her voice takes on a rib-kicking cadence. It elicits a moan from Sawtooth, like the lowing cry of a sea cow.

"*You* love me?" she keeps asking, her voice flat and piti-less. Sawtooth tries to speak, but can only make little stran-gled noises. A thin stream of spittle trickles down one side of his mouth.

"You love *me*?" Her voice tightens, and Sawtooth thinks of a hand squeezing some dumb animal's udders.

"Yes!"

"No," she says with a bitter little laugh. "No. I don't think so, Pops. How could you?" She shakes her head angrily, as if Sawtooth is the one who has committed a stupid, indefensi-ble crime. "How *could* you?" As if to echo her own question, she scoops a few yellow pills up from the crease in his flaccid trouser leg and pockets them. Then she strides onto the dock without a backwards glance.

Sawtooth flops back onto the floor. A small puddle seeps into the rug, his empty trouser leg dripping toilet water. He can feel the gravelly pills pressing into his back. He sees no reason to struggle, to get up.

Eventually, Sawtooth dozes off. He has a nightmare about the stingrays. He is lying on his back, naked and whole, on a velvety carpet of rays. There are dozens, hundreds of them, undulating beneath him. They do a cartilaginous dance through the warm salt water. The tips of their wings smooth against his wrinkled skin like bruising kisses. They brush-stroke Sawtooth's pebbly spine, his scrawny ass, the hollows of both knees: all the soft, forgotten places that haven't been touched for decades. He can't enjoy it. He lies there, holding his breath with a terrible anticipation. His spinal cord screams like a silver wire. His whole body tenses, waiting for the stinger. In the dream he can see Undersea Mary watching him from the opposite deck, her cheeks shining with painted-on compassion.

When he wakes up, night has already fallen. He goes and peers nervously over the side of his boat. It's too dark to tell what's under the surface of the water. Gherkin must have repaired the Wave Assuager, because he can seen Zenaida's Medicaid Lifeboat bobbing alongside her slip. Sawtooth slumps into his deck chair and stares up at the sky. It's a drunken sky, the stars hiccupping light. Great gusty clouds go spinning past the moon. The bright planets feel like pinpricks to Sawtooth's old eyes. Tonight, the phantom pain banshees through him with a pointless fury. He considers taking one of his pills, then thinks better of it. The doctor is reluctant to give him refills. And the girl might come back. He massages the roaring space where his leg used to be. If she needs the pills badly enough, he thinks, she just might.

When he was a boy growing up on the swamp, Sawtooth used to know all of the constellations, but now he has forgotten how to find them. Overhead, the sky lurches in unfamiliar, opalescent swirls. All around him, the muted yellow lamps of his neighbors' boats blink off quietly, one by one, until Sawtooth is left bobbing alone in the darkness.

Accident Brief,
Occurrence # 00/422

"Hooey," Mr. Oamaru says, working his fork with a silly urgency. A single pea is caught between his square front teeth. "That boy can sing. The boy just needs a friend is all. You be that, Tek. You be that friend."

My mother's prim smile confirms that I should be that friend. My Christian sisters nod their earnest, brunette heads. Makeup is forbidden in our household, but my sisters have slathered their lips with beeswax so that each syllable emerges at a blinding wattage:

"Be that friend!"

My sisters all have Bible names that start with a pious growl, "Rrrachel, Rrrebecca, Rrruth." They eat unbuttered peas and fatty gristle and leave the choicest, glaziest cuts of the ham for Mr. Oamaru and me. They are pretty, and this means that charity comes easy to them. They don't understand the real cost of what they are asking me.

There is a long silence full of bright, expectant stares and chewing sounds, gulping sounds, tiny metal clinking sounds. Jesus. Peas roll around and around my selfish mouth. Outside, I can hear the reindeer rubbing antlers against the fence wood. Snow waits in the high clouds. Our kitchen window fills with cold early stars.

"Why should I have to do it? Rangi is creepy, Mom. He's Moa. He's mute."

"Son," Mr. Oamaru answers for her. I don't look over at him, but I can feel his radiant disapproval. "Why shouldn't you have to do it? The boy is very nearly your cousin."

That's a cheap trick. Everybody in Waitiki Valley is almost a cousin. Marriage here requires an actuary to make sure you're not blood kin.

"Rangi Gibson is not my cousin."

"He's your brother," Rebecca says unhelpfully, "in Christ."

"He hasn't had your advantages, Tek." Mr. Oamaru twirls a pea on the tine of his fork. "To be orphaned at that age! And Digger Gibson is a heathen and a drunk. He can't even keep the cemetery grass mowed, much less care for a bastard child."

My mother winces at the word "bastard." *Some advantages,* I think angrily.

"Why should I have to be part of the stupid Avalanche at all? Why should I have to freeze my ass off and pop my ears to sing a shitty untrue song about pirates?"

"Don't curse, Tek." Mr. Oamaru raises his eyebrows at my mother. "I wonder who he learned that language from? Nobody in this family, that's for sure."

There it is, the rustle of dead leaves. Dried sap, a branch crack, the whirring teeth of Mr. Oamaru's saw. My father—

my real father—is a limb that got axed off the family tree a long time ago now. My mother coughs and cleans phantom juices off her silver with a cloth doily. My sisters clench their knives.

"Listen, don't you bring my father into this. . . ."

"The Avalanche," peacemaker Rachel recites, "is *very important*. It's a privilege to sing it. It's a celebration of our past." Everybody around the table smiles at her.

"Yeah? Well, I've seen how easily the past can get rewritten." I glare at Mr. Oamaru. "Lyrics change. New authors come along."

We are flying to the Aokeora Glacier to sing down the snows. It's one of those rituals whose true meaning is lost in antiquity, a ritual that we continue because of blind tradition and our parents' desire to booze. You can see the Aokeora Glacier from the red roof of our silo, rising some thousands of feet above our valley. We bake and sell moonpies all year to pay for our trip to the top. (The Waitiki Valley Boys Choir is fiscally dependent on the pity of mothers. Our moonpies look and taste like shoe heels.) The ice planes we hire are four-seaters, and it takes several trips to fly the entire Waitiki Valley Boys Choir up there. It's a funny sort of concert. We leave our audience so far below us, out of earshot.

Our families gather at the base of Aokeora and synchronize their watches. They can't hear us, of course, and they certainly can't see us, but they crane their necks and imagine. At precisely ten o'clock, the crowd slurs along in rough jolly voices: "Ho! Ho! Ho! Ho! The Piii-raates' Conquest!" For our finale, the choir hits the high C that triggers the

Avalanche. We hold that single note for as long as we can. Sometimes the weather cooperates. Then our voices send rocks crunching down the side of the glacier. Snowbursts explode off the cliffs like white fireworks. Chunks of ice plummet into the moat around Aokeora, shooting up whale flukes of water. Two years ago, we sang so well that melt-water hosed our parents' faces. It's a way for the parents to hear us, I guess, albeit indirectly. Everybody gets a little sniffly about it, especially the mothers. For some of us, it's the last year that we can goad our voices to that altitude.

The Waitiki Valley Boys Choir Proudly Presents

10:00	*A Stirring Rendition of*
	"The Pirates' Conquest,"
	Conducted by Franz Josef
10:12	*Avalanche*
10:13	*Punch and Moonpies*

In Waitiki Valley, most everyone is a descendant of the Inland Pirates. Our great-great-grandparents sailed along the glacial river, burned their thieving boats, and then moved inland to meet the locals. The Moa were a peaceful, station-ary people, who only killed one another. And then our pirate forebears arrived, swilling brandy and sneezing Mainland diseases all over them. We sing a ra-ra tribute to the pirates every year at the Winter Concert, "The Pirates' Conquest." It's our local anthem, these squirrelly arpeggios that cele-brate our pirate forebears' every ancient offense. Verse 1: The quick extinction of the Moa's sacred red penguins. Verse 2: The depletion of their greenstone quarries. Verse 3: The invasion of their mothers' bodies. Verse 4: Their stolen treasure. And what did we bring the Moa in return? Grog and possums. Quail pox. Whores.

It's a weird thing to harmonize about.

Verse 4 is the worst. It's a lamentation for the pirates' lost treasure. (Formerly the Moa's holy relics, although we downplay this detail in "The Pirates' Conquest.") Captain Walley and his men hid the profits they'd swashbuckled in the mountains. These pirates assumed, with typical pirate arrogance, that their plunder would stay safely frozen away for an eternity. But maps don't work in a country of glaciers. The treasure got lost on calved icebergs and crushed into the impasse of moraines. By the time our great-great-grandfathers returned to recover the treasure, X marked a spot that had long since melted into the sea. Bar fights still break out over it every once in a while, the product of our grandparents' bloody and useless nostalgia.

The grandparents, hoarse and contemptuous, like to remind us of the true Avalanches, their Avalanches, from the early century. They have a knack for making you feel like you are betraying your pirate lineage just by sitting in a car. "How do you like that city-boy juice, city boy?" they'll ask, watching you pour berry cocktail from a carton. Our grandparents juiced frozen berries with their own teeth. They sang more sweetly than we ever will. They never sold a single moonpie. They got to the top of Aokeora with blood and gumption, crescent axes, and it took them five days. It wasn't uncommon for boys to die.

All *you* have to do, they wheeze, is nudge a snow lump over the edge with your voice. Easy.

Our Avalanche is a setup. It's a show for the cheap seats.

The choir director, Franz Josef, flies up a few days in advance and takes a hatchet to the powder. He picks out snow that's survived the melt season: loosened with crampons, in regular contact with sunlight, eager to be sung apart or sunk into our valley. We sing, and we pretend that it's our frail voices that fracture the glacier. Theoretically, the snow could ball up and fall on us, but our parents encourage this death risk with words like *tradition, heritage,* and *rite of passage.* They like to believe in the old, boulder-rolling power of our songs. They like to see the evidence of our voices, even if they can't hear them.

With any luck, this will be my last Winter Concert. I'm hoping my voice will change later on this summer, and then I will never have to sing down another Avalanche. I ask God to grant me this wish every night. "God," I pray, "please deliver me from the choir." I kneel beside my attic bed on bare, hairless knees, and tune a hopeful ear for damage in my voice. I can hear my prayer coming true in the shower, where I sing test syllables. My voice sounds like the doorbell to a condemned building. Shrill, with a new hollowness behind it.

When I was a much younger boy, my mother was beautiful, but it was a sewn-up tulip kind of beauty. Then my father left. We curled in and blackened. We were heathens, you know, before Mr. Oamaru and his piratical, body-soul conquest of my mother. Mr. Oamaru has had a soft opening effect. He paid her mortage and made my sisters. He made her beautiful again. Everyone notices. Other mothers pay her incredulous compliments, peppered with real jealousy: "Why, you look like a new person, Leila. You look so *happy.*"

And you know what? I hate him for it.

If you've seen me in town, I guarantee you don't remember. Dark eyes, a red lick of hair under a dark hat. I'm not a lacy saint like my sisters, but I don't think I'm an exceptionally bad kid, either. I love my mother and my sisters, and I do my barn chores enough of the time. My stepdad, Mr. Oamaru, seems most proud of me for the sins that I resist: I don't chew tobacco, I don't fake sick, I don't vandalize silos. Once, he actually complimented me for not "diddling with" the reindeer, as the Tau boys have been rumored to do. These are tough victories to take pride in.

Like most men in the valley, Mr. Oamaru is a reindeer farmer. He grazes his blue-gray stock on ancestral Moa land. He is a good man who takes good care of my mother. He claims he loves to watch me sing. When we sang down the Avalanche last year, Mr. Oamaru collected an eyedropper of the glacial snow. He wears it under his plaids on a fraying noose knot, a vial of melted time. "You sang well, Tek. You make a father proud." I wanted to smash that vial on sight. Everybody knows that I'm a lousy singer. On my best days, my voice melts into the other boys' and I swallow my mistakes.

"Dad sure loves your singing," Ruth told me once, her own voice squeaky with jealousy. "He wears that eyedropper everyplace."

"That's just faucet water, dummy," I heard myself lying. "That eyedropper stuff is all an act. Your dad thinks his pregnant cows sing better than I do. Your dad couldn't pick my voice out of the choir."

And then Ruth was crying and I felt like a monster. But everybody knows that Mr. Oamaru is not my real father. Mr. Oamaru is my mother's husband. He is my sisters' father. Not mine.

Your father left us because he was in a bad way, my mother used to tell me.

Tek's father left us because he is a bad man, she tells everybody now. She says it again and again. She's snowing down a new past for Mr. Oamaru, a tough rock of ice in a sea of time. A new memory for our family to stand on. *Tek's father is a bad, bad man.* It was hard enough to lose my father the first time. Now I can't even hold on to my memory of him as a basically good person. Mr. Oamaru has taught me that loss isn't just limited to the present; it can happen in any direction. Even what's done and vanished can be taken from you. Other, earlier memories that we made of my father sink and revert to water. The past shifts its crystals inside me.

> *To be in the Waitiki Valley Boys Choir, you need a good attitude, and the ability to sing in a pleasant, undamaged, unchanged singing voice.*
> —Franz Josef

On Saturday, Mr. Oamaru drops me off on the tarmac in the purple-gray predawn. We argue about "The Pirates' Conquest" on the car ride over:

"Honestly! Half that stuff is only in there because it rhymes with conquest."

Any fool can hear, from the first verse onward, how Waitiki's history has been retrofitted to the demands of rhyme and meter.

"Bronze *breast,* ice *chest,* crow's *nest,* laid to *rest,* Captain Walley's scarlet *vest.* Do you really think that Captain Walley wore a *vest*?"

"That song's truer than you are. Why, we've been singing it for longer than you've been alive! It's *history*. . . ."

It's freezing out. A wreath of icicles forms on the dash. We reach a short airstrip where a bunch of sullen, sleepy choirboys are huddled together, flanked by a small fleet of ice planes. The choir director nods at me and checks a box. Franz Josef has a thick, twitchy mustache and no wife. There's no magic to his conducting. He waves the metal wand with a grim, efficient panic, as if he's directing traffic. I miss my cue again.

"Tek Oamaru! You're a beat behind us. Chin up, eh? Enunciate, eh? You're singing down into your chest."

Just Tek, I whisper under my breath. I hate rehearsing this evil stuff. It makes me feel like "The Pirates' Conquest" is still happening. Usually I just lip sync the part about the rapes and fires. If I were braver, I wouldn't sing at all. I have a secret admiration for Rangi, his genius refusal to carry the tune.

Rangi's been in the choir longer than any other boy. If his voice has changed, it's done so in secret, with the stealth of wine in a dark bottle. If you ask me, it's a perverse charity to make the mute boy rehearse with the choir. But Franz Josef says there is music like water frozen inside him. He says he wants the Waitiki Valley Boys Choir to be the heat that melts the blocks of song in Rangi. We think that Franz Josef has fantasies of a TV special, or at least a write-up in the *Waitiki Gazette:*

Local Choir Director Hailed as Miracle Worker! Mute Moa Youth Has the Music in Him!

"Sing it with us, Rangi!" Franz Josef says now. He kneels down and pushes his gloved hand into Rangi's diaphragm, as if he is a doctor fighting for the life of an infant sound. "Me-me-me-ME-me-me-me!"

Rangi looks as if he might bite Franz Josef.

Rangi's a Moa orphan. His adopted father, Digger Gibson, is the cemetery warden. Digger never comes to our concerts. Most days he spends dreaming in the ditches. White face, gray knuckles around a bottle. On his chest you can watch the shovel rising, the shovel falling, a graveyard metronome.

We know that Rangi can at least mutter because Digger Gibson says he used to talk to the bear. In his group home for orphaned Moa boys, Rangi had a pet cinnamon bear. I saw her once. She was just a wet-nosed cub, a cuff of pure white around her neck. Rangi found her on the banks of the Waitiki River and walked her around on a leash. He filed her claws and fed her tiny, smelly fishes. They shot her the day his new father, Digger, came to pick him up.

"Burying that bear," I overheard Digger tell Mr. Oamaru once. "The first thing we ever did together as father and son."

Rangi's given us this global silent treatment ever since, a silence he extends to people, animals, ice. Doctors say it's an elective mutism; they can't detect trauma, can't find a gauze of sickness on his tongue. Rangi has tried to run away from our choir four times now, although he never gets very far— the Valley is walled in on every side by glacial mountains. We think he's on an insane quest to unearth the bear. He always gets "rescued" at some anonymous spot in the forest, spading up dark triangles of dirt. There are no physical markers to help him to locate the burial mound, no clues to the bear's whereabouts outside of Rangi's childhood memory. Digger never put down a stone. Rangi could dig forever and find

only yellow bromide and shallow roots. *Stubborn,* the grand-
fathers say. *Ungrateful. Typical Moa.* This diagnosis has always
troubled me. Sometimes Rangi's gaze darkens and rolls inward,
and then I think he must be seeing something that nobody's
invented the words for yet. A slick world that no sound will
adhere to.

"Me-me-me-ME-me-me-me!" Franz Josef keeps prompt-
ing. His hand pushes down with more encouragement. "Me-
me-me-omph!"

Franz Josef's head snaps forward. His wire spectacles and
conductor's wand go flying. There's a moment of shocked
silence, and then the clearing erupts with laughter. Brauser
has nailed Franz Josef in the back of the head with a mam-
moth snowball. Brauser's a sociopath with a pleasant tenor.
He spends most rehearsals around back, torturing stray penguins or pissing his name in the snow. Now he's smirking at
us from the treeline, scooping up more powder. It's unclear
whether Brauser was trying to hit Franz Josef or Rangi. I
hope it was the former. That's one difference between a bully
and a hero, I guess: good aim. If Brauser was trying to hit
Franz to help Rangi, then maybe there's more to his malice
than I thought.

Then Brauser starts pelting the altos with indiscriminate
glee, making my hero theory less tenable. They cry out in
terror. Franz calls a stern halt to our rehearsal. He searches
the snow for his wand.

Rangi, meanwhile, has wandered away from the choir.
He is sitting on a low fence at the edge of the airstrip and
staring off into the trees. I take one step towards him, then
another. *Be that friend* becomes the wind pushing me forward.

"Hey Rangi? Listen, I'm sorry for . . . you know, I have

this stepfather, too. . . ." I trail off. Rangi turns and stares at me with a mirror's flat assessment, merciless and impersonal. I can see how stupid I must look to him. "I just wanted to say that I'm sorry." I shrug. Then some secret life flames in Rangi's eyes and for an instant I feel an identical ache quivering between us. It's over so quickly that I wonder if I imagined it. Rangi goes back to studying invisible symmetries in the snow. I jog through the light flurries, hoping that Brauser and the others didn't see me back here.

A few minutes later, the planes begin to roll forward, the white egg of the sun reflected in their dark windows. On the glacier, the sun is so violently bright that, without special lenses, ice pilots can burn through their corneas within half an hour. Today there are four pilots on the tarmac, all with matching ski suits and identical lavender eyes. Each ice pilot walks around and whumps the red belly of his fuselage. They introduce themselves: Steve and Steve and Steve and Hone Te Kauriki-himi. "Call me Steve," Hone says, with a bitter curl to his lips, and we all laugh with relief. Hone's eyes are lavender, too, but you can see their true tea color behind the contacts.

Hone comes around with a bucket of eel-yellow transponders. He goes from boy to boy and loops them around our necks.

"These willies need to be jiggered at all times."

"Why?"

"In case something goes less-than-good with the Avalanche." The cold, calloused pads of Hone's fingers brush my neck. He flips the switch to ON. "We need to be able to find you boys if you get buried."

The transponder feels stone-heavy around my neck. I wish that Honc would make just one more joke.

Steve #2 hands us an ice axe and a sack lunch. My ice axe is crusted with triangles of rust or blood. My sack lunch is salami. The ice pilots start to load up the planes. Steve #3 does a head count and frowns down at the manifest.

"Franz Josef? There are some names missing on the manifest."

A whispered conference. Brows furrow in our direction. Franz smiles at us, and I catch a whiff of conspiracy.

"Mr. Gibson, Mr. Oamaru, Mr. Brauser, there's been an, ah, error of logistics. You boys don't mind waiting for an extra plane? Very sure? Most certain? Well."

The substitute pilot forgot his contacts at the lodge. He seems momentarily flustered, blinking out the cockpit window. Then he winks one naked blue eye at us and flashes us a terrifying grin.

"Can you boys keep a secret?"

"Rangi can!" Brauser laughs. He is rendered apoplectic by his own wit. "That's the only thing Rangi's good for! Because he's *dumb*.

"Ritardaaaando!" He flicks at Rangi's left earlobe. "Figaro, figaro, you fuckin' psycho . . ."

"He's not deaf, you know." I am careful to say this in a coward's voice, too soft for Brauser to hear.

"It's okay for me to call Ritardando dumb"—Brauser's face goes crumple smug—"like how it's okay to call a female dog a bitch. Because it's the truth."

The substitute pilot's smile broadens. "Good news! Nothing wrong with keeping your quiet." He gives Rangi a friendly thump on the back. "Same goes for you two. No reason to go blabbling to the Steves that I flew you up without my lenses."

Rangi's expression remains flat and illegible.

"Dumb-dumb-dumb-dumb biiitch!" Brauser really does have a lovely contralto. He can hit, color, and hold a note like a buxom Viking princess. Otherwise Franz Josef would have kicked him out of the choir a long time ago. I'm sure it's no coincidence that Brauser, Rangi, and I got volunteered for the last flight up here. Franz often refers to us as his "problem" voices. He's probably overjoyed for an excuse to begin the concert without us.

Brauser's melodic insults fill the cabin, *dumb-dumb-dumb-dumb,* a song that thuds into us like a steady rain laced with hailstones. He sings it until I want to scream. Rangi listens like someone locked indoors, watching the weather outside his cell window.

During the flight up, I close my eyes and try to ignore the tremors of the cabin. It's a perilous ascent. We rise through a low, gold-limned dross of clouds. The valley falls away from us in waves. Then nothing but frost and seracs, freckled with shale. The plane has to do all sorts of dubious maneuvers to enter the openings in the Southwest Icefalls, a dozen squint-thin eyes in the glassy rock face. Up here it's cratered and lifeless terrain. Mount Kei looks like a cloud volcano in the rising sun, bubbling ocher and maroon. Brauser is telling some stupid joke about my father and a female reindeer. Rangi's staring into the cockpit at the giddy, spinning controls. He gnaws on all four of his fingers. Clouds stream around the small windows. The substitute pilot is massaging his temples with his two free hands.

Everybody is injured in the crash. The wind screams across the flat snowfields. Both skis snap off on impact, and the plane slides to a stop on its belly. The substitute pilot makes it out first, kicking through the cockpit door. I ignore the pilot's outstretched hand and tumble face-first into the snow. It's four feet of fresh powder. There is nothing up here, no points of reference. Just snow forever, pocked with these turquoise holes like painted whirlpools. Crevasses, I shudder, deep enough to gulp us whole. On a glacier, the ground is just an illusion, a slick disguise for a million chasms. I try to get up on my knees and let out a whimper. Brauser has rolled a few meters away from me, and I wait for him to resume cursing. But Brauser is lying fish-eyed in the snow. Not moving. Not blinking. I follow his blank gaze and see nothing. No choir director, no altos, no tenors, no planes.

We are alone on the glacier.

"Excuse me, sir . . . ?" Etiquette and panic duel in each syllable. "Where are, um, the other planes?"

Is it possible, I wonder, that we have wrecked on another glacier, the *wrong* glacier? Usually, the planes do a smooth glissando right into the Ice Amphitheater. Franz Josef conducts during touchdown, keeping ¾ time. When I turn around, I see that the substitute pilot's smile has started to run like gravy. His face looks sick and yellow in the light. He yells something and points behind us.

As we watch, the ski plane starts to slide backwards.

"Fuck."

The substitute pilot stands there for what feels like a very long time. Then he starts running, falling and running and running and falling, so slowly, through the deep virgin snow.

"Fuck. Fuck."

The plane skids faster and faster. It slides at a whistling speed. A dazzling wake of frost explodes up around the body of the plane.

"Fuck!"

And then it slides, soundless and dreamlike, over the ridge.

On his way back to the boys, the substitute pilot falls into a small blue crevasse. He has to lift one leg out and then the other. Even at this altitude, the substitute pilot's bathed in sweat, sweat running down his chin and neck. Fear must be the fountain of youth, because the substitute pilot now looks younger than any of us, doughy and flushed with horror.

"Help!" The substitute pilot waves his arms. He's up to his waist in snow. At a lower altitude, this would have made me laugh out loud.

"Help me! Don't just stand there, kid."

I just stand there. I know better than to walk over there. Somehow, I intuit that if I extend my hand now, I will get infected by the pilot's helplessness, his gibbering fear. The help can't be me; the help needs to come from some other direction. I hear myself barking orders, full of an iron contempt for the pilot. What a crybaby. What a true fuckup. It's an angry feeling that I used to use on the farm when my father first left, late at night, to immunize myself against my mother's terror.

"Just lift your legs, one at a time. We need your help over *here*."

Behind us, Brauser is moaning. His cries swell and sky-crawl. It's a wordless sound, a wild sound, this animal pain that can't be haltered and led to meaning. It reminds me of the time that Mr. Oamaru had to shoot a two-headed reindeer calf, and for a horrid instant both heads lowed in tandem. They sang their way across some abominable threshold. I still hear them screaming in nightmares. For months afterwards, I plugged up my ears with my mother's *Dolly Nutmeg Reads the Bible!* cassettes and refused to enter the barn alone. This is the worst sound, I think, the very worst sound in the whole world.

Then the moaning stops. Brauser's movement stops. And I regret all my hastier judgments. Any sound is better than this.

"Brauser? Brauser!"

Where are the others? My head is throbbing. *Where are the other planes?*

"Where's your hat, Brauser?"

Already, Brauser's marigold hair has become hoary with snow. With his bare white head and his curled-in spine, Brauser looks like a rapidly aging man. He blows crimson spit bubbles that I pop immediately, scared and weirdly embarrassed. Rangi sits in a shocked, straight-backed silence in the bowl left by the vanished wreck, still holding tight to his sack lunch. The soggy bottom's torn apart. His sandwich bread and apple slices litter the snow.

The substitute pilot manages to hoist himself out of the crevasse and stumble over. "Boys," he says, but he directs every word at me. He holds up a hissless walkie-talkie. "I need to slide down to where I can get reception. I'm going to call for a helicopter rescue. Don't go anywhere until that heli comes, eh? Don't move a muscle."

I nod. Brauser twitches once, then stops.

The substitute pilot is already half crawling, half sliding down the empty snowfield.

"Wait up, I'll come with you!" I start after him, unsteady in my boots, and fall sideways into the snow. "Wait for me!"

Halfway down the run, the ice pilot turns around and shouts something:

"———!"

His words break apart on the ice. Then he scoots down the gentle snowfield on his back, shooting into a sterling ice cave like a pinball.

"What? What was that? Hey, buddy, we can't hear you. . . ."

Brauser is slumped half dead in the snow. Rangi exhales plumes of silence. I crawl a few feet away and slam a shallow hole in the powder. I open the cramped fist of my stomach, squeeze my eyes shut, and retch.

> *Music is pleasant not only because of the sound of many voices,*
> *but because of the silence that is in it.*
> —Franz Josef

Weep! Weep! All of our transponders beep in tandem. There's a silence of five seconds between each tiny sonic burst. I fiddle with the black knob. Together, the transponders sound like panicked crickets. How, exactly, will the rescue helicopter use these tiny chirps to find us?

"Brauser?"

Something necessary is ebbing out of Brauser's eyes. Snow collects between his lashes. A trickle of strawberry-red blood dribbles out of the corner of his mouth.

After some experimentation, I discover that if I poke Brauser to the right of his belly button, he'll make a sound. A gargle. Poke! A burp of despair. There's something pitiable and terrifying about the unconscious bully. His crumpled nose and hat.

Brauser opens one blue eye and stares at me. I look away. I brush the snow off Brauser's cold earlobes. This is the first true thing that Brauser and I have ever shared, this fear, besides dog-eared songbooks and cafeteria noodles.

"Hold on, Brauser," I say without conviction. "Help is on the way."

I wonder, briefly, if I could eat Brauser if it came to that. At this point, we have been alone on the glacier for fourteen minutes.

Brauser's face is a raw, freckly pink. I fix his hat. The shadow of my hand moves back and forth over Brauser's open eyes. Pupils expanding, pupils contracting. A dark blue ring around the world. In between breaths, I realize that something incredible is happening at this new elevation. Up here you can hear everything—the orange *ping* of light on metal, the purr of water melting. These blue ocean contractions in Brauser's eyes. His pupils make a faint tidal *whooshing*. Shadows sound like feed pouring out of a cloth sack. When I move my hand, millions of shadow grains bounce along the hard snow. That's my sound, I think, birdseed raining out of a sack. It shakes out across the empty snowfields. I look up at the sky, nervous. What sort of bird, I wonder, is my shadow designed to be food for?

Above us, the sun bounces orange and yellow. The silence changes. We bump noses, but I can't hear Brauser's eyes anymore, or his shadow. I tug his hat down harder.

Rangi's air pulses red like a swallow's breast. Brauser's quiet is coma white. My own silence hums with these black-and-yellow bee stripes of fear:

> *YOU ARE*
>   *GOING*
>   *TO DIE UP*
> *HERE*
> *NOBODY KNOWS*
> *WHERE*
>   *YOU ARE*
> *THERE IS*
>   *NO MORE DOWN*
> *THERE*

I snap out of it when I realize that Rangi has started walking away from us. He pushes through the shallow crater left by the ice plane, stabbing his crampons into the jellied snow. Then he climbs over a ridge of wind-scoured shale and disappears.

"Rangi! Wait up!"

It takes me a full five minutes to cover the short distance between us and clamber over the wedge of shale. Rangi is waiting for me on the other side. "Why did you—" The question dies on my lips. No explanation is forthcoming from Rangi. We lie flat on our bellies, taking labored breaths and watching the sky, two soldiers in the trenches. Then Rangi starts making a sound. Nothing quite so deliberate as speech, but a dense fizz of noise, like bubbles zipping up to the surface of a tall glass.

"— — — . . . — — —, " he says, pointing into the clouds.

We both look up. A helicopter is coming for us, the sun pinging off its blades.

"We're saved!"

Rangi and I peer over the ridge and watch as the helicopter touches down on the glacier. Two men leap like flames out of the cockpit. Their vests glow red against the pure white backdrop. The glare off the snow makes their faces look like taupe holes.

The men unload three stretchers from the helicopter and lay them flat across the powder. They heave Brauser onto the first stretcher. One of the rescuers is whistling a cheery tune. It's a scary, incongruous sound in this landscape. Each whistled syllable hacks flat into the wind like a cleaver. I can see the dark fissures between his teeth.

"Help!" I jump up and pull Rangi out of the powder, puppet-jerk him to life. "Here!" I start to wave and shout. "Here! We're over he-e-ere!"

The ice pilot is still whistling, oblivious of us. I think I can just make out a softer, inner whistle, under the word: *Run.*

"Run," Rangi says.

Then I am facedown in the snow. Rangi's kneeling on my back, digging his whole weight into the base of my spine. Something thunks against the back of my head, and for a moment red stars cluster in front of my vision. Rangi grabs me by the legs and starts dragging me across the ice gully. I'm stunned but still conscious, too shocked to struggle. Then he yanks me over a snowbank and out of sight. The world goes blue-white-blue for a series of hills. I yelp and try to kick away, but Rangi's got me. He presses me to his chest in a murderous bear hug as we roll. We slide down the slope together and bang our way into an ice cave. In the lunar shadows, it looks as if our cheeks are sweating blue light. The altitude here manifests itself as a pernicious thirst, and my throat burns in the desiccated air of the cave. Inside, a twinkling, chandelier light fills every ablation. Even seated, I can touch the cold ceiling. I touch my tongue to the cold roof of my mouth.

The helicopter is taking off without us. It makes three buzzard circles above us, and I'm surprised to find myself cowering with Rangi in the cave. I should be jumping up and down, screaming at its metal belly. I think about Franz Josef's hand pressing hard on my diaphragm. Up here I can't untangle it, the word-strangle of it, the twisted umbilical that binds deep panic to sound. I open my mouth and release dead air. Snip, snip! go the scissors of the wind.

Rangi holds his hands over his ears and buries his face in my side. He doesn't speak again. The helicopter shrinks into a dense red pinprick of noise above us, lost in the sun. Then it's gone. After a few moments, the silence reconstitutes itself. I can hear our shadows again, spilling up the walls. It's a scary freedom.

When I look down and see Rangi staring up at me, I feel my stomach heave again.

"W-what-what the hell were you thinking?" My teeth are chattering uncontrollably. "Do you enjoy being stuck up here? Those men were here to *rescue* us, Rangi!"

Rangi closes his eyes and he *smiles*. He beams at me with ghastly relief. I move away from him, horrified.

"Who knows how long it will take before they send another helicopter? It could be *hours*!"

Anger flames through me and my muscles tense to hit him, a violence that clenches once and then vanishes. My fists uncurl without my conscious intervention. I stare down at my open palms with real surprise, feeling shaky and defeated. It's as if my body knows before I do that it's too dangerous to feel this way towards Rangi. Right now, he's the only other human around for thousands of vertical miles.

"Rangi? What are you doing?"

Rangi is on his hands and knees, crawling towards me, his face flickering in the cavelight. His black eyes sparkle with intent.

"Ran-gi?"

My voice has a wobble in the middle—like a tightrope strung between two fears. It sounds as if a sly little demon is bouncing across it.

"Come on, Rangi!" I say nervously. "Let's go back to the snowfield. Don't you want to get down from here? Don't you want to get home?"

Rangi holds a finger to his lips. His breathing comes quick and adenoidal when he reaches over and turns off my transponder. Before I can even process what's happening, Rangi rips it off my neck and lobs it, with a casual madness, into the blue maw of the crevasse.

Then Rangi flicks off his own transponder. He slips it over his neck.

"No!"

He sails it into a narrow opening in the ice.

"Oh no—oh no—oh *God*—oh no *why* did you do that? Now you've done it, Ritardando, now you've really done it. . . ."

I belly-squirm out of the cave and peer over the lip of the crevasse. The chasm glows with the loveliest, least hospitable colors: cold white stars, the green of interstellar vapors. It reminds me of the old stories, kids' stuff, about sirens who swam in the deep pools and thrashed up snowstorms with their merscales. Pirate lore. X-marks-the-spot stuff. I'm in no position to appreciate the fantasy shades of white and green inside the chasm. The only color that I want to see is the plastic yellow of my transponder.

This is when I plunge my hand into the ice hole, up to my elbow, fishing around a ledge for the transponder, and come up with a fistful of treasure.

It's really true, then, the part about the treasure. I can't wait to tell Mr. Oamaru that I was wrong, that "The Pirates' Conquest" isn't all lies and stupid rhymes; there are at least a few bars of truth in our song. Verse 4.

It's the stolen Moa patrimony: greenstone, river pearls, whale-tooth combs. The crevasse has swallowed our transponders, but the ice ledges inside are heaped with old plunder. Soon I've amassed a tall stack of greenstone. I wonder if I'm looking at the Moa's holy relics, melted down by our great-great-grandfathers into these anonymous nephrite bricks. I pull out coins, too, orange and red metal. They must have been here for a century or more. The coins are frozen. Each is chiseled with a historic profile, a numismatic portrait of the old Moa leaders. Nobody we sing about in "The Pirates' Conquest." You can't even make out their gender anymore, just high collars, proud noses, stout asparagus braids in the green copper. Men and women from some past that never made it into our music. I would have preferred a miracle that benefited us more directly.

"Here you go, Rangi!" And suddenly I'm laughing, I'm shaking all over now, in total hysterics. My body feels like a great chattering tooth. "We'll split it! Fifty/fifty . . ."

Rangi refuses to touch the treasure. I grab him by the elbows and twist open his palms. I place a brick of the luminious nephrite in each of his hands. It's enough that, if Rangi ever gets back to town, he could become the cemetery's sole proprietor. He could employ Digger Gibson.

"Take it!" I scream. "It's yours, it's yours, take it!"

What a small, cold fortune. Rangi lets it sink into the snow. He just wants a fistful of bear fur. I want my father.

I try to remember the chorus of "The Pirates' Conquest," and I'm frightened to discover that I've forgotten how it goes. No words, no melody, just a white, blank space. Sun sparkles above us. The walls of the ice caves are melting together—too softly, this time, for me to hear. I touch a drop of the wall to my tongue. A clear braid of liquid trickles across the caves, snow that fell in 1947, 1812, earlier still, released all at once like tears from a body. Rangi crawls over and crouches in front of me. The solar glare is sculpting the ice into glass fangs and tall blue scythes.

"Well, I hope you're happy," I hiss. "No one's going to save us now."

Rangi doesn't look happy; his face is still a mask of old fury. I wonder what it feels like to be angry at everyone except for a dead bear. It scares me to think about it. I picture the dead bear loping and slathering forever inside of Rangi, a long-toothed loyal animal, his one memory of love. Digger Gibson should never have adopted him. Who wants salvation when it just orphans you further?

I lean my cheek against the translucent outer wall of one of the caves. Water whispers inside: *You are going to die up here—nobody knows where you are.* . . . Any place, then, can become a cemetery. All it takes is your body. It's not fair, I think, and I get this petulant wish for ugly flowers and mourners, my mother's old familiar grief. Somebody I love to tend my future grave. Probably this is the wrong thing to be wishing for.

I jerk away from the trickly whisper of the snowmelt. This is the wrong thing to be wishing for. I don't want to die on this glacier. This accident is nothing I volunteered for. Below us, the ground rolls with sluiced water. In the Valley, it's easy to forget that the ground is moving, that we're traveling on a frozen river. But up here I can hear it happening. Centuries of water are melting in the heart of the glacier, a constant interior roar that calves icebergs into the black sea. Even now, we're moving away from Waitiki Valley. And suddenly I'd give anything to be back in my kitchen with Mr. Oamaru, swapping lies about my father. I'd pay any price to open my eyes and find myself in the Ice Amphitheater with the boys choir, all of us holding that single note.

And then I get a hero idea. This is my solo. If I can sing down an Avalanche on my own, the families at the base of the glacier will see it and send help. Mr. Oamaru's weathered face floats in front of my vision, and I make it a target for my anger. I pitch my voice so high that my forehead starts throbbing. Higher, and higher still. Breath floods out of my lungs. The note beckons and retreats above me, a round luminous note, like the sun viewed from the bottom of the Waitiki River. My voice rises like a hand struggling to break the surface of that water. I wonder if it's like this for Rangi, too; if Rangi's mutism just means that he has sunk several fathoms farther down than the rest of us, and given up on swimming.

If this were a local interest story, some square of uplift in the *Gazette,* I'd send down a tremendous Avalanche, an S.O.S. I'd hit that high C, or, in a fluted miracle, the C above it. Somebody below us would see it and send help. But that's not what's happening. My voice is cracking. It suffers up and fails and surges again. It breaks eons before the ice ever will. Now I'm breathless and covered in freezing spittle. Rangi watches and never even opens his mouth.

I hear myself echoing Franz Josef: "Sing it with me, Rangi! Forget Franz. Forget Digger. It's okay to sing now, Rangi. Or scream if you have to, anything. . . ." Our voices are the only hatchet that we have up here. But Rangi, if you can believe this, has fallen backwards into the snow. He's settled into his own snow angel. When I kneel and shake him, Rangi looks up at me with a mild surprise, as if he's forgotten that I am still here. Then his gaze shifts inward. A new shape is running in Rangi's eyes now. A brown-gold speck, at such a distance. Its black snout opens in a soundless, joyful roar.

Somewhere, an Avalanche is about to happen without us. Rangi must know this before I do, and the dead bear in his eyes comes racing towards us across old snow. At the base of Aokeora, Mr. Oamaru is fiddling with the flashbulb, the black drape of the box camera billowing around him. He is snapping picture after picture of white sludge rolling down an ice shelf. My mother is pointing to the ridge where I'm supposed to be and making good-natured jokes about my weight gain. Ruth, Rachel, Rebecca are sending up a prayer for my success. They'll eat stale lemon moonpies and listen for a happy hallucination of my voice. In a few minutes, the town will stand up and applaud. I feel as if I'm looking down at my own funeral, only nobody knows that I'm dead. It's a frightening, lonely feeling.

Even so, I can't silence a small chirp of hope. Who knows? Maybe my transponder hit a ledge that jarred the switch back to ON. Maybe it's still emitting a signal. A part of me feels certain that my family will hear my absence at the bottom of Aokeora, thousands of feet below us, and know that I am lost.

St. Lucy's Home for Girls Raised by Wolves

Stage 1: The initial period is one in which everything is new, exciting, and interesting for your students. It is fun for your students to explore their new environment.

—from *The Jesuit Handbook on Lycanthropic Culture Shock*

At first, our pack was all hair and snarl and floor-thumping joy. We forgot the barked cautions of our mothers and fathers, all the promises we'd made to be civilized and lady-like, couth and kempt. We tore through the austere rooms, overturning dresser drawers, pawing through the neat piles of the Stage 3 girls' starched underwear, smashing lightbulbs with our bare fists. Things felt less foreign in the dark. The dim bedroom was windowless and odorless. We remedied this by spraying exuberant yellow streams all over the bunks. We jumped from bunk to bunk, spraying. We nosed each other midair, our bodies buckling in kinetic laughter. The nuns watched us from the corner of the bedroom, their tiny faces pinched with displeasure.

"*Ay caramba,*" Sister Maria de la Guardia sighed. "*Que barbaridad!*" She made the Sign of the Cross. Sister Maria came to St. Lucy's from a halfway home in Copacabana. In Copacabana, the girls are fat and languid and eat pink slivers of guava right out of your hand. Even at Stage 1, their pelts are silky, sun-bleached to near invisibility. Our pack was hirsute and sinewy and mostly brunette. We had terrible posture. We went knuckling along the wooden floor on the calloused pads of our fists, baring row after row of tiny, wood-rotted teeth. Sister Josephine sucked in her breath. She removed a yellow wheel of floss from under her robes, looping it like a miniature lasso.

"The girls at our facility are *backwoods,*" Sister Josephine whispered to Sister Maria de la Guardia with a beatific smile. "You must be patient with them." I clamped down on her ankle, straining to close my jaws around the woolly XXL sock. Sister Josephine tasted like sweat and freckles. She smelled easy to kill.

We'd arrived at St. Lucy's that morning, part of a pack fifteen-strong. We were accompanied by a mousy, nervous-smelling social worker; the baby-faced deacon; Bartholomew, the blue wolfhound; and four burly woodsmen. The deacon handed out some stale cupcakes and said a quick prayer. Then he led us through the woods. We ran past the wild apiary, past the felled oaks, until we could see the white steeple of St. Lucy's rising out of the forest. We stopped short at the edge of a muddy lake. Then the deacon took our brothers. Bartholomew helped him to herd the boys up the ramp of a small ferry. We girls ran along the shore, tearing at our new jumpers in a plaid agitation. Our brothers stood on the deck, looking small and confused.

Our mothers and fathers were werewolves. They lived an outsider's existence in caves at the edge of the forest, threatened by frost and pitchforks. They had been ostracized by the local farmers for eating their silled fruit pies and terrorizing the heifers. They had ostracized the local wolves by having sometimes-thumbs, and regrets, and human children. (Their condition skips a generation.) Our pack grew up in a green purgatory. We couldn't keep up with the purebred wolves, but we never stopped crawling. We spoke a slab-tongued pidgin in the cave, inflected with frequent howls. Our parents wanted something better for us; they wanted us to get braces, use towels, be fully bilingual. When the nuns showed up, our parents couldn't refuse their offer. The nuns, they said, would make us naturalized citizens of human society. We would go to St. Lucy's to study a better culture. We didn't know at the time that our parents were sending us away for good. Neither did they.

That first afternoon, the nuns gave us free rein of the grounds. Everything was new, exciting, and interesting. A low granite wall surrounded St. Lucy's, the blue woods humming for miles behind it. There was a stone fountain full of delectable birds. There was a statue of St. Lucy. Her marble skin was colder than our mother's nose, her pupil-less eyes rolled heavenward. Doomed squirrels gamboled around her stony toes. Our diminished pack threw back our heads in a celebratory howl—an exultant and terrible noise, even without a chorus of wolf brothers in the background. There were holes everywhere!

We supplemented these holes by digging some of our own. We interred sticks, and our itchy new jumpers, and the bones of the friendly, unfortunate squirrels. Our noses ached beneath an invisible assault. Everything was smudged with a human odor: baking bread, petrol, the nuns' faint woman-smell sweating out beneath a dark perfume of tallow and incense. We smelled one another, too, with the same astounded fascination. Our own scent had become foreign in this strange place.

We had just sprawled out in the sun for an afternoon nap, yawning into the warm dirt, when the nuns reappeared. They conferred in the shadow of the juniper tree, whispering and pointing. Then they started towards us. The oldest sister had spent the past hour twitching in her sleep, dreaming of fatty and infirm elk. (The pack used to dream the same dreams back then, as naturally as we drank the same water and slept on the same red scree.) When our oldest sister saw the nuns approaching, she instinctively bristled. It was an improvised bristle, given her new, human limitations. She took clumps of her scraggly, nut-brown hair and held it straight out from her head.

Sister Maria gave her a brave smile.

"And what is your name?" she asked.

The oldest sister howled something awful and inarticulable, a distillate of hurt and panic, half-forgotten hunts and eclipsed moons. Sister Maria nodded and scribbled on a yellow legal pad. She slapped on a name tag: HELLO, MY NAME IS _____! "Jeanette it is."

The rest of the pack ran in a loose, uncertain circle, torn between our instinct to help her and our new fear. We sensed some subtler danger afoot, written in a language we didn't understand.

Our littlest sister had the quickest reflexes. She used her hands to flatten her ears to the side of her head. She backed towards the far corner of the garden, snarling in the most menacing register that an eight-year-old wolf-girl can muster. Then she ran. It took them two hours to pin her down and tag her: HELLO, MY NAME IS MIRABELLA!

"Stage 1," Sister Maria sighed, taking careful aim with her tranquilizer dart. "It can be a little overstimulating."

> Stage 2: After a time, your students realize that they must work to adjust to the new culture. This work may be stressful and students may experience a strong sense of dislocation. They may miss certain foods. They may spend a lot of time daydreaming during this period. Many students feel isolated, irritated, bewildered, depressed, or generally uncomfortable.

Those were the days when we dreamed of rivers and meat. The full-moon nights were the worst! Worse than cold toilet seats and boiled tomatoes, worse than trying to will our tongues to curl around our false new names. We would snarl at one another for no reason. I remember how disorienting it was to look down and see two square-toed shoes instead of my own four feet. Keep your mouth shut, I repeated during our walking drills, staring straight ahead. Keep your shoes on your feet. Mouth shut, shoes on feet. Do not chew on your new penny loafers. Do not. I stumbled around in a daze, my mouth black with shoe polish. The whole pack was irritated, bewildered, depressed. We were all uncomfortable, and between languages. We had never wanted to run away so badly in our lives; but who did we have to run back to? Only the curled black grimace of the mother. Only the father, holding his tawny head between his paws. Could we betray our parents by going back to them? After they'd given us the choicest part of the woodchuck, loved us at our hairless worst, nosed us across the ice floes and abandoned us at St. Lucy's for our own betterment?

Physically, we were all easily capable of clearing the low stone walls. Sister Josephine left the wooden gates wide open. They unslatted the windows at night so that long fingers of moonlight beckoned us from the woods. But we knew we couldn't return to the woods; not till we were civilized, not if we didn't want to break the mother's heart. It all felt like a sly, human taunt.

It was impossible to make the blank, chilly bedroom feel like home. In the beginning, we drank gallons of bathwater as part of a collaborative effort to mark our territory. We puddled up the yellow carpet of old newspapers. But later, when we returned to the bedroom, we were dismayed to find all trace of the pack musk had vanished. Someone was coming in and erasing us. We sprayed and sprayed every morning; and every night, we returned to the same ammonia eradication. We couldn't make our scent stick here; it made us feel invisible. Eventually we gave up. Still, the pack seemed to be adjusting on the same timetable. The advanced girls could already alternate between two speeds: "slouch" and "amble." Almost everybody was fully bipedal.

Almost.

The pack was worried about Mirabella.

Mirabella would rip foamy chunks out of the church pews and replace them with ham bones and girl dander. She loved to roam the grounds wagging her invisible tail. (We all had a hard time giving that up. When we got excited, we would fall to the ground and start pumping our backsides.

Back in those days we could pump at rabbity velocities. *Que horror!* Sister Maria frowned, looking more than a little jealous.) We'd give her scolding pinches. "Mirabella," we hissed, imitating the nuns. "No." Mirabella cocked her ears at us, hurt and confused.

Still, some things remained the same. The main commandment of wolf life is Know Your Place, and that translated perfectly. Being around other humans had awakened a slavish-dog affection in us. An abasing, belly-to-the-ground desire to please. As soon as we realized that someone higher up in the food chain was watching us, we wanted only to be pleasing in their sight. Mouth shut, I repeated, shoes on feet. But if Mirabella had this latent instinct, the nuns couldn't figure out how to activate it. She'd go bounding around, gleefully spraying on their gilded statue of St. Lucy, mad-scratching at the virulent fleas that survived all of their powders and baths. At Sister Maria's tearful insistence, she'd stand upright for roll call, her knobby, oddly muscled legs quivering from the effort. Then she'd collapse right back to the ground with an ecstatic *oomph!* She was still loping around on all fours (which the nuns had taught us to see looked unnatural and ridiculous—we could barely believe it now, the shame of it, that we used to locomote like that!), her fists blue-white from the strain. As if she were holding a secret tight to the ground. Sister Maria de la Guardia would sigh every time she saw her. *"Caramba!"* She'd sit down with Mirabella and pry her fingers apart. "You see?" she'd say softly, again and again. "What are you holding on to? Nothing, little one. Nothing."

Then she would sing out the standard chorus, "Why can't you be more like your sister Jeanette?"

The pack hated Jeanette. She was the most successful of us, the one furthest removed from her origins. Her real name was GWARR!, but she wouldn't respond to this anymore. Jeanette spiffed her penny loafers until her very shoes seemed to gloat. (Linguists have since traced the colloquial origins of "goody two-shoes" back to our facilities.) She could even growl out a demonic-sounding precursor to "Pleased to meet you." She'd delicately extend her former paws to visitors, wearing white kid gloves.

"Our little wolf, disguised in sheep's clothing!" Sister Ignatius liked to joke with the visiting deacons, and Jeanette would surprise everyone by laughing along with them, a harsh, inhuman, barking sound. Her hearing was still twig-snap sharp. Jeanette was the first among us to apologize; to drink apple juice out of a sippy cup; to quit eyeballing the cleric's jugular in a disconcerting fashion. She curled her lips back into a cousin of a smile as the traveling barber cut her pelt into bangs. Then she swept her coarse black curls under the rug. When we entered a room, our nostrils flared beneath the new odors: onion and bleach, candle wax, the turnipy smell of unwashed bodies. Not Jeanette. Jeanette smiled and pretended like she couldn't smell a thing.

I was one of the good girls. Not great and not terrible, solidly middle of the pack. But I had an ear for languages, and I could read before I could adequately wash myself. I probably could have vied with Jeanette for the number one spot, but I'd seen what happened if you gave in to your natural aptitudes. This wasn't like the woods, where you had to be your fastest and your strongest and your bravest self. Different sorts of calculations were required to survive at the home.

The pack hated Jeanette, but we hated Mirabella more. We began to avoid her, but sometimes she'd surprise us, curled up beneath the beds or gnawing on a scapula in the garden. It was scary to be ambushed by your sister. I'd bristle and growl, the way that I'd begun to snarl at my own reflection as if it were a stranger.

"Whatever will become of Mirabella?" we asked, gulping back our own fear. We'd heard rumors about former wolf-girls who never adapted to their new culture. It was assumed that they were returned to our native country, the vanishing woods. We liked to speculate about this before bedtime, scaring ourselves with stories of catastrophic bliss. It was the disgrace, the failure that we all guiltily hoped for in our hard beds. Twitching with the shadow question: *Whatever will become of me?*

We spent a lot of time daydreaming during this period. Even Jeanette. Sometimes I'd see her looking out at the woods in a vacant way. If you interrupted her in the midst of one of these reveries, she would lunge at you with an elder-sister ferocity, momentarily forgetting her human catechism. We liked her better then, startled back into being foamy old Jeanette.

In school, they showed us the St. Francis of Assisi slide show, again and again. Then the nuns would give us bags of bread. They never announced these things as a test; it was only much later that I realized that we were under constant examination. "Go feed the ducks," they urged us. "Go practice compassion for all God's creatures." *Don't pair me with Mirabella,* I prayed, *anybody but Mirabella.* "Claudette"—Sister Josephine beamed—"why don't you and Mirabella take some pumpernickel down to the ducks?"

"Ohhkaaythankyou," I said. (It took me a long time to say anything; first I had to translate it in my head from the Wolf.) It wasn't fair. They knew Mirabella couldn't make bread balls yet. She couldn't even undo the twist tie of the bag. She was sure to eat the birds; Mirabella didn't even try to curb her desire to kill things—and then who would get blamed for the dark spots of duck blood on our Peter Pan collars? Who would get penalized with negative Skill Points? Exactly.

As soon as we were beyond the wooden gates, I snatched the bread away from Mirabella and ran off to the duck pond on my own. Mirabella gave chase, nipping at my heels. She thought it was a game. "Stop it," I growled. I ran faster, but it was Stage 2 and I was still unsteady on my two feet. I fell sideways into a leaf pile, and then all I could see was my sister's blurry form, bounding towards me. In a moment, she was on top of me, barking the old word for tug-of-war. When she tried to steal the bread out of my hands, I whirled around and snarled at her, pushing my ears back from my head. I bit her shoulder, once, twice, the only language she would respond to. I used my new motor skills. I threw dirt, I threw stones. "Get away!" I screamed, long after she had made a cringing retreat into the shadows of the purple saplings. "Get away, get away!"

Much later, they found Mirabella wading in the shallows of a distant river, trying to strangle a mallard with her rosary beads. I was at the lake; I'd been sitting there for hours. Hunched in the long cattails, my yellow eyes flashing, shoving ragged hunks of bread into my mouth.

I don't know what they did to Mirabella. Me they separated from my sisters. They made me watch another slide show. This one showed images of former wolf-girls, the ones who had failed to be rehabilitated. Long-haired, sad-eyed women, limping after their former wolf packs in white tennis shoes and pleated culottes. A wolf-girl bank teller, her makeup smeared in oily rainbows, eating a raw steak on the deposit slips while her colleagues looked on in disgust. Our parents. The final slide was a bolded sentence in St. Lucy's prim script: DO YOU WANT TO END UP SHUNNED BY BOTH SPECIES?

After that, I spent less time with Mirabella. One night she came to me, holding her hand out. She was covered with splinters, keening a high, whining noise through her nostrils. Of course I understood what she wanted; I wasn't that far removed from our language (even though I was reading at a fifth-grade level, halfway into Jack London's *The Son of the Wolf*).

"Lick your own wounds," I said, not unkindly. It was what the nuns had instructed us to say; wound licking was not something you did in polite company. Etiquette was so confounding in this country. Still, looking at Mirabella—her fists balled together like small, white porcupines, her brows knitted in animal confusion—I felt a throb of compassion. *How can people live like they do?* I wondered. Then I congratulated myself. This was a Stage 3 thought.

> Stage 3: It is common that students who start living in a new and different culture come to a point where they reject the host culture and withdraw into themselves. During this period, they make generalizations about the host culture and wonder how the people can live like they do. Your students may feel that their own culture's lifestyle and customs are far superior to those of the host country.

The nuns were worried about Mirabella, too. To correct a failing, you must first be aware of it as a failing. And there was Mirabella, shucking her plaid jumper in full view of the visiting cardinal. Mirabella, battling a raccoon under the dinner table while the rest of us took dainty bites of peas and borscht. Mirabella, doing belly flops into compost.

"You have to pull your weight around here," we overheard Sister Josephine saying one night. We paused below the vestry window and peered inside.

"Does Mirabella try to earn Skill Points by shelling walnuts and polishing Saint-in-the-Box? No. Does Mirabella even know how to say the word *walnut*? Has she learned how to say anything besides a sinful 'HraaaHA!' as she commits frottage against the organ pipes? No."

There was a long silence.

"Something must be done," Sister Ignatius said firmly. The other nuns nodded, a sea of thin, colorless lips and kettle-black brows. "Something must be done," they intoned. That ominously passive construction; a something so awful that nobody wanted to assume responsibility for it.

I could have warned her. If we were back home, and Mirabella had come under attack by territorial beavers or snow-blind bears, I would have warned her. But the truth is that by Stage 3 I wanted her gone. Mirabella's inability to adapt was taking a visible toll. Her teeth were ground down to nubbins; her hair was falling out. She hated the spongy, long-dead foods we were served, and it showed— her ribs were poking through her uniform. Her bright eyes had dulled to a sour whiskey color. But you couldn't show Mirabella the slightest kindness anymore—she'd never leave you alone! You'd have to sit across from her at meals, shoving her away as she begged for your scraps. I slept fitfully during that period, unable to forget that Mirabella was living under my bed, gnawing on my loafers.

It was during Stage 3 that we met our first purebred girls. These were girls raised in captivity, volunteers from St. Lucy's School for Girls. The apple-cheeked fourth-grade class came to tutor us in playing. They had long golden braids or short, severe bobs. They had frilly-duvet names like Felicity and Beulah; and pert, bunny noses; and terrified smiles. We grinned back at them with genuine ferocity. It made us nervous to meet new humans. There were so many things that we could do wrong! And the rules here were different depending on which humans we were with: dancing or no dancing, checkers playing or no checkers playing, pumping or no pumping.

The purebred girls played checkers with us.

"These girl-girls sure is dumb," my sister Lavash panted to me between games. "I win it again! Five to none."

She was right. The purebred girls were making mistakes on purpose, in order to give us an advantage. "King me," I growled, out of turn. *"I say king me!"* and Felicity meekly complied. Beulah pretended not to mind when we got frustrated with the oblique, fussy movement from square to square and shredded the board to ribbons. I felt sorry for them. I wondered what it would be like to be bred in captivity, and always homesick for a dimly sensed forest, the trees you've never seen.

Jeanette was learning how to dance. On Holy Thursday, she mastered a rudimentary form of the Charleston. *"Brava!"* The nuns clapped. *"Brava!"*

Every Friday, the girls who had learned how to ride a

bicycle celebrated by going on chaperoned trips into town. The purebred girls sold seven hundred rolls of gift-wrap paper and used the proceeds to buy us a yellow fleet of bicycles built for two. We'd ride the bicycles uphill, a sanctioned pumping, a grim-faced nun pedaling behind each one of us. "Congratulations!" the nuns would huff. "Being human is like riding this bicycle. Once you've learned how, you'll never forget." Mirabella would run after the bicycles, growling out our old names. HWRAA! GWARR! TRRRRRRR! We pedaled faster.

At this point, we'd had six weeks of lessons, and still nobody could do the Sausalito but Jeanette. The nuns decided we needed an inducement to dance. They announced that we would celebrate our successful rehabilitations with a Debutante Ball. There would be brothers, ferried over from the Home for Man-Boys Raised by Wolves. There would be a photographer from the *Gazette Sophisticate*. There would be a three-piece jazz band from West Toowoomba, and root beer in tiny plastic cups. The brothers! We'd almost forgotten about them. Our invisible tails went limp. I should have been excited; instead, I felt a low mad anger at the nuns. They knew we weren't ready to dance with the brothers; we weren't even ready to talk to them. Things had been so much simpler in the woods. That night I waited until my sisters were asleep. Then I slunk into the closet and practiced the Sausalito two-step in secret, a private mass of twitch and foam. Mouth shut—shoes on feet! Mouth shut—shoes on feet! Mouthshutmouthshut . . .

One night I came back early from the closet and stumbled on Jeanette. She was sitting in a patch of moonlight on the windowsill, reading from one of her library books. (She was the first of us to sign for her library card, too.) Her cheeks looked dewy.

"Why you cry?" I asked her, instinctively reaching over to lick Jeanette's cheek and catching myself in the nick of time.

Jeanette blew her nose into a nearby curtain. (Even her mistakes annoyed us—they were always so well intentioned.) She sniffled and pointed to a line in her book: "The lake-water was reinventing the forest and the white moon above it, and wolves lapped up the cold reflection of the sky." But none of the pack besides me could read yet, and I wasn't ready to claim a common language with Jeanette.

The following day, Jeanette golfed. The nuns set up a miniature putt-putt course in the garden. Sister Maria dug four sandtraps and got old Walter, the groundskeeper, to make a windmill out of a lawn mower engine. The eighteenth hole was what they called a "doozy," a minuscule crack in St. Lucy's marble dress. Jeanette got a hole in one.

On Sundays, the pretending felt almost as natural as nature. The chapel was our favorite place. Long before we could understand what the priest was saying, the music instructed us in how to feel. The choir director—aggressively perfumed Mrs. Valuchi, gold necklaces like pineapple rings around her neck—taught us more than the nuns ever did. She showed us how to pattern the old hunger into arias. Clouds moved behind the frosted oculus of the nave, glass shadows that reminded me of my mother. The mother, I'd think, struggling to conjure up a picture. A black shadow, running behind the watery screen of pines.

We sang at the chapel annexed to the home every morning. We understood that this was the humans' moon, the place for howling beyond purpose. Not for mating, not for hunting, not for fighting, not for anything but the sound itself. And we'd howl along with the choir, hurling every pitted thing within us at the stained glass. "Sotto voce." The nuns would frown. But you could tell that they were pleased.

> Stage 4: As a more thorough understanding of the host culture is acquired, your students will begin to feel more comfortable in their new environment. Your students feel more at home, and their self-confidence grows. Everything begins to make sense.

"Hey, Claudette," Jeanette growled to me on the day before the ball. "Have you noticed that everything's beginning to make sense?"

Before I could answer, Mirabella sprang out of the hall closet and snapped through Jeanette's homework binder. Pages and pages of words swirled around the stone corridor, like dead leaves off trees.

"What about you, Mirabella?" Jeanette asked politely, stooping to pick up her erasers. She was the only one of us who would still talk to Mirabella; she was high enough in the rankings that she could afford to talk to the scruggliest wolf-girl. "Has everything begun to make more sense, Mirabella?"

Mirabella let out a whimper. She scratched at us and scratched at us, raking her nails along our shins so hard that she drew blood. Then she rolled belly-up on the cold stone floor, squirming on a bed of spelling-bee worksheets. Above us, small pearls of light dotted the high, tinted window.

Jeanette frowned. "You are a late bloomer, Mirabella! Usually, everything's begun to make more sense by Month

Twelve at the latest." I noticed that she stumbled on the word *bloomer*. HraaaHA! Jeanette could never fully shake our accent. She'd talk like that her whole life, I thought with a gloomy satisfaction, each word winced out like an apology for itself.

"Claudette, help me," she yelped. Mirabella had closed her jaws around Jeanette's bald ankle and was dragging her towards the closet. "Please. Help me to mop up Mirabella's mess."

I ignored her and continued down the hall. I had only four more hours to perfect the Sausalito. I was worried only about myself. By that stage, I was no longer certain of how the pack felt about anything.

At seven o'clock on the dot, Sister Ignatius blew her whistle and frog-marched us into the ball. The nuns had transformed the rectory into a very scary place. Purple and silver balloons started popping all around us. Black streamers swooped down from the eaves and got stuck in our hair like bats. A full yellow moon smirked outside the window. We were greeted by blasts of a saxophone, and fizzy pink drinks, and the brothers.

The brothers didn't smell like our brothers anymore. They smelled like pomade and cold, sterile sweat. They looked like little boys. Someone had washed behind their ears and made them wear suspendered dungarees. Kyle used to be a blustery alpha male, BTWWWR!, chewing through rattlesnakes, spooking badgers, snatching a live trout out of a grizzly's mouth. He stood by the punch bowl, looking pained and out of place.

"My stars!" I growled. "What lovely weather we've been having!"

"Yeees," Kyle growled back. "It is beginning to look a lot like Christmas." All around the room, boys and girls raised by wolves were having the same conversation. Actually, it had been an unseasonably warm and brown winter, and just that morning a freak hailstorm had sent Sister Josephina to an early grave. But we had only gotten up to Unit 7: Party Dialogue; we hadn't yet learned the vocabulary for Unit 12: How to Tactfully Acknowledge Disaster. Instead, we wore pink party hats and sucked olives on little sticks, inured to our own strangeness.

The nuns swept our hair back into high, bouffant hairstyles. This made us look more girlish and less inclined to eat people, the way that squirrels are saved from looking like rodents by their poofy tails. I was wearing a white organdy dress with orange polka dots. Jeanette was wearing a mauve organdy dress with blue polka dots. Linette was wearing a red organdy dress with white polka dots. Mirabella was in a dark corner, wearing a muzzle. Her party culottes were duct-taped to her knees. The nuns had tied little bows on the muzzle to make it more festive. Even so, the jazz band from West Toowoomba kept glancing nervously her way.

"You smell astoooounding!" Kyle was saying, accidentally stretching the diphthong into a howl and then blushing. "I mean—"

"Yes, I know what it is that you mean," I snapped. (That's probably a little narrative embellishment on my part; it must have been months before I could really "snap" out words.) I didn't smell astounding. I had rubbed a pumpkin muffin all over my body earlier that morning to mask my natural, feral scent. Now I smelled like a purebred girl, easy to kill. I narrowed my eyes at Kyle and flattened my ears, something I hadn't done for months. Kyle looked panicked, trying to remember the words that would make me act like a girl again. I felt hot, oily tears squeezing out of the red corners of my eyes. *Shoesonfeet!* I barked at myself. I tried again. "My! What lovely weather—"

The jazz band struck up a tune.

"The time has come to do the Sausalito," Sister Maria announced, beaming into the microphone. "Every sister grab a brother!" She switched on Walter's industrial flashlight, struggling beneath its weight, and aimed the beam in the center of the room.

Uh-oh. I tried to skulk off into Mirabella's corner, but Kyle pushed me into the spotlight. "No," I moaned through my teeth, "noooooo." All of a sudden the only thing my body could remember how to do was pump and pump. In a flash of white-hot light, my months at St. Lucy's had vanished, and I was just a terrified animal again. As if of their own accord, my feet started to wiggle out of my shoes. *Mouth shut,* I gasped, staring down at my naked toes, *mouthshutmouthshut.*

"Ahem. The time has come," Sister Maria coughed, "to do the Sausalito." She paused. "The Sausalito," she added helpfully, "does not in any way resemble the thing that you are doing."

Beads of sweat stood out on my forehead. I could feel my jaws gaping open, my tongue lolling out of the left side of my mouth. What were the steps? I looked frantically for Jeanette; she would help me, she would tell me what to do.

Jeanette was sitting in the corner, sipping punch through a long straw and watching me pant. I locked eyes with her, pleading with the mute intensity that I had used to beg her for weasel bones in the forest. "What are the steps?" I mouthed.

"The steps!"

"The steps?" Then Jeanette gave me a wide, true wolf smile. For an instant, she looked just like our mother. "Not for you," she mouthed back.

I threw my head back, a howl clawing its way up my throat. I was about to lose all my Skill Points, I was about to fail my Adaptive Dancing test. But before the air could burst from my lungs, the wind got knocked out of me. *Oomph!* I fell to the ground, my skirt falling softly over my head. Mirabella had intercepted my eye-cry for help. She'd chewed through her restraints and tackled me from behind, barking at unseen cougars, trying to shield me with her tiny body. *"Caramba!"* Sister Maria squealed, dropping the flashlight. The music ground to a halt. And I have never loved someone so much, before or since, as I loved my littlest sister at that moment. I wanted to roll over and lick her ears, I wanted to kill a dozen spotted fawns and let her eat first.

But everybody was watching; everybody was waiting to see what I would do. "I wasn't talking to you," I grunted from underneath her. "I didn't want your help. Now you have ruined the Sausalito! You have ruined the ball!" I said more loudly, hoping the nuns would hear how much my enunciation had improved.

"You have ruined it!" my sisters panted, circling around us, eager to close ranks. "Mirabella has ruined it!" Every girl was wild-eyed and itching under her polka dots, punch froth dribbling down her chin. The pack had been waiting for this moment for some time. "Mirabella cannot adapt! Back to the woods, back to the woods!"

The band from West Toowoomba had quietly packed their instruments into black suitcases and were sneaking out the back. The boys had fled back towards the lake, bow ties spinning, snapping suspenders in their haste. Mirabella was still snarling in the center of it all, trying to figure out where the danger was so that she could defend me against it. The nuns exchanged glances.

In the morning, Mirabella was gone. We checked under all the beds. I pretended to be surprised. I'd known she would have to be expelled the minute I felt her weight on my back. Walter came and told me this in secret after the ball, "So you can say yer good-byes." I didn't want to face Mirabella. Instead, I packed a tin lunch pail for her: two jelly sandwiches on saltine crackers, a chloroformed squirrel, a gilt-edged placard of St. Bolio. I left it for her with Sister Ignatius, with a little note: "Best wishes!" I told myself I'd done everything I could.

"Hooray!" the pack crowed. "Something has been done!"

We raced outside into the bright sunlight, knowing full well that our sister had been turned loose, that we'd never find her. A low roar rippled through us and surged up and up, disappearing into the trees. I listened for an answering howl from Mirabella, heart thumping—what if she heard us and came back? But there was nothing.

We graduated from St. Lucy's shortly thereafter. As far as I can recollect, that was our last communal howl.

Stage 5: At this point your students are able to interact effectively in the new cultural environment. They find it easy to move between the two cultures.

One Sunday, near the end of my time at St. Lucy's, the sisters gave me a special pass to go visit the parents. The woodsman had to accompany me; I couldn't remember how to find the way back on my own. I wore my best dress and brought along some prosciutto and dill pickles in a picnic basket. We crunched through the fall leaves in silence, and every step made me sadder. "I'll wait out here," the woodsman said, leaning on a blue elm and lighting a cigarette.

The cave looked so much smaller than I remembered it. I had to duck my head to enter. Everybody was eating when I walked in. They all looked up from the bull moose at the same time, my aunts and uncles, my sloe-eyed, lolling cousins, the parents. My uncle dropped a thighbone from his mouth. My littlest brother, a cross-eyed wolf-boy who has since been successfully rehabilitated and is now a dour, balding children's book author, started whining in terror. My mother recoiled from me, as if I was a stranger. TRRR? She sniffed me for a long moment. Then she sank her teeth into my ankle, looking proud and sad. After all the tail wagging and perfunctory barking had died down, the parents sat back on their hind legs. They stared up at me expectantly, panting in the cool gray envelope of the cave, waiting for a display of what I had learned.

"So," I said, telling my first human lie. "I'm home."

Acknowledgments

I would like to thank Denise Shannon, my sorcerous agent; my brilliant and endlessly supportive editor, Jordan Pavlin; Sarah Gelman and the excellent team at Knopf; the all-star poet and editor Carin Besser; all of my teachers, with a special debt of gratitude to Ben Marcus, Sam Lipsyte, Stephen O'Connor, Jaime Manrique, Sheila Donohue, Brian Bouldrey, Marie Hayes, and Edith Skom; and my workshop groups at Columbia University and Northwestern, who inspired me with their own terrific writing and were the first readers for many of these stories. Without you guys, this book would not exist.

To the editors that I was blessed to work with this past year, for their lightning-insights and wonderful suggestions: Fatema Ahmed, Bradford Morrow, Michael Ray, and Carol Ann Fitzgerald.

A huge thank-you to my incredible friends, who have stuck it out with me in Miami, in Chi-town, and here in the Big Apple—I love you guys so much. To my family, the Russells and the Romanchucks, you make me feel like the luckiest kid alive. Thank you for the swamp trips, Papa! Finally, I'd like to thank the faculty and students of the Writing Division at Columbia University and the Henfield/Transatlantic Foundation for giving me the time and the courage to write.

And a big hug and high-five for Madeleine Timmis, the world's greatest seventh-grade teacher.

"How I wish these were my own words, instead of breakneck demon writer
Karen Russell's, whose stories begin, in prose form, where the jabberwock
left off. . . . Run for your life. This girl is on fire."
—Susan Salter Reynolds, *Los Angeles Times Book Review*

In these ten glittering stories, debut author Karen Russell takes us to the
ghostly and magical swamps of the Florida Everglades. Here wolflike
girls are reformed by nuns, a family makes their living wrestling alligators in a theme park, and little girls sail away on crab shells. Filled with
inventiveness and heart, *St. Lucy's Home for Girls Raised by Wolves* introduces
a radiant new writer.

"Karen Russell is a storyteller with a voice
like no other. . . . Laced with humor and
compassion." —Lauren Gallo, *People*

"One of the strangest, creepiest, most
surreal collections of tales published in
recent memory. . . . Her writing bristles
with confidence." —June Sawyers,
San Francisco Chronicle

"Twenty-five-year-old wunderkind
Karen Russell . . . proves herself a mythol-
ogist of the darkest and most disturbing . . .
often unforgettable, gorgeously . . .
tales." —Jenny Feldman, *Elle*